1

Praise for

A SKELETON IN THE FAMILY

"Dr. Georgia Thackery is smart, resourceful, and determined to be a great single mom to her teenager. Georgia is normal in every respect—except that her best friend happens to be a skeleton named Sid. You'll love the adventures of this unexpected mystery-solving duo."
—Charlaine Harris, #1 *New York Times* bestselling author

"Adjunct English professor Georgia Thackery makes a charming debut in *A Skeleton in the Family*. Georgia is fiercely loyal to her best friend, Sid, an actual skeleton who is somehow still 'alive.' When Sid see someone he remembers from his past life—who later turns up dead—Georgia finds herself trying to put together the pieces of Sid's past as she works to hunt down a killer. Amateur sleuth Georgia and her sidekick, Sid, are just plain fun!"
—Sofie Kelly, *New York Times* bestselling author of *Cat Trick*

"No bones about it, Leigh Perry hooked me right from the beginning. An unusual premise, quirky characters, and smart, dry humor season this well-told mystery that kept me guessing until the very end. It's too bad Perry's sleuth is fictional—I'd invite Georgia over for dinner in a heartbeat."
—Bailey Cates, national bestselling author of *Bewitched, Bothered, and Biscotti*

"A delightful cozy with a skeleton who will tickle your funny bone."
—Paige Shelton, national bestselling author of *If Bread Could Rise to the Occasion*

Berkley Prime Crime titles by Leigh Perry

A SKELETON IN THE FAMILY
THE SKELETON TAKES A BOW
THE SKELETON HAUNTS A HOUSE

A SKELETON IN THE FAMILY

Leigh Perry

BERKLEY PRIME CRIME, NEW YORK

THE BERKLEY PUBLISHING GROUP
Published by the Penguin Group
Penguin Group (USA)
375 Hudson Street, New York, New York 10014, USA

USA | Canada | UK | Ireland | Australia | New Zealand | India | South Africa | China

Penguin Books Ltd., Registered Offices: 80 Strand, London WC2R 0RL, England
For more information about the Penguin Group, visit penguin.com.

A SKELETON IN THE FAMILY

A Berkley Prime Crime Book / published by arrangement with the author

Berkley Prime Crime Books are published by The Berkley Publishing Group.
BERKLEY® PRIME CRIME and the PRIME CRIME logo are trademarks of
Penguin Group (USA).

For information, address: The Berkley Publishing Group,
a division of Penguin Group (USA).
375 Hudson Street, New York, New York 10014.

ISBN: 978-0-425-25584-1

PUBLISHING HISTORY
Berkley Prime Crime mass-market edition / September 2013

PRINTED IN THE UNITED STATES OF AMERICA

10 9 8 7 6 5 4 3 2 1

Cover photos by Shutterstock.
Cover design by George Long.
Interior text design by Kelly Lipovich.

To John W. Holt. Technically you're only a brother by marriage, but after all these years, I'm keeping you.

Acknowledgments

It's always a challenge to start a new series and create a new world, so I need to thank a whole lot of people for their help:

My husband, Stephen P. Kelner, Jr., who I can always count on.

Charlaine Harris and Dana Cameron, the fastest beta readers in the West. Or East.

My daughters, Maggie and Valerie, for putting up with it all.

My agent, Joshua Bilmes, for endless support.

My editor, Ginjer Buchanan, for ideas I never would have thought of myself.

Dana Cameron again for insight into anthropology, knowledge of reference collections at universities and museums, and experiences from her life in academia.

B. K. Stevens, Rhea Paniesin, and Sara Weiss for sharing their knowledge of the trials and tribulations of adjunct faculty members.

Sue Senden for answering every stupid question about skeletons I could come up with.

David Kronen at Bone Clones, Inc. (www.boneclones .com) and Diana at The Bone Room (www.boneroom.com) for providing gloriously icky details about denuding skeletons. (Sadly, I didn't get all those details into this book, but there's always next time.)

Jan Dumas, for introducing me to her adorable keeshond, Byron, who inspired the fictional Akita of the same name.

My Facebook friends, who never failed when I needed to know about Angry Birds, pet doors, housebreaking dogs, and other gaps in my knowledge needed for this book.

I

Saturday Evening

If I'd ever had reason to consider the notion, I'd have been willing to bet that if I walked into a room that held a dead body, the body would have been the first thing I noticed. As it turned out, it wasn't even close.

In my defense, to say that the room was cluttered would have been an understatement. The bookshelves had overflowed and slopped books onto the floor, the walls were covered with maps and diagrams, and there were stacks of paper everywhere.

Besides, I hadn't gone looking for a corpse. Or rather, I hadn't gone looking for a whole one. I'd just wanted an arm bone, an ulna to be precise. Since said ulna had last been seen in the possession of a fluffy red dog with a creamy white tummy, my attention was initially all for that dog, who was comfortably situated in a doggy bed on the floor just by the door. The bed was made of wicker, with a plaid cushion, and I think the fact that I took note of that proves that I'm really not an unobservant person.

"Sid!" I called out. "I found the dog."

"Finally!" he replied, clattering down the hall. We were trying to be at least semi-stealthy, but Sid can't help rattling when he walks.

I know that every family has secrets. From friends I've heard whispered tales of ancestral bootleggers, draft dodgers, illegitimate offspring, and even more colorful characters. But somehow my family hit the jackpot. Our skeleton in the closet is literally a skeleton. A skeleton named Sid, who refuses to stay in the closet. He walks, he talks, and he makes bad bone jokes.

So naturally he finds it hard to walk quietly.

He stopped right behind me. "Uh, Georgia?"

"Don't worry—I'll get it." Sid isn't fond of any dog, for obvious reasons, and he was definitely not a fan of this particular one. The ulna it was chewing on was Sid's, and he needed it back.

I knelt down and patted the dog, who seemed pleased by the attention, at least enough to quit gnawing for a moment. One paw was still holding the ulna down, so I had to slide it out while patting with the other hand. It let the bone go a lot more easily than I'd expected, but then again, it's not like there was any meat left to hold canine interest for long.

Still patting, I held the ulna out behind my back so Sid could reach it, like passing the baton in a really strange relay race. A long moment later, he hadn't taken it from me. "Sid? You want this or not?"

"Georgia, stand up."

I did so, hoping the dog wouldn't make a grab for the ulna.

"Now look at the desk."

"What?" It was also covered with papers, surrounding an open laptop.

"The other side of the desk."

I leaned over, and when I saw somebody lying on the floor, I froze in place. Nobody was supposed to be home. Then I realized the woman wasn't moving. Her eyes were open and unblinking, and her face was bloodied.

All I could think of was that any minute a horde of cops was going to rush in, and I was going to have to explain what I was doing there with two dead people: a fresh one in front of me and a skeletal one behind me.

2

Sunday, Thirteen Days Earlier

The front door lock opened smoothly when I inserted the key, even though my parents had been out of the country for several months. Of course, my sister, Deborah, had been in to check on things, and she would never have allowed the front door of her own parents' house to squeak.

"Honey, we're home!" I sang out as I stepped into the foyer.

"One of these days somebody is going to answer you when you do that," Madison said as she followed me inside, "and you are going to have a heart attack."

"Then it's a good thing you learned CPR," I said. This time I'd had a particular reason for announcing our presence, but Madison didn't know that.

"It smells okay," she said, sniffing. "I thought it would be stuffy from being closed up."

"Your aunt has been keeping an eye on the place. She must have aired it out." Or somebody had.

Normally when we move into a new place, my teenage

daughter and I make a thorough inspection, planning where to put our belongings and checking for items we'll need, like curtains, rugs, and, in one memorable instance, a working toilet. This time we were already familiar with the layout of the old yellow Victorian house, from the comfortably worn living room furniture to the recently renovated downstairs bathroom to the wall of family photos hung in the dining room. After all, I'd grown up in the place.

My parents, both tenured English professors, were off on a dual sabbatical, and when they heard I'd landed a job at McQuaid University, they'd offered to let us live at the house. I'd only argued a little bit about their insistence that it be rent free—it was the second week of September, and I'd been without a job since the spring semester, so my bank account was getting a little lean.

Madison and I started bringing in our stuff and emptied the U-Haul trailer attached to my green minivan in fairly short order, partially because we'd done it so many times before and partially because we didn't really have that much stuff. Moving frequently has that effect.

Also, since we'd known the house had plenty of furniture, we'd sold or given away the junkiest of our stuff and were planning to store the rest in the basement.

"Why not use the attic?" Madison wanted to know on our third trip down the uneven concrete stairs. "Won't stuff mildew down here?"

"There's a dehumidifier, and it's better to climb one flight of steps down than two up," I said. "Besides, there's too much stored up there already." There was one particular thing in the attic that I wasn't going to be talking about.

Once everything was at least in the house, if not put away, we went to see if there was anything edible in the kitchen and found sandwich fixings, fresh fruit, and diet soda in the refrigerator; a loaf of bread in the breadbox; and a selection of basic supplies in the cabinet. As with the well-maintained lock, I recognized my sister's handiwork.

"It's going to be so cool living near Aunt Deb," Madison said as she reached for ham and mayonnaise.

"Fabulous," I said with far less enthusiasm.

"Hey, you know I love you best of all, Scarecrow!"

"Thanks for the reassurance, but that's not the problem. As an only child, you've been spared the experience of having a perfect big sister."

Deborah had her own successful business, never carried a balance on her credit cards, kept her car serviced and washed, and each year she had her tax returns sent in by the time the groundhog went looking for its shadow—all of which was in distinct contrast to my lifestyle. True, I'd pleased our parents by following their footsteps into the halls of academe, but being perennially untenured had tainted my image. The whole unwed-mother thing might have bothered them, too, had they not adored Madison unreservedly. Of course, Deborah claimed that Madison took after her.

After we'd eaten sandwiches with apples for dessert and had cleaned up nearly to Deborah's standards, we took the trailer back to the closest U-Haul depot to ensure there were no late charges. When we got back, I assumed we'd continue to unpack, but Madison asked, "Do you mind if I take a ride?" Her bike was always the last thing packed and the first thing unpacked, and not just because of logistics.

"I think what you're really wondering is: 'Can I toddle around and figure out where the cool kids hang out?'"

"Mom, we've been in Pennycross a jillion times. I already know where the cool kids hang out—or where they would if anybody used the word *cool* anymore. Let alone 'toddle.' Besides which, I have no interest in cool kids. I'm looking for my fellow nerds."

"Then you're going to Wray's." The combination comic-book store and game shop had been there since I was buying X-Men comics and twenty-sided dice. "Since that just happens to be next to Arturo's, you can bring your tired old mother some ice cream when you come back." I reached into my pocket and pulled out some money.

"Dark chocolate?"

"Do they make other flavors?"

"Rumor has it."

"These newfangled inventions . . . Speaking of which, be sure to take your cell phone."

"Please."

"Sorry." As if Madison wouldn't sooner leave the house without her jeans than without her phone. She gave me a quick kiss on the cheek and scooted out.

3

Once she was gone, I set up my laptop on the coffee table in the living room to make sure my parents' Internet connection was up and running and ended up getting caught in a flurry of e-mail. That meant I was concentrating on the screen and didn't see the door to the armoire behind me slowly drift open, and the noise of my typing masked the sound of movement as the skeletal figure emerged from the gaping blackness.

Had the worn oriental carpet not muffled the footsteps, I would have heard the feet scraping against the floor as the creature stepped into the room, even though his feet were bare.

In fact, they couldn't have been any more bare—bare of clothing, bare of skin, bare of anything—there was only bleached white bone from head to toe. Or rather, from skull to phalanges. Like something out of a nightmare, the skeleton moved across the floor.

It stepped toward my unprotected back, one fleshless arm reaching for me, but an instant before that mockery of a human hand touched my shoulder, I saw his reflection on my computer screen. "Sid! I'm working here."

"How did you know?" the skeleton demanded.

"How long have I known you?" I wasn't about to tell him about the reflection or he'd think of a way around it next time.

"Hey, can you blame me for wanting to jump your bones? Get it? Jump your *bones*?"

"I got it the first thousand times you made that joke, Sid, and it hasn't been funny since the first time." Then I reconsidered. "No, I giggled the second time, too." I sent off the e-mail I'd just finished typing, and said, "So do I get a hug or what?"

"I wasn't sure you'd care, since you didn't even bother to come up to the attic to see me."

"You weren't in the attic, were you?"

"But you didn't know that."

"I suspected," I lied. Years back, my parents had bought the battered but sturdy armoire for Sid to use as an emergency hiding place for those times when he couldn't get upstairs to the attic without being seen, and Deborah had installed locks inside and out so nobody could open it unexpectedly. In addition to hiding in there, Sid wasn't above using it for a spot of eavesdropping—his hearing was excellent despite his lack of ears.

"I had to wait to make sure that the coast was clear, which is your fault, since you're the one who wants to keep Madison from finding out about you."

He sniffed as if to say he suspected I'd been stalling.

It made no sense for a skeleton to sniff, but of course there wasn't anything about Sid that did make sense. When your best friend is a walking, talking human skeleton, you pretty much give up the expectation of logical explanations and just stick with the reality of his existence.

If I'd been older when Sid rescued me, I'd probably have been traumatized for life, but as a six-year-old I'd still firmly believed in Santa Claus, the Easter Bunny, and the Tooth Fairy. Adding an ambulatory skeleton to my roster of childhood heroes wasn't that much of a stretch. Though later evidence had proven to me that those other guys weren't real, Sid was still a part of my life.

I repeated, "Do I get a hug or not?"

"I suppose," he said, but the hug was more sincere than his words.

Hugging Sid is an unusual sensation. The closest thing I've ever felt to it was wrapping my arms around a really dried-out Christmas tree so I could lug it out to the street. Sid didn't have that nice a scent, but then again, he didn't leave an annoying trail of pine needles either.

"Did you lock the front door in case Madison comes back early?" Sid asked.

"No, but I will." I did so. "Sid, are you sure you want to play it like this? I know Madison is ready to hear about you."

Sid and I had agreed when Madison was born that it would be best if we waited to let them meet face-to-skull. It wasn't that he was overly terrifying in appearance—my father's great-aunt Margaret, who used a pound of white face powder a week and dyed her hair to the darkness of a black hole, was much scarier. We just didn't want to rely on a child to keep the secret of Sid's existence. But when Madison turned a mature ten, I was ready to introduce them during our annual visit to my parents. Sid vetoed it, and had continued to do so. He said he didn't want to disturb the status quo, that it was too much to put on her, that Madison was too young, that Madison was too old. The reasons just kept on coming, and I'd reluctantly respected his wishes, even if I didn't understand them. That didn't mean I'd given up, of course.

"Besides," I said, "it's going to be tough hiding you long-term without my parents to run interference if Madison hears anything suspicious from the attic. It'll be hard on you, too."

"Don't worry about me. I'll be extra quiet."

"But there's no reason to keep you secret. Madison isn't a little kid anymore. She can be trusted. Just wait until you get to know her."

"I'd like to," he said wistfully, "but let's not pile too much on her at once. Making new friends and settling into a new school is more than enough for a girl her age."

"She's used to changing schools, Sid." Though I wasn't proud of the fact that my employment record had meant she'd had to switch schools midyear more than once, I was glad that she didn't seem to have suffered from it. "She can handle—"

"How was the move?" Sid asked, firmly changing the subject.

I sighed. He was one stubborn bag of bones. "About the same as usual. We threw out as much as we kept, and I dropped a box of books on my foot. Then the landlord tried to stiff me on the security deposit, but I had photos of the day we moved in and could prove that the stains on the carpet predated us."

I'd had far too much experience with sneaky landlord tricks. Not that all landlords I'd had were bad people—we still exchanged Christmas cards with a couple—but because of my job, Madison and I usually lived in college towns, and dealing with college students can make even the most hospitable landlord turn cynical. "He finally admitted the place looked better than it had before we rented it and said he'd mail the deposit back, but when I pointed out that our lease said he had to pay on the day we moved out, he just happened to have a check in his pocket. Which I cashed before leaving town, just in case he tried to pull a fast one." Well, that and the fact that I needed the money to pay the VISA bill.

Before I could return to the subject of introducing Sid to Madison, he asked, "Ready to start your new job?"

"You have no idea." I'd nearly given up on finding a

teaching job for the fall—I'd thought I was all set for another year at the previous college, so being let go after writing up lesson plans for the summer session had caught me off guard.

"Why weren't you on tenure track, anyway?"

"You sound like Deborah."

"Sorry."

I waved it away. "It was the same old story. They gave me five sections of freshman expository writing each semester, with a textbook I hadn't worked with before, and I had a hundred essays to grade every week. With no assistant, of course. And even though I got top marks from the students and peer review, all they wanted to know was why I hadn't published any papers during the two years I was there. Apparently 'because I had to sleep' wasn't considered a legitimate excuse."

"That's insane. I have no brains at all—literally—and I can see that's insane."

"That's life in academia." Though I'd networked like crazy, I'd had no luck lining up a new job for the fall and had been filling in the gap by teaching high school students how to improve their SAT scores. Then one of McQuaid's instructors got an offer from a corporate education center that was lucrative enough to make her leave on short notice. I'd exchanged small talk and business cards with the department chair at a campus function last year, which is why he'd called me.

Since I was more than ready to leave that subject behind, I said, "Anyway, about Madison—" But, as if she'd heard my voice, I got a text from the fourteen-year-old herself: *On the way.* "Madison will be back in a few minutes. Are you sure . . . ?"

But Sid was already heading for the stairs. "Come up tomorrow after work. I want to know how it goes."

"Will do. You know—"

"I think she's here!"

He zipped up the stairs, and I zipped toward the door, but there was no Madison to be seen. He'd fooled me.

Time was when I could see right through Sid, metaphorically as well as physically, but somehow my best friend was hiding something.

4

The next day felt all too familiar.

I spent the first part of the morning getting Madison enrolled at Pennycross High School. The school was technically my alma mater, but they'd abandoned the century-old building where I'd attended classes some years back. So instead of nostalgia, I got déjà vu—the new building could have been half the schools Madison had attended. On the plus side, we knew everything we needed to know about the red tape involved in the transfer of paperwork and enrolling in classes. In fact, we knew the procedure better than the school's vice principal, who was looking a bit dazed by the time Madison gave me a big hug and kiss good-bye. Well, actually she waved, and said, "Later!" but for a teenager, that was a display of affection to be treasured and posted about on Facebook.

Thanks to our efficiency, it was still early when I got to the McQuaid campus, which was considerably more recognizable to me than the high school. Unlike me, my parents had both been granted tenure early on in their careers, which meant that they'd been teaching at the same college since I was in junior high school.

They'd been trying to get me a job there for years, but the timing had never worked out—either I had what I thought would be a long-term position when something opened up at McQuaid, or McQuaid had just hired somebody when I was looking for work, or one of my parents had been serving in some capacity in which the hiring of their own daughter would be suspect.

I hadn't been overly disturbed by the situation because I wasn't convinced that I wanted to teach in the same department where my parents were regarded as twin pinnacles of academic achievement. This time, it was different. For one thing, my parents were on sabbatical for several more months and, given my luck, I might be gone before they got back. For another, there was nothing like the prospect of a year of coaching anxious high school students in test-taking techniques to shift my standards.

That edge of desperation was part of why I was wearing my best navy blue suit for this meeting, even though the adjunct job was supposed to be in the bag—I didn't want Dr. Hardison Parker to think I was cocky. The shiny red leather briefcase I was carrying instead of my usual soft-sided bag was to convince him that I wasn't desperate.

Parking is a perennial problem at any college, and McQuaid had it worse than most. They'd recently embarked on a massive building campaign, so a good chunk of the parking was currently being taken up by construction equipment. Fortunately I'd noticed my parents' parking hang tags in the basket of mail that Deborah had been collecting for them, and I'd grabbed one. So I parked in one of the conveniently located faculty spaces instead of tromping across campus in heels, hoping not to sweat in the surprisingly warm fall day.

Since the English Department was one of the largest departments at McQuaid, it had its offices in a prime spot in Benson Hall, the most picturesque building on campus. It was, in fact, pretty much the only picturesque building. McQuaid had never had a school of architecture, and it showed in the brick-and-concrete monstrosities that made up most of the campus. Therefore Benson was featured on the college letterhead and on every year's brochure for freshmen because it had all the traditional trappings of a New England college building—the clapboard, the columns, the ivy. Unfortunately it also had the steep stairs, antiquated electrical system, and tiny bathrooms. Charm doesn't come cheap.

Mrs. Speed, the English Department secretary, who was only slightly younger than the building, was looking discontentedly at her computer screen when I stepped inside the office. I'd always thought she figured that if she looked happy, people might ask her to do more work.

"Hello, Mrs. Speed," I said. "I'm here for my appointment with Dr. Parker."

After I'd stood there an awkward minute, she said, "Want me to tell him you're here?"

"Yes, please."

She turned her head almost half an inch, and said loudly, "The Thackery girl is here." In a slightly lower voice she said, "Go on in."

Dr. Parker offered a reasonably firm, low-moisture handshake from across his desk. He was a slender man with the large forehead and carefully gelled hair of a man trying to disguise a receding hairline. His eyes bulged just a touch more than was ideal.

We exchanged greetings, and Parker said, "Good to see you again, Ms. Thackery. It is still Thackery?"

"Yes, sir." It was still *Doctor*, too, but I wasn't going to press the point.

"Perhaps we should begin with you explaining your background and qualifications."

"Certainly. If it will help, I have a copy of my CV." I

pulled it out of my briefcase and handed it to him, not bringing up the fact that I'd sent him one the previous week. Printing out fresh copies of my curriculum vitae was a habit forged by experience.

The next hour was standard for such interviews. He asked a bevy of questions about my specialty in literature—contemporary American, with particular interest in popular culture—even though it was completely meaningless for the job. Except for very rare instances, adjuncts were stuck with freshman composition courses.

I'd be teaching the usual five sections: three one-hour sections meeting on Mondays, Wednesdays, and Fridays; and two one-and-a-half hour sections on Tuesdays and Thursdays. Though five sections were going to be a lot of work, I would have loved one more. Six sections would have meant full-time pay and benefits, even if I wasn't in a tenure track job, but with five, I got nearly as much work without any benefits. If I weren't living in my parents' house, I'd have had to teach online courses, too, just to make ends meet.

At least Parker didn't try to play games with my pay—prices for adjunct faculty are standard, and in no way dependent on experience or level of skill. I'd make the same pitiful amount per credit hour if I was still working on my dissertation or if I'd been teaching for twenty years.

After that lukewarm welcome, Parker sent me to the university human resources office to deal with the requisite paperwork, and after a solid hour of filling out forms, I was officially McQuaid faculty. I stopped at the school's Hamburger Haven, making use of my brand-new faculty ID to get a discount. The food was fine, but I was almost certain I detected a sniff of disdain when the cashier saw ADJUNCT on my ID.

I keep expecting some college to adopt the idea of a big red A embroidered on the bosom of each adjunct. It would be both demeaning and literary, which was a rare combination.

While eating, I read over the packet labeled *Welcome Aboard, Adjunct!* In a cloying style, it told me how glad McQuaid was to have me and outlined the responsibilities and benefits of the job. There were far more responsibilities, of course, with required office hours and time sheets to be filled out weekly and grades to be turned in seconds after the last class ended. The benefits section mostly described the food discount I was already taking advantage of, the faculty parking hang tag that could be used by me and nobody else but me, and my choice of desks in the office I'd be sharing with the university's other adjunct faculty members.

The adjunct office was my next stop. It was in the basement of the student center, a location that was equally inconvenient for all departments. The door was wooden, with a small panel of translucent glass and a badly printed sign. There was a battered coatrack on one side of the door and a row of office mailboxes on the other. Judging from the wide variety of name labels stuck, taped, and stapled onto the mail slots, apparently I was going to have to provide my own.

I stopped to look at the names, hoping for a few familiar ones. A bonus to being an adjunct was that I rarely worked at a college where I didn't know somebody, or at least have connections. In this case, I recognized the names of four friendly acquaintances from previous jobs before I realized somebody was standing next to me.

"Dr. Thackery," a man said in a pleased baritone. "What a delightful surprise."

"Dr. Peyton. You're looking as dapper as ever."

Dapper isn't a word I use every day, but it's pretty much the only way to describe Charles Peyton. He was wearing a tweed suit and vest with an honest-to-God watch chain hanging out of one pocket. His hair was perfectly arranged without visible use of product, and the streaks of gray only added to his look of distinction. His shoes were shined to a blinding gloss, and his mustache was neatly trimmed. In a word: *dapper*.

He made a slight bow that would have looked either mocking or coy if performed by anybody else. "A man does what he must in order not to be completely overshadowed by beauty like yours."

"Charles, you are a boon to womankind." That's the kind of guy Charles is—he had me using the word *boon*. "If I'd known you were teaching here, I'd have come sooner."

"Dear lady, you make my day complete."

"What classes did they stick you with?"

"Here at McQuaid, two sections of Colonial American, one Revolutionary American. At Joshua Tay University, I've got one Vietnam era, and one Scandinavian."

Charles was a historian who specialized in the Pax Britannica, 1815 to 1914, so naturally he ended up teaching courses for every era and country but that. Having to divide his time between two different campuses made it even more annoying, but sometimes it was the only way for an adjunct to get a full course load. I'd had to do the same one long year.

"I've got composition," I said. "Again."

"I'm sure you'll teach it admirably. Have you been made aware of our customs here at McQuaid?"

"I just got here."

"Then please, let me assist you. Obviously, these are our mailboxes. If you don't have a label of your own, I would be happy to provide one."

"I think Mrs. Speed from the English Department is planning to take care of that right away."

He raised one eyebrow.

"I know. As if. A label would be great."

Charles said, "The coatrack is reasonably secure for coats and hats, but I would hesitate to leave anything more than that. Umbrellas tend to disappear."

"Thanks for the warning."

"Now let us proceed into our humble abode. Emphasis on humble, I'm afraid."

As Charles and I went inside, the noise level rose to

alarming levels. Inside the large room were rows of desks of differing vintages, either scarred wood, dented metal, or chipped Formica. There was a hodgepodge of chairs, trash-cans, and other office furnishings, and I estimated that the walls hadn't been painted in ten years. About half of the thirty desks were currently occupied with people working on their laptops, talking on cell phones, or grading papers. One poor guy was trying to meet with a student in the back corner.

Having a desk of one's own is in the mid-range for adjunct treatment. The best schools provide private offices, even if they're tiny. One step down is two or three adjuncts to an office. A step below the assigned desk at McQuaid would be a shared office with unassigned tables recycled from the cafeteria, in which one would have to arm wrestle for work space, and bribery would be needed to get an outlet for a laptop.

Sadly that isn't even the bottom rung. One school hadn't provided me with any kind of office space, which forced me to work in a corner of the library.

Charles said, "The desk chart is here. Feel free to claim any empty square."

On the wall was a white board with a shaky floor plan of the office on it, which I suspected was drawn by some-body other than an adjunct from the Art Department. Names were scrawled on most of the blocks representing desks, but I saw three empty spots. "Any advice?" I asked Charles.

"Hmm . . ." He put his hand on his chin. "I wouldn't recommend the one in the back. The instructors to either side have rather strong voices."

In other words, they were loud enough to disrupt my work.

He went on. "The one in the center has a tendency to be encroached upon." He didn't need to tell me that people had been known to expand their areas an inch at a time in order to grab a little extra real estate. "I'd choose this one. It's next to the wall, giving you a modicum of privacy, and the desk is in decent shape. The chair isn't, but if you trade with the chair from the desk in the back, it should be adequate."

"Sounds good," I said, and found a marker to put my name on the grid. "I'm surprised somebody hasn't moved up to it. Looks like a prime location."

"Ah, yes, well . . ." He looked significantly at a brunette with shoulder-length hair sitting in the desk in front of the one I'd just picked. Charles rarely says something negative about another adjunct, so his silence said all I needed to know. The woman—Sara Weiss, according to the desk grid—was not going to be an ideal neighbor.

I lowered my voice. "What's the downside?"

"Oh, she's a fine scholar, I'm sure, but she can be a tad . . . inquisitive."

"I can deal." I'd had nosy office-mates before.

"Then let me introduce you." Charles walked me over and said, "Dr. Weiss, may I introduce Dr. Thackery?"

"Hi," she said, looking me over. "What department?"

"English. And you?"

"Biology."

Not only did Sara have a plum desk location, she even had a hook on which to hang her coat. Her desk wasn't bad, either.

"You've been here awhile," I guessed.

"Six years. How many classes did they give you?"

"Five."

"The usual."

Charles said, "Let me trade chairs for you." He rolled away the lopsided one that had been behind my desk.

"You hooked up with Charley pretty quick," Sara said, making it sound distasteful.

"Charles and I go way back. I think this is the third time we've been at the same school. No, the fourth."

"Is it true that he's rich and only teaches for fun?"

"That's the rumor." It wasn't true, but I'd never bothered to enlighten anybody with the real story.

"He must be rich," she said. "Look at how he dresses, how he acts. And his car! He's taking the bread out of the mouths of people who need it."

"He's an excellent teacher, and he does the work," I said. "Why shouldn't he get paid for it? It's not like any of us get paid all that much anyway."

"She speaks the truth!" said a scrawny specimen with hipster glasses who was passing by. "New hire?"

"Georgia Thackery, English."

"Bob Hewitt, Español."

"Buenos días."

"Not even a little bueno. I've got to give an oral test to twenty of the worst linguists I've ever encountered. Welcome aboard, and here's hoping you escape soon."

"Bob is having a bad week," Charles said diplomatically after the other man scurried away. He'd returned with a chair that looked a lot more comfortable than the previous one, and a label on which he'd already written my name in beautiful cursive. I was willing to bet he'd used a fountain pen, too. "I'll affix this to a mailbox while you settle in. I would very much enjoy catching up with you further, but I have to attend to some test papers. How about lunch on Thursday?"

"That sounds great."

He went out long enough to put the sticker on for me, then proceeded to his desk, nodding amiably at everybody he passed.

I looked over my new desk. On top were a stack of composition books, a bunch of papers, and three empty Starbucks cups.

"Excuse me, but do these things belong to anybody?" I said to the room at large.

Nobody answered, and Sara was looking at her computer screen with exaggerated concentration.

"Does anybody know who this stuff belongs to?" I said more loudly.

Still no response.

"Okay." I grabbed the comp books and papers and carried them outside to leave next to the mailboxes. The coffee cups I tossed in the nearest trash can.

Then I looked through the desk drawers. All of the useful supplies were long gone, of course, but I did find that my file drawer was half-filled with stuffed hanging folders. "Does anybody know—?" I started to say.

Sara said, "Those are mine. I'm short on file room. You don't mind if I leave them there, do you?"

"Sorry, but I need the space," I said, trying to sound sympathetic even though I wasn't. If Sara had been an adjunct for six years, then she knew darned well it wasn't acceptable to poach on other people's desk space. Shared offices get territorial, and I'd long since learned that it was best to lift my leg and lay claim to my territory right off the bat.

I pulled out the whole bundle, and tried to hand it to her, but she wouldn't take it.

"Do we have to do this now?" she snapped. "I'm busy!"

"No problem. Do you want them on top of your desk or on the floor?"

She gave me an evil look, flung open her own file drawer, and pulled out her purse, of all things. Once that was gone, there was plenty of room for the files. "Just put them in here!"

I was tempted to put them in backward, but in the interest of our new friendship, I put them in properly, even straightening a folder that had become misaligned in transit. She was still glaring at me, so I don't think she appreciated my forbearance.

I went back to my desk and pulled out my laptop to check e-mail and found that Mrs. Speed had already sent me class times and locations, lesson plans, and student records for the classes I was going to teach. Dr. Parker had wanted me to start that very day, but I'd pointed out that I didn't know what the classes were working on, so I'd need a couple of days to get up to speed. Since it was Monday, I would start first thing on Wednesday.

First thing meant eight thirty in the morning—adjuncts get all the early morning classes. I'd be teaching classes at eight thirty, two o'clock, and four o'clock on Mondays, Wednesdays, and Fridays, and at eight thirty and ten thirty on Tuesdays and Thursdays. So much for sleeping in.

Fortunately for my class planning, my predecessor hadn't done anything particularly tricky in her lesson plans—she'd been sticking with the vanilla synopses in the textbook. That would make it easy for me, if not particularly interesting, and I was making notes about upcoming assignments when Sara said, "Thackery . . . Aren't there some other Thackerys teaching here?"

"My parents are in the English Department, too, but they're on sabbatical this year."

"Tenured, of course," she said, which was obvious. Adjuncts don't get sabbaticals. When we take time off from work, it's without benefit of pay or the knowledge that our jobs will be waiting for us. "I'm surprised they didn't pull strings to get you on full-time."

It wasn't really a question, so I didn't feel the need to answer. The fact was I'd never asked Mom and Phil to pull strings. Some days I wasn't sure if I was principled or just an idiot.

"And don't they have an office you could use so you wouldn't have to be in here?" Sara pressed.

"What, and miss the fun of being with you guys?" I said. I probably would end up using Mom and Phil's adjoining offices at some point, but I knew it was important to maintain ties with my fellow adjuncts. Besides which, I knew Sara just wanted my file drawer back, and I didn't want to give her the satisfaction.

"Why are my comp books out in the hall?" a voice suddenly boomed.

Sara smirked and pretended to go back to what she'd been doing.

A man much less dapper than Charles stomped in,

carrying the detritus I'd left by the mailboxes. He was around my age, with black hair and dark eyes, and would have been cute if he hadn't been scowling. Actually, he was pretty cute with the scowl, though I doubted he'd appreciate being told that.

"Oh, are those yours?" I asked as he made his way to the desk next to mine, which was nearly covered with books and papers. "I asked, but nobody seemed to know."

He shot a look at Sara, whose smirk melted. "I was told the space was available," he said.

"I was told the same thing, which is why I put my name on the desk grid and moved in." I stuck out my hand. "Georgia Thackery, English."

He looked at his desk, then put the books onto his chair to offer his hand in return. "Fletcher Wildman, journalism."

"Fletcher is only teaching one class," Sara said. "He's got a full-time reporting job at the *Pennycross Gazette*."

"First adjunct job?" I asked.

"How can you tell?"

"It doesn't take us long to either learn how to squeeze our stuff in or to find storage space at home. Don't worry. You'll pick it up." I patted one corner of my desk. "You can stack those comp books here for now. I won't need the space for a couple of days." Then I raised my voice to make sure Sara heard me as I said, "I'll be moving my files in right away, of course." I could forgive Fletcher for making a rookie mistake, but she had no excuse.

"No, thanks—I'll manage," he said, sounding miffed.

"Suit yourself." I went back to my work. Fifteen minutes later, I saw that Fletcher was standing with a bunch of folders in one hand and that same stack of composition books in the other. "Um, Georgia?" he said. "If you're sure you don't mind . . ."

"No problem," I said.

"Thanks."

I shouldn't have enjoyed watching him trying to organize

his desk, but I did, and it wasn't just schadenfreude. I couldn't help but wonder how he'd accumulated so much stuff in less than a semester, when he was only teaching one class. I probably wouldn't have that much with my five.

I checked my watch, decided it was time to skedaddle, and packed up my laptop. "Later, folks," I said to the room at large. Nobody answered, but then again, we'd hardly had time to bond.

Fletcher did say, "Georgia, I take it you've been an adjunct before."

"Oh, yes, I'm a longtime proponent of the adjunct lifestyle."

"Do you think we could talk sometime? I could use some pointers."

I couldn't tell if he was just asking for help with work or something more personal, but I was willing to roll with either. "Sure. You can leave me a message in my mailbox, of course, or you can call me." I glanced at his desk just long enough to see that it was a lost cause, then pulled a pad out of my briefcase to write down my number.

I noticed that Sara was looking even crankier than before, and I assumed that Fletcher hadn't asked her for pointers. That put a bit of a spring in my step. Unfortunately, it didn't last. On the long walk back to my van, all I could think of was that I was most definitely getting to be an old hand at being an adjunct. The way things were going, I was likely to be one forever.

5

I wouldn't always be able to pick Madison up from school—most of the time she'd have to walk or bike—but since it was her first day, I'd promised her a ride home. Besides, I wanted to hear about her day.

"Hi, Mom," Madison said, jumping into the van with her backpack far more filled than it had been that morning.

"How'd it go?"

"Great! I love this school. It's only a couple of years old, and most of the tech actually works. Only I guess the chemistry teacher doesn't like the smart board—supposedly he spilled some chemicals on it by accident, but Samantha says everybody knows he did it on purpose."

"Samantha?"

"You'll love her. She was the first one who spoke to me at lunch, and she was wearing a Studio Ghibli T-shirt and had a Totoro backpack. She said there are other *otaku* in school, too, and she's going to introduce me to them."

Fortunately for my relationship with my daughter, I speak a few phrases of manga and anime, enough to recognize a famous Japanese animator, his most beloved character, and the Japanese word for anime and manga fans.

"Did you meet any teachers, or were they not wearing the right T-shirts?"

She gave me her best exasperated look, which was quite good, thanks to years of practice. "I like all of the teachers so far, except for the French teacher, so I'm going to see if I can switch to Spanish, which Samantha says is more fun. And yes, my English teacher is the best one."

"All English teachers are the best."

"Anyway, Ms. Rad—Nobody can pronounce her last name, so they call her Ms. Rad. And she's really funny and perky, which nobody understands because she specializes in Holocaust literature."

"Not *The Boy in the Striped Pajamas* again!" One of the curses of switching schools was that there were some books Madison had missed completely, while others she'd read multiple times.

"They did it for summer reading, so I'm in the clear, but we're doing *The Crucible* in the spring."

"Second time?"

"Third."

"Yow."

"It's okay—I'll deal. Ms. Rad is so much better than the last two teachers."

She chattered on about the people she'd met, joining the drama club, and how the cafeteria was much better than most. And with every bit of excitement, my heart sank. It wasn't that I didn't like her to be happy, but it killed me to see her put down roots, knowing they'd be ripped up when I had to change jobs.

We stopped at the grocery store on the way home to pick up dinner supplies, and Madison's cell phone rang just as we got back to the house. Samantha, of course. I let Madison off the hook for unloading duties, so she ran off to her room to talk while I put things away. Then I unpacked a few more boxes while she did her homework, all the while wondering if it was worth the trouble if I was going to have to repack everything in a few months.

I tried to pull myself out of my funk by fixing sloppy joes, one of Madison's favorites. It was a pleasure to have a full-size kitchen to ramble around in, rather than the tiny kitchenettes I usually got stuck with as an apartment dweller. Even better, every single eye on the stove actually worked.

While the sloppy joe mix was simmering, I toasted rolls and tossed a fresh-from-a-bag salad. Then it was time to ring the dinner bell. Which is to say that I texted Madison—since she did homework with her headphones on, yelling wouldn't have done the job, but she always had her phone within reach.

A minute later she clomped down the stairs. "Mom, great news!"

"You finished your homework?"

"Better!"

"You finished your homework for the week? The month? The year?"

"Mom!"

"Tell me while you set the table."

She got silverware out from the drawer. "Samantha says Mangachusetts is this weekend!"

"That's fabulous! Or it would be if I knew what you were talking about."

"Mangachusetts is a local manga and anime conference, and Samantha wants me to come and meet her there."

At first it had amused me that my strawberry blonde, green-eyed daughter was so enamored of Japanese comic books and animation, but I soon found that manga and anime heroines actually resembled Madison as often as not. Though I didn't share her fondness for the form, we had a mutual respect pact: I didn't mock Naruto or Goku and she didn't mock the X-Men.

"Where is it?" I said. Travel expenses and a weekend at a hotel did not have a place in my current budget.

"Here in town! At McQuaid!"

She went on to tell me who the guests were going to be, how many people she'd be able to meet, and what fun it would be, winding up with the fact that the registration fee was terribly reasonable when I took into account that it was two whole days' worth of entertainment.

As it turned out, the price really was semi-reasonable, and I was able to give permission without having to check the bottom of my purse for spare change. In fact, Madison's excitement was so contagious that I decided to attend, too. It's always been my view that families should geek out together.

The rest of the evening was taken up with homework for her and unpacking for me. That meant I never got a chance to visit Sid, but I was sure he'd understand.

6

S id didn't understand.

"So what if I waited for hours, hoping you'd find a few spare seconds for me?" Sid said in an aggrieved tone. "There's no need to worry about me staying up all night."

I'd gone upstairs as soon as Madison had biked off to school, and I was just as aggrieved that he didn't appreciate it. "Number one, you don't sleep. Number two, you were reading the Harry Potter series again, so you weren't exactly bored." The stack of books was teetering right next to his chair, so it hadn't been hard to figure that out.

"Coccyx, I meant to put those up!" When I'd been a kid, my mother had told Sid his language was too salty, so he'd come up with his own invective. If a bone's name just happened to sound dirtier than it was, so much the better.

"Anyway, you know it's not going to be easy for me to sneak up here with Madison in the house. If you'd just let me introduce you two—"

"I'm not ready for that."

"But why—?"

"Tell me about the job! Did Parker put you on the tenure track right away, or does he want you to prove yourself for a while first?"

As distractions went, it was a good one. I sighed, and said, "Don't get too used to having me around, bone boy. I'm good for the rest of this semester, and I think next, but after that there's no telling where I'll be."

"Don't give up yet! A tenure-track job could open up at any moment."

"As much as I would like to see that, and to put a video of the event on YouTube, it wouldn't make any difference. Once you're an adjunct, that's all you ever are."

"I don't believe it! You're smart, you're a fabulous teacher, and you are going to get your dream job soon. I just know it."

"You're awfully optimistic for a dead guy."

"I can't help it. It's the time of year. The first day of school. New books and crayons. The smell of chalk and freshly varnished floors!"

"Dude, it's not even close to the first day of school, nobody uses chalk in college, and I don't think anybody varnishes tile floors."

"Then what does it smell like?"

"Desperation. Students who want to do well, grad students finishing their dissertations, researchers who need results to keep their grants—"

"Adjuncts who are afraid they won't have a job next semester?"

I nodded. "God, Sid, I hate this. Madison is already settling in and I know she's hoping to keep the same batch of friends for two years in a row. I'm afraid she's going to ask for a dog again."

"A dog?" he said, sounding worried, as well he might.

We tend to keep Sid away from dogs, because dogs tend to have one of two reactions to him. The most common is stark terror, as the dog recognizes that something is walking around that really shouldn't be. Less frequently, we encoun-

ter a dog who thinks that he and Sid should have the traditional dog-bone relationship.

I said, "Most kids want games and clothes and computers—
all my kid wants is a freaking home, and I can't even give her
that."

"Come on, Georgia, it'll work out—it always does."

"My life doesn't work out, Sid. I scrape by, that's all. I
wouldn't even be doing that if Mom and Phil and Deborah
weren't helping me all the time."

"I'd help if I could—"

"You do help! You're the only one I can blow off steam
with. I would have exploded years ago if it weren't for you."
The fact that I'd moved so often meant I didn't have many
close friends, and while my family was supportive, they
didn't understand what I was up against. My parents thought
all I had to do was work hard, and maybe whip out a research
project, and a school would snap me up in a second. Deborah
thought I should get a job doing something else, which might
be reasonable if I knew how to do anything else.

"I know what you need," Sid said. "You need a movie!
Toy Story? Toy Story 2? We haven't had a chance to watch
Toy Story 3 together."

"Sid, I have work to do. I don't have time for a movie."

But he'd already turned on the TV and stuck in a DVD.

"Fine," I said grudgingly. "I'll watch part of it with you,
but don't expect me to cheer up." I watched it all, of course,
and damned if it didn't cheer me up.

Though I'd intended to go over to McQuaid to work, I
ended up lugging my laptop to the attic and hanging with
Sid while I prepped for my first batch of classes.

It was cozy being up in the attic with him, actually. Sid
has a comfortable setup, better than many of my apartments.
He doesn't need a bed, but he has a couch, an armchair, a
table, and an attic's worth of storage. For entertainment he
has a TV with a DVD player, a boom box, and plenty of
books.

Sid was clearly delighted to have company for the day. Technically, of course, he was always smiling, because he didn't have lips, and he was short on facial expressions in general for obvious reasons. But I know how to read him, and I could tell he was happy. I did my best to be happy, too, and not think about him being somebody else I'd disappoint if I had to move to find another job.

7

By the end of the day Wednesday, Madison and I were feeling comfortably at home. I'd seen her off to school, had a quick visit with Sid, and gone to meet my first crew of students. Since I was picking up the class in midstream, I didn't have to explain much in the way of a syllabus or expectations, but I did announce my office hours. After seeing that adjunct trying to meet with a student in the middle of the cattle pen, I'd decided to use my parents' office for such occasions. As nepotism went, it was fairly mild.

There was some grumbling in the morning class about them having to turn in an essay that week, what with the change in regime and having missed a class on Monday. So after a little wrangling, I let them off the hook. They left feeling happy and listened to, and I was just as glad that I'd have less work while I got into the swing of things. To ensure the other classes felt equally empowered, I allowed them to grumble their way to the same compromise.

In between classes, I made a couple of appearances at the adjunct office to drop off some stuff I'd brought from home, and saw with approval that Fletcher had found a way to handle his storage problems that did not involve my space.

I also took the opportunity to renew acquaintances with a physicist I'd worked with the year before and a psychologist I'd dated one term a few years earlier. It had just been an adjunct romance, and had ended amicably when he'd gotten a new job. Though he was a nice guy and a skilled kisser, I wasn't particularly interested in renewing the relationship and was just as happy when he mentioned he was seeing a French instructor.

All in all I was pleased with the day's accomplishments, enough so that when Madison swore she'd finished her homework and asked permission to accompany new BFF Samantha to Wray's for the weekly Yu-Gi-Oh! tournament, I cheerfully gave permission and money for her to grab a sub for dinner. I thought it would give me a chance to get some work done. Unfortunately, it also gave Sid another chance to try to sneak up on me as I worked at the coffee table.

This time I heard him coming down the stairs from the attic—those bony feet of his aren't exactly stealthy on bare wood steps.

I waited until he was just a couple of feet behind me before saying, "Hi, Sid."

"Coccyx! Why won't your parents carpet the stairs?"

"How many times have you tried to sneak up on them?"

"None," he said. "They're no fun to surprise."

I stopped typing for a second—that had sounded a bit forlorn. "Are you not getting along with Mom and Phil?"

"Of course I am. They're great. So, what are you working on?"

"Subtle segue there."

"I get along fine with your parents," he said firmly. "They're just busy, that's all."

"If you say so," I said, resolving to ask my mother what was going on the first chance I got. "Anyway, I'm just putting together some notes for my next class."

"Let me help." He removed his skull from atop his shoulders and placed it onto my more normally fleshed version. "You know what they say: two heads are better than one."

"Sid!"

"You missed a word in the second sentence." Unlike most people, Sid could continue to talk when his head was detached.

"I was just about to fix that," I said, "and I'd get this done a lot faster if you'd stop bugging me."

"Okay, okay." Sid put his skull back onto his neck, but continued to watch. "You misspelled *accommodate*."

"Coccyx!" Great. I was reverting—I could curse whenever I wanted to. Whenever the *hell* I wanted to. I made the correction as Sid wandered over to where my mother had covered the wall with an assortment of framed family pictures. There were pictures of Deborah and me growing up, my parents at academic functions, school pictures of Madison, and of course shots of Madison's bravura performances in *The Sound of Music* and *Guys and Dolls*.

"You and Madison need to get a new picture," Sid said.

"Uh-huh," I said, still trying to work.

"She's really grown."

"Uh-huh."

"I think she's turning green."

"No, she's not, and yes, I'm listening." I typed a last bit of punctuation and announced, "I'm done. What do you want, Sid?"

"Can't I just come down to visit?"

"Theoretically, but if there's one thing being a mother has taught me, it's when somebody wants something. And you want something."

"Actually, I did want to ask a favor. I heard you and Madison talking about that anime convention—"

"Do you have the house miked?"

"Eavesdropping is my hobby. Anyway, I was wondering if you'd take me, too."

"Since when do you know anything about that stuff?"

"Since Madison left all her manga here last summer."

With our frequent moves, Mom and Phil let both Madison and me use their house to store anything too big or too heavy to lug along from apartment to apartment. Madison's collection of Japanese comics was both, and once it had been left in the house, it was fair game for Sid.

"I've got a costume all worked out," Sid said. "I can be Shinigami from *Soul Eater*. You know who that is, right?"

"Nope. Manga is Madison's thing. If you want to talk X-Men—"

"I haven't got the build for Wolverine or Emma Frost, thanks just the same, but I can do Shinigami. He's Lord Death. So, skull head, which I've already got, and all I need you to get for the rest is some black cloth to make a robe, some wire, and some foam rubber."

"Sid, I know you like getting out of the house, but this isn't like Halloween." While I'd lived at home, I'd taken Sid out trick-or-treating every year. "It'll be inside and well-lit and crowded. Plus Madison will be there. I don't think—"

I stopped when he started making Bambi eyes at me—which shouldn't have worked, since he hasn't got eyes—but he was doing a creditable job until we heard somebody at the front door.

Sid immediately skittered into his armoire.

I went into the hall, expecting to see Madison. Instead my sister Deborah was closing the door behind her.

"It's just Deborah," I called out to Sid.

"Glad to see you, too," Deborah said.

"I'm always glad to see a guest who rings the door like a normal person. People who walk into my home uninvited, not so much."

"It's my parents' house, too."

"Granted, but they are not currently in residence, and I am. Gimme the key."

"Fine," she said, handing it over. "I don't need it anyway."

That was true enough—she could probably pick the lock as quickly as I could find a key in my purse.

"So, are you going to invite me in?"

"Oh, elder sister, how blessed am I that you condescend to grace my humble abode with your most bountiful presence. Pray step in and take full part of those small pleasures that I delight in offering you."

"That's more like it." She went into the living room and plopped down in the most comfortable chair.

It's not that I don't like Deborah, and probably vice versa, but we don't have a Hallmark-card kind of relationship.

Sid climbed out of the armoire and sat on the couch. "Deb! How do you like my new haircut?"

She ignored him, as usual. I don't think I'd seen my sister directly address Sid since she graduated from high school, at which point she'd apparently decided that Sid's existence was impossible and therefore not worth acknowledging, but Sid never gave up. I gave him a sympathetic pat as I sat next to him.

To me, Deborah said, "You and Madison all settled in?"

"Pretty much. She's off checking out the Yu-Gi-Oh! competition at the games store. Not playing mind you, just watching the other players to see who might be worth her time."

"That's my girl!" Deborah said, and I resisted the impulse to snap that she was *my* girl. Deborah and Madison were as affectionate as Deborah and I weren't, and I didn't want to get between them. Well, maybe I did, but I knew I shouldn't.

"Thanks for stocking the kitchen for us. What do I owe you for groceries?"

"My treat. I wasn't sure when you'd get your first paycheck, and I wanted to make sure you two wouldn't go hungry."

"I'm not broke, Deborah."

"It's been a while between jobs, right?"

"Yes, but I've been doing some test-prep tutoring—"

She waved it away. "Don't sweat it. Business is booming, thanks to our spree of break-ins." Only locksmiths like Deborah and the local newspaper cheered at break-ins. "You can return the favor if our positions are ever reversed."

The words were right, but I could have done without the unspoken follow-up of *as if that would ever happen*. Since I wasn't sure if it was Deborah who wasn't saying it or me, I did say, "Thank you. It is appreciated."

"You never bring me groceries, Deb," Sid said. "And just look at me. I'm down to skin and bones! Minus the skin."

Again, she didn't so much as look at him, and he threw up his hands in disgust. Literally. He managed to catch the right one again, but the left one hit the floor, so I picked it up and handed it back to him.

"How was the locksmith convention?" I asked. Had it not been for the convention taking her to Chicago, she'd have been around to help Madison and me move in. And by *help*, I meant that she'd have tried to get us to do it her way. Violence might have ensued. I was very grateful for that convention.

"Not bad. Met some people, picked up some swag, learned some things, and got drunk. The usual."

"Have you eaten? Madison ate out, and I was thinking about calling for pizza."

"I'd die for an order of ribs," Sid tossed in.

"No, thanks," Deborah said. "I just stopped by on the way home. I've got to get caught up on paperwork. I was behind even before the trip, and my assistant is great, but he can't work a spreadsheet to save his life."

"I'm always available for data entry," Sid offered. No response, but Sid was nothing if not persistent. "Hey, why don't you hang around and help me design my costume for Mangachusetts? I'm going to be Lord Death, and—"

"Sid!" I said. He knew I hadn't agreed to take him to the con, but Deborah spoke up before I could say so.

"Seriously, Georgia? You're going to hang out with that crowd of costumed weirdos?"

"Including your niece," I said icily.

"It's fine for kids," she conceded, "but you're not a kid. It's going to be at the college, right? What if somebody sees you there? How is that going to look?"

"Actually there's some serious scholarship going on in that area. At last year's Popular Culture Association conference, there were more than a dozen talks about manga and anime."

"Yeah, and if you ever start publishing papers, that'll mean something."

That stung, mostly because it was true. Deborah may have run as far as she could from the halls of academe, but not before she'd absorbed the mantra of *publish or perish.* I had much more practice at perishing, but would have argued the point if she hadn't gone on.

"Besides," she said, "what if you get caught with . . . ? What if somebody sees . . . ? What if somebody sees *him*?"

"You mean Sid?"

"You know who I mean."

"Then use his name." Naturally, since Deborah was arguing against it, I instantly changed my mind about taking him to the con. "Anyway, you heard *Sid*—he'll be in costume. I used to take him out for Halloween every year and it was never a problem, so what's the big deal? You can come with us if you like."

"Please. I've got better things to do with my time." She started toward the door. "Lock up when I'm gone. You can't be too careful in the house alone."

"She's not alone!" Sid said. "What am I, chopped liver? I mean, I don't even have a liver!"

Once again, she ignored him, and I was getting tired of it. "Deborah, why are you so rude to Sid?"

"Because the only skeleton I want hanging around is a skeleton key," she said, and made her exit.

"Wow, Deborah made a pun," Sid said. "I'm impressed."

"Sid! She totally dissed you!"

He shrugged, which is pretty noisy the way he does it, and said, "I'm used to it. Shall we discuss costume construction?"

Having talked myself into letting him go just to spite Deborah, I couldn't very well back out of it, but if I was going to be springing for costume materials, I should skip the pizza. "Let me make a sandwich first. Then you can tell me what you need."

8

The next couple of days were pleasantly occupied. I met with my Tuesday-Thursday classes, had lunch with Charles, and visited a craft store to pick up supplies for Sid. Madison stayed busy with homework and texting friends new and old, while Sid worked on his ensemble. All three of us were up bright and early Saturday morning to go to McQuaid for the con.

Fortunately for my budget, Madison had decided not to cosplay, or as most people would say, she wasn't going in costume. Instead she would be wearing jeans and a carefully chosen geek-chic T-shirt—specifically the one with the Pokémon/My Little Pony crossover character My Little Ponyta. To further identify her favored fandoms, she had a messenger bag with an assortment of pin-back badges.

As for Sid, I stashed his costume and Sid himself in the back of the minivan while Madison was in the shower. He and I had concocted a detailed plan for getting him into the convention without her seeing him, but we needn't have bothered. I'd barely pulled into the parking lot when Madison hopped out of the van, and said, "Cosplay chess is starting, and I've got to go meet people! I'll text you!" Then she was gone.

That meant I could save my ninja skills for another time, and instead openly pulled out the garment bag and the wheeled suitcase from the van before heading for my parents' office. Once I was inside with the door locked and window blinds down, I zipped open the suitcase. "The coast is clear."

"Thank goodness," Sid said with an audible gasp. "I couldn't breathe in there!"

He really hated riding in the suitcase. It was a hard-sided bag with a pattern that had been advertised as antelope, but looked like bacon to me.

"Coming to the con was your idea," I reminded him. "And since when do you breathe?"

He ignored me as he pulled himself together, something I hadn't seen for a while, and it never ceases to amaze me. One second he was a pile of bones, and the next he was connected again and climbing out of the suitcase. It only took him a few minutes and a little help from me to put on his costume.

Shinigami from *Soul Eater*, also known as Lord Death, wears a black-hooded robe with lots of jagged edges and a kind of black lightning bolt on top of his head. The robe covers everything but his face and hands, which was why the character was a great choice for Sid.

In a touch of irony that made me snicker, Sid was actually wearing a stylized skull mask over his normal skull face because Shinigami is a cartoon. Besides which, he needed to disguise the fact that there was nothing in his skull but dust.

Shinigami's hands are flat, oversized, and have only four fingers—I think they look more like hockey gloves than anything else—and he uses them to administer his signature move: the Direct Noggin Shinigami Chop. Since Sid was hoping to do some chopping in order to stay in character, he'd made his hands out of foam rubber to avoid damaging anybody.

The shoes were the hardest part. Sid's bony feet are close to the length of a normal person's, but don't have the meat to fill up a shoe, so we'd had to pad them with more foam rubber, put socks over them, then jam them into my father's black snow boots. It didn't look stable, but Sid managed it well enough.

"How do I look?" he said when he had it all on.

"Like death."

"Perfect!"

I handed him his name badge. I'd gone to the convention's registration table Friday afternoon to sign up the three of us, telling Madison it was to avoid standing in line on Saturday when in fact it was to hide the fact that I was buying three badges instead of just two. So as soon as Sid and I made arrangements to meet later on, he was ready to go, and after I made sure the coast was clear, he slipped out of the office. I waited a few minutes before I followed to make sure nobody knew we were together.

As I walked across the quad several yards behind him, I could tell from the spring in his step that Sid was having a wonderful time being out of the house. I'd really neglected him for the past few years, but it wasn't easy for me to tend to him when I was living elsewhere, not to mention the fact that Madison was my priority for tending to. From some of the things Sid had said—and hadn't said—I was realizing that while Mom and Phil hadn't exactly ignored him, neither had they made lots of time for him. He was lonely.

Watching him as he encountered his first batch of fellow cosplayers on the quad, I decided I was going to have to get him out more, no matter how much of a pain it was going to be. By the time we both reached the student center, the building where most of the con's events were being held, Sid was surrounded by people and he was posing for photos and happily performing the Shinigami chop. He was having so much fun he didn't even notice me passing by.

I picked up a program book and found a quiet corner in which to look over the schedule of events. There were signing sessions by people I'd never heard of, panels on manga and anime with which I was unfamiliar, and classes in creating costumes. I decided to forgo those pleasures to visit the artists' alley, where artists of all skill levels were hawking wares ranging from prints of anime characters, pin-back badges with obscure jokes, crocheted Pokémon characters, handcrafted jewelry, and an amazing assortment of T-shirts.

I took my time making the rounds, not that I had much of a choice. The room was packed solid with excited otaku. It must have taken me a solid hour to make my way past all the tables, and I was on my way out when I ran into Madison and a group of friends clustered around a table labeled Interrobang Studios.

"Mom," she said, "Kevin Bolk is here!"

I racked my brains, trying to remember why the presence of Kevin Bolk was so wondrous. Fortunately for my mom cred, I caught a glimpse of a picture of a character I recognized from a book Madison had left lying around. "The guy who does *Ensign Sue Must Die*?"

She nodded. "He's taking commissions for sketches, but he's almost booked up. Do you think we can—?"

"How much?"

She told me. "Can we afford it?"

I probably shouldn't have, but I am nothing if not a rapid rationalizer. I'd just started a new job, the security deposit for my old apartment had taken care of my most pressing bills, and we were going to be saving a lot of money by living in my parents' house. "Sure, we can swing it." I pulled the money out of my wallet and got the requisite kiss before she turned away to talk to the revered artist.

I escaped to the hallway, where there was actually enough air to breathe, then made a circuit of the dealers' room.

Another glance at the program book confirmed that I wasn't missing anything I wanted to see, so I found a table at the campus deli counter—creatively named Campus Deli— where I could pull out my laptop and pretend to work while I watched people go by.

Despite my ignorance about most manga—my experience was pretty much limited to Pokémon, Sailor Moon, and Speed Racer—I felt at home in the crowd. I was an old-school nerd myself: *Star Trek*, Robert Heinlein, and Ursula K. Le Guin. Still, a nerd is a nerd is a nerd. I idly speculated for a few minutes about putting together a research project about generational nerd culture—which books were considered essential to different age groups. Then I remembered how many papers I'd be grading for the next few months and the concept seemed much less compelling.

Deborah wasn't wrong when she tried to push me to publish more—along with attracting fat grants, publishing research was the tried-and-true way for achieving tenure. I'd just never been able to manage the research in addition to the heavy adjunct teaching loads in addition to being a single parent. Sleeping took up an unreasonable amount of my time, too. So instead of outlining a brilliant project, I spent the next few hours reading up on the next month's classes so I could be more than one day ahead of my students.

I saw Sid go by a few times, and he even gave me a friendly chop, to the amusement of the other attendees. Madison wandered by, too, but just long enough to grab half the order of nachos I'd intended to hog all to myself. My daughter has a highly effective radar system for sensing when I've scored junk food. Fortunately I'm used to her methods, so I kept the M&M's hidden until she'd zoomed off again.

About mid-afternoon, as I was wondering if there were more comfortable seats available elsewhere in the building, I saw adjunct-slash-reporter Fletcher Wildman making his way through the crowded hall, stopping now and then to take photos. I waited to wave until his viewfinder was aimed in my general direction, and he came over.

"May I join you?" he asked.

"Please do." I shoved my accumulating trash to one side so he wouldn't feel like he was sitting down at a garbage heap. "Are you here as an otaku or as a reporter?"

"Definitely as a reporter, and I'm hoping otaku isn't some obscure insult."

"Yes and no, actually. In Japan, it's a derogatory term for anime and manga fans—like a nerd or a geek—but American fans call themselves otaku proudly. So no insult was intended."

"That's good to know." He pulled out a long, spiral-bound pad labeled *Reporter's Notebook*. "How do you spell that?"

I told him.

"Can I assume you're an otaku yourself?"

"I'm afraid not. I've never mastered the technique of reading books backwards, which limits my enjoyment of manga substantially. I'm here with my daughter."

"Damn, I was hoping for a guide to this strange new world in which I've found myself."

"I can help you with the basics—I've taken Madison to quite a few anime cons."

"That would be great," he said and, with a total lack of subtlety, checked my left hand for a wedding band, earning points by looking pleased by the seductive sight of my bare finger.

I gave him the same treatment, and was glad to see that his ring finger was equally exposed.

Fletcher said, "I'm really out of my comfort zone, and I'm not at all sure what these people are dressed as. They are photogenic, though."

"Cosplay is a big part of the anime/manga scene," I said, and launched into an overview of the tropes of the field, mentioning some of the most popular fandoms and identifying some of the characters walking by, including Sid in his robe. Fletcher scribbled furiously, and suddenly I realized I'd been talking for a solid half an hour. "I'm sorry—I went into lecture mode, didn't I?"

"No, no, this is great. My editor wants a long feature, and I didn't know where to start. Can I buy you a drink to thank you?"

"A Diet Coke would be great." After all, I'd been talking a long time.

"You got it." When he returned, he bought a couple of extra-large chocolate chip cookies, too, and since it would have been churlish of me to reject his offering, I graciously accepted one.

"I take it that anime conventions aren't part of your usual beat," I said in between bites.

"My editor doesn't believe in beats—she thinks a reporter should be able to cover anything from a car crash to a city council meeting to a high school football game."

"Which means she doesn't have to hire as many reporters."

He nodded. "Back when I had a beat of my own, it was business. I'm a whiz at IPOs, zoning legislation, and retail strategy. Ask me anything."

"I'll take your word for it. How did you end up at the Gazette?"

"Newspapers aren't exactly a growth market. I got laid off, and had to decide if I wanted to try TV, learn to blog, or go for a smaller paper. I thought I'd prefer the newspaper, but I don't know if I'm cut out to be a general reporter. Next weekend I'm covering a kids' soccer tournament and I know less about soccer than I now know about anime. I don't suppose you—?"

"Sorry, Madison always took drama classes during soccer season. But if I might make a suggestion?"

"Please."

"You've got a class full of would-be journalists, and chances are that several of them play or have played soccer.

Give it to them as a class assignment. You might have to do some editing, but still, you'll get the article and they'll get a publication credit."

"That's brilliant!"

"Moderately," I conceded, "but it's an old adjunct trick. I've let students critique one anothers' compositions to cut down on my grading, and let them guest lecture on short stories and poems. They learn a lot, and it saves me work. A win-win situation. I've even worked deals with other adjuncts. I realized I had a class full of kids who didn't know what it meant to fact-check, so I had my students critique papers for a bunch of history students, who then helped my students learn basic research techniques. It took some coordinating, but both classes started producing better work."

"Wow. You know all the tricks."

"Only because I've been an adjunct ever since I got out of grad school. McQuaid is my—" I paused to count it out on my fingers. "McQuaid is my seventh college."

"And I thought college professors had it easy with the tenure system."

"Once upon a time, sure, but more and more schools are using adjuncts to save money. They don't pay us as much, they can hire and fire as class sizes change, and they only provide minimal benefits. From a business perspective, it makes all kinds of sense."

"What about the adjunct's perspective?"

"Most of us would kill for tenure."

Fletcher blinked.

"Well, we'd maim for it, anyway."

"I had no idea. You know, this would make a great article. Something meaty, with depth."

"I can't see the *Gazette* running it. McQuaid is one of their regular advertisers."

"True, but there are other places I could try." He glanced at his watch. "Unfortunately, I've got to get going to make today's deadline. I'm so glad I ran into you. This has been really helpful."

"My pleasure. Thanks for the cookie."

He gathered his things, got up, and then said, "Would you like to get together sometime?"

"For an interview about adjunct trials and tribulations?"

"Actually I was thinking dinner and a movie. Unless there's another man in the picture?"

"No, my picture is currently without male embellishment." We exchanged smiles, and he left.

To add to my pleasure, Madison wandered by just then. She looked at me with a questioning expression, and when I put on a look of studied nonchalance, she checked Fletcher out from the rear and gave me a thumbs-up.

I had to agree with her grading. Not only was Fletcher more than presentable from the front, he had an excellent rear view.

The rest of the day went by quickly, even without further visits from attractive reporters. Since the con was being held on campus rather than at a hotel, it had to shut down earlier in the day than was the norm for cons, and the last panels ended at seven.

The plan had been for me to meet Sid back at my office at six so I could get him back out to the van before coming back inside to drag Madison away from her friends. But I'd been sidetracked by a particularly tricky level of Angry Birds, and I didn't get back to my office until quarter after. I'd been worried Sid would also have lost track of time since his costume hadn't included a watch, but as it turned out he was already in the office, and had packed up his costume and most of himself.

"Sorry I'm late," I said.

"No problem."

"Did you have a good time?"

"Yeah."

I waited for more, but that was it and there wasn't time to talk anyway, so I zipped up the suitcase and got him and his costume out to the car.

We made it by the skin of my teeth. I'd just slammed the back of the van shut when I caught sight of Madison and a trio of new friends heading my way. When she introduced me to Nikko, Liam, and Chelsea, at first I thought she was just being polite and thoughtful, when in fact, she had offered them all rides home and knew it would be tougher for me to refuse with them standing there. Before we'd gotten out of the parking lot, that had morphed into an invite for them to come to our house, after a short stop for sustenance at the Aquarius Drive-In, the burger joint that had been an institution even when I was in high school.

Most of the conversation during the drive was incomprehensible to me, but I did smile when I heard Madison say, "Did you guys see the guy dressed as Shinigami?"

"Could you annotate that for me?" I said, pretending ignorance.

"Lord Death from *Soul Eater*. He was awesome! He stayed in character all day long, and he was chopping people right and left. It was so funny!"

"Oh, him," I said offhandedly. "He chopped me, too." I hoped Sid could hear about the good impression he'd made.

Unfortunately, Madison's new coterie hung at the house until after midnight, which meant that I didn't get a chance to debrief with Sid. I had to wait until Madison went to bed to get his suitcase out of the van, and left him at the bottom of the attic stairs to make his way up by himself.

"I'll come get you tomorrow morning," I whispered as he reassembled himself.

"Don't bother," he said. "I think I'll stay home."

"Didn't you have fun?"

"It was fine. It was good. I just think one day is plenty."

"But—"

I heard Madison's bedroom door open, and slammed the attic door shut.

"What are you doing?" she asked.

"I thought I saw a bug." Which was the first thing I could think of.

"G-mom and G-dad must have bug spray."

"I'll take care of it tomorrow. You better get to bed if you want to go back to the con tomorrow."

"Just getting a drink of water."

With Madison wakeful, I didn't dare risk speaking to Sid again that night, and though I checked with him again the next morning, he insisted he didn't want to come along. So I hung out near the deli for most of the day, playing Angry Birds and hoping in vain to see Fletcher again.

9

Monday was one minor disaster after another: Madison had forgotten to take her school clothes out of the drier, which meant they were a wrinkled mess; I spilled most of a carton of orange juice on the kitchen floor; my right rear tire had gone flat and I'd let my AAA membership lapse; my students were unexpectedly surly; and just before dinner, Madison announced that she needed poster board for a project that was due the next day. In other words, I had no time for Sid.

Tuesday wasn't much better, and Madison and I snarked at each other most of the day. I wasn't sure if it was her fault or mine or a combination, but when Deborah called and asked if I minded her running off with my daughter for the evening, I was delighted to give my blessing. I'd have given her my VISA card to pay for dinner, too, if I weren't nudging the credit limit.

As soon as they were out of the driveway, I headed up to the attic and knocked on the door. "Sid? The coast is clear!"

There was no response.

"Sid?"

"I'm reading."

"You can read anytime. Come down and visit."

"I'm getting to a really good part."

Now I was partially suspicious, and partially worried. Sid loved to read, but he could read all day and night, whereas I'd never known him to pass up a chance to gossip.

I tried again. "I'll put on your *Bone Songs* mix disc so we can dance."

"I'm not in the mood."

"We could watch *The Nightmare Before Christmas.*"

"No, thanks."

Passing up music and his favorite movie. "Come on, Sid, I want to talk to you."

"I told you I'm reading."

I bent over to check the crack under the door. "With no light on?"

"Are you worried I'll ruin my eyes?"

It was an invasion of his privacy that I knew I'd feel guilty about later, but I tried the doorknob anyway. Alas, it was wasted guilt. Locked. "Unlock the door and come out or else!"

"Or else what?"

"Or else I'm going to get the screwdriver and take the hinges off the door, probably breaking every one of my fingernails in the process and getting half a dozen bruises."

"Yeah? I don't have much trouble with fingernails and bruises."

"I'll never get the door back up by myself, which will mean that you'll have to hide if Madison comes near the attic, which means that you won't be able to eavesdrop. And we'll either have to get Deborah to come fix it, which she won't make a priority, or wait until my parents get back from sabbatical, or hire somebody I can't afford to pay. Is your sulk really worth all that trouble?"

A few seconds passed, but finally Sid unlocked the door and opened it.

"I'm not sulking," he said. "I'm thinking." He turned to go back up.

Now I knew something was wrong. When Sid was in a good mood, all his bones were tightly connected as if still fastened by invisible tendons, but when he was down, the connections were loose, as if it weren't worth the trouble it took to hold himself together. He occasionally left behind a metatarsal if upset, like when I went to Europe for a month, and the day Deborah announced that she didn't want to talk to him anymore, he left two finger bones on the couch. This time, as I followed him up, I saw no fewer than a dozen tiny bones left on the stairs. I collected them as I went.

When I got upstairs, he'd collapsed on the chair, looking more like a pile of bones than he'd been when stuffed into his suitcase. I put the pieces he'd dropped next to him, but he didn't even bother to put them back into place.

"Talk to me, Sid. Why are you upset?"

"Who said I was upset?"

"Come on, spill your guts." With his love of straight lines, he should have responded *They're already spilled*, or maybe *There's nothing left to spill*. Instead he just shrugged. Given that he'd been acting odd as early as Saturday, I made an educated guess. "Did something happen at the con?"

"No," he said in a tone that any parent would have recognized as a lie.

"What happened?"

"Nothing happened."

I waited him out.

"It's something I saw. Some*one*, I mean. I recognized somebody."

"Okay. Was it one of Mom and Phil's friends or what?"

"No. I remember her from before."

"From before what?"

"From before I was . . . like this. Georgia, I recognized a woman from when I was alive."

10

"From when you were alive?" I said stupidly. "Are you sure?"

"I think so. Yeah. Only she looked older."

"That stands to reason. I mean, you've been living with us for thirty years."

"Maybe I've been here that long, but I haven't been living here. I am dead, you know."

"Mom always says you're in a different state of consciousness."

"Yeah, the dead kind."

"Whatever you call it, you've been part of this family for that long, so if you remember that woman from before, she would have to be older."

"Even if I'm not."

"So, who was she?"

Sid shrugged with a careless clatter. "I don't know. It's just that when I saw her, I felt . . . something."

"Happiness? Sadness? Love? Hate?"

"Fear."

"You were afraid of her?"

"Not exactly, but seeing her made me afraid. Like a flashback. You remember that time you slammed your finger in the car door and had to go to the emergency room? For months afterward, you flinched every time somebody shut a car door."

"I still do."

"Well, it was like that. Seeing her reminded me of being scared."

"But you don't know why?"

He shook his head, his skull rattling alarmingly. "How can I be afraid of something I don't remember? There was something else. I felt guilty, too, as if I'd done something I shouldn't have or hadn't done something I should have. What if I did something bad when I was alive, Georgia?"

"The statute of limitations has run out for anything you could have done," I said, trying to make a joke and failing miserably. The fact was, we really didn't know who Sid had been before he was Sid.

It wasn't as though my family hadn't wondered who he was or where he'd come from, but he'd never been able to remember anything about his past. He knew how to walk, talk, and read, and his knowledge of current events and popular culture was no more than a year or so out of date, but that was it. Though Phil had quizzed him about the experiences of death and his bony rebirth, his earliest memory was the first moment he saw me.

Mom and Phil had spent quite a lot of time theorizing about his origins, deciding that he was either a ghost haunting his own skeleton, a vegetarian zombie, a government project gone very wrong, or the most amazing shared delusion ever. None of the explanations stood up to scrutiny, of course, but I hadn't really cared where Sid came from and Sid didn't seem to, either. Sid was just . . . Sid. As I told my parents, I could always count on him, even if I couldn't account for him.

And right now he was upset and in danger of falling apart. Unlike most people, when he fell apart, he really fell apart.

"Tell me about this woman," I said while there were still enough pieces hanging together for us to carry on a conversation. "What did she look like?"

"Tall. Older—like in her sixties. Jeans and a down jacket. Outdoorsy looking."

"Did you talk to her?"

"No!"

"Could you read her name tag?"

"She wasn't wearing one."

"Really?" Security at the con had been kind of tight—I was surprised they'd let anybody into the building without a tag.

"I don't think she was attending the con. She was looking around like she was confused, not turning her nose up or anything, but she clearly just didn't get it."

"Then what?"

"That's it. She walked through the main hallway looking around, and I saw her meet some young guy and they left. And before you ask, I didn't recognize the guy and he didn't have a name tag, either."

"That's it?"

"That's it."

"And that's why you didn't want to go back to the con Sunday."

"Yeah. I was afraid I'd see her again." He paused, drumming his fingers noisily. "Now I don't know what to do."

"You don't have to do anything," I pointed out. "As long as you stay away from campus, you'll probably never see her again."

"Maybe, but now I know she's out there. I've kind of got

memories." He shook his head. "Not exactly memories, but a feeling. It's like there's another person inside me, and I don't know who that person is. I don't like it."

"Sid, there are two choices. One, forget it ever happened. Two, we try to find out who that woman is."

"We?"

"Well you don't think I'd leave you alone with this, do you?"

"But you've got so much going on. It's not fair for me to ask you."

"Did you ask? Unless you don't want me to—"

"No! I want you to."

"Okay, then."

"So . . . What do we do first?"

Never have I been so grateful to be interrupted as I was in the next second—I didn't have the slightest idea of how to start.

"Mom! Mom!" Not only was Madison home, but she was on her way up the stairs.

"Shit! I've got to go." I practically ran down the attic stairs, and was grateful I didn't fall down them. I got the door slammed behind me just in time.

"Another bug?" Madison asked.

"No, but I thought I heard a squirrel up there—I may need to get a trap." Before she could object, I added, "A humane one."

"Good."

"Why are you home from dinner so early? Did you and Aunt Deb have a fight?"

"I never fight with Aunt Deb."

"Right, that's me."

She rolled her eyes. "Aunt Deb got an emergency call from somebody who'd forgotten the code for his alarm system, so we ate fast and she dropped me off on her way."

"And you came running to find me because you missed me?"

"No, look! I made Kevin Bolk's Tumblr!" She waved her

phone at me, and I had to take it to hold it still long enough to see the photo of her standing next to Bolk, proudly holding the sketch she'd commissioned from him.

I thanked the powers that be for Kevin Bolk's Tumblr—now I had a suggestion for Sid. "I guess there must be a lot of pictures from Mangachusetts on the Web," I said loudly, assuming that he was eavesdropping.

"Oh, sure. I've put some up on Facebook myself, and Samantha took a lot of pictures for her blog."

"I'll have to go Web surfing and see if I can spot some of the people I saw there."

"I'll send you some links," she promised.

I didn't actually get to my computer until after Madison went to bed, but when I logged on, there was an e-mail from her with a dozen links. Many of those led to more, and I soon decided that I was the only attendee who hadn't taken and posted pictures. My original plan had been to print out any promising photos or group shots, but given the sheer numbers, I gave up that idea—there wasn't enough toner in the house to print that many. Instead, I tiptoed up to the attic and lent my laptop to Sid.

Though he'd rarely had reason to use a computer, he picked up the basics of Web surfing surprisingly quickly. As he smugly said, watching all those TV shows and movies of people using their laptops must have paid off. I just hoped he wouldn't somehow erase my hard drive or start World War III while I was asleep.

The next day, my laptop was outside my bedroom door with a sad note from Sid that had only two words: *NO LUCK.*

II

I felt terrible for Sid, so once my morning class was over and I'd spent a few minutes answering student questions, I decided to devote some time to his problem. Since I had a couple of spare hours, I spent it at the adjunct office looking through photos from Mangachusetts until the normal clothing of the adjuncts started to look odd to me.

There must have been fifty different sites with photos for Mangachusetts, including quite a few shots of Sid as Shinigami. I kept hunting through them for a woman who fit Sid's description, but as far as I could tell, she was the only person at the convention who didn't appear in pictures. There were even shots of me at the deli.

Just when I was about to give up, Fletcher came in, sat down at his desk, then swiveled his chair toward me.

He said, "Hey, I really owe you one! I told my class I was looking for people to cover the soccer tourney for extra credit, and I got enough volunteers to cover every single one of the playoff games. All I'm going to have to do is take pictures."

"That's great," I said. Then one word he'd said sank in: *pictures*. "I read your article about Mangachusetts in Sunday's paper. Nice job."

"Thanks. I think I captured some of the experience."

"Definitely." Of course, Madison had turned her nose up at his obvious unfamiliarity with manga and anime, but I'd thought he'd done a decent—and most importantly, respectful—job. "Good pictures, too, but I was expecting more, given what you said Saturday."

"Oh, I had far more than I could use."

"I'd love to see them," I said, trying to put just the right touch of admiration into it.

"All of them?"

"I was hoping to find some photos of my daughter and her friends to send to my parents. They're dying to see how she's settling in. So I've been checking the Web, but I haven't had any luck." Other than that extremely good shot of Madison on Kevin Bolk's Tumblr, but my legs were crossed, so it didn't count as a fib. "Unless there's a rule about showing them."

"No, it's just that there are a *lot* of them. The best way to get publishable photos is to take a bucket load of shots. I filled up most of a memory card."

"I have a gadget I can plug into my laptop to look at memory cards," I said. A former boyfriend who'd been a fan of computer gadgetry had given it to me after watching me spend half an hour hunting for the right cord to transfer photos from my camera to my computer.

"Yeah, okay, then." He rummaged around in his leather backpack to find the memory card while I dug around in my satchel to find the gadget. We emerged victorious at about the same time, and Fletcher rolled his chair over to my desk so we could look at the photos together.

"I'm really not that great a photographer," Fletcher warned me as we started, and I had to admit he was being honest. A lot of the pictures were no better than what I took with my phone, and many were far worse. There were more images of his thumb than of the Sailor Scouts.

Still, it was kind of cozy to flip through them together, and I liked the way Fletcher was willing to laugh at his own photography skills. I liked it even more when Sara came by and gave us a remarkably dirty look—if I'd had a camera handy, it would have made a terrific photo.

About two thirds through the directory of files, I finally found what I was looking for. At least, I thought I had. There were four shots of an older woman without a Mangachusetts name badge who looked like the woman Sid had described.

"Who's that?" I asked, hoping I sounded nonchalant. "That's not a costume I recognize."

"Oh, I remember her. She's dressed as Eminent Scholar, but it's not a costume."

"Okay, now you've got me curious."

"She was there to meet somebody and got caught up in the festivities."

"Her face does have that 'what an interesting specimen' expression, with just a hint of 'I hope they don't bite,'" I said.

"When I realized she knew even less about manga than I did, I figured I didn't need the picture for my story."

"It's a nice shot, though. What's her name? Now that I look at her, she looks kind of familiar. Maybe she's a friend of my parents."

"I'd have to check my notes." He rummaged some more, pulled out a notebook, and flipped through it. While all that was going on, I surreptitiously copied the photos of the woman to my hard drive.

"Here we go. Dr. Jocasta Kirkland. Is that the one you're thinking of?"

"I'm not sure. What is she a doctor of?"

"No idea."

"Does she teach here?"

"I don't know."

"Isn't finding stuff out your job?"

He shrugged. "Once I found out I couldn't use her for the story, I lost interest. Call it journalistic tunnel vision."

I must have been suffering from a bit of tunnel vision myself. I was thinking so hard about getting the picture to Sid so he could verify if that was the right person that I almost missed Fletcher's next words, which were an invitation to dinner and a movie on Friday night. Fortunately I realized what he was saying quickly enough to enthusiastically accept.

I had to leave for my afternoon classes after that, and went straight home afterward. Madison was there, which made it awkward to go up to the attic, so I printed the best picture of Dr. Kirkland, slid the printout and a note under the attic door, and tapped a couple of times to get Sid's attention. A few minutes later, I got a note back: *THAT'S HER!*

12

Sid and I really needed to talk that night, so I had to come up with a way to manage it without arousing Madison's suspicions. Though I admit my method was inelegant, I categorically denied his subsequent accusation that I was going out of my way to annoy him so he'd let me tell Madison about him. As I reminded him, I'd been annoying him for years without a hidden agenda.

What I did was put the laundry basket inside the attic door. It was empty except for a blanket and a note telling Sid to climb in and pull the blanket around him. Then he was to tap on the door for me so I'd know to come carry him into my room. He weighed about twenty-five pounds, which was heavier than the average load of laundry, but well within my carrying capacity.

As it turned out, when we made our move, Madison was downstairs watching TV and texting while playing Minecraft on her laptop. He could have walked past in slow motion with a dramatic soundtrack and she wouldn't have noticed. Once I had him in my room, I yelled down, "I'm working—emergency interruptions only!" and locked the door. She may even have heard me.

Sid untangled himself from the blanket with the picture of Dr. Kirkland in his hand. "That's her, that's her, that's her!"

"Do you remember anything else?"

He stared at the picture unblinkingly. Well, he never blinked, but he looked at it intently enough that, even if he'd been a blinking kind of guy, he still wouldn't have blinked. "Not really."

"Well, we've got a name: Dr. Jocasta Kirkland. That's a start." I went to the McQuaid Web site but didn't find her listed as faculty or staff. "I suppose it would have been too easy if she worked someplace handy. Let's try Google." I entered in her name. "Okay, she's a zooarchaeologist, whatever that is."

"A zooarchaeologist studies animals that lived at the same time as early peoples," Sid said.

"How did you know that?"

"Hey, I read."

"I read, too, and I've spent my whole life around academics, and I didn't know that one. Maybe you remember more about Kirkland than you thought." Since I didn't know anything about zooarchaeology, I opened another window to search for more information. "According to this, she studies faunal remains like antlers, teeth, shells—"

"And bones."

"Which may or may not be a coincidence. She's apparently a grand dame of her field and a winner of the prestigious Mejia Medal for Anthropological Studies."

"Why anthropology and not archaeology?"

"Archaeology and zooarchaeology are subsets of anthropology," I explained, and went on, "Kirkland is a professor emeritus at JTU."

Joshua Tay University, which was two towns over in North Ashfield, was a semi-friendly rival school to McQuaid. Our programs and backgrounds were similar, so we competed for the same students. It was one of the few schools in the area that I'd never taught at.

"She only retired from teaching a few months ago and is now living here in Pennycross."

"What was she doing at the con?"

"Fletcher said she was on campus to meet somebody, and found herself in otaku country."

"Fletcher?"

"I told you about Fletcher."

"No, you didn't."

"Well, I would have if you hadn't been sulking. You remember seeing that guy sitting with me at Mangachusetts? He's a part-time adjunct in journalism who works at the *Gazette*. He was covering the con for the paper, and took that picture of Dr. Kirkland, but when he found out she wasn't there for the con, he wasn't interested in her anymore."

"Was he interested in you?"

"Absolutely. After sharing a soda and cookie with me, he swore his undying devotion and pledged his life and fortune to me and me alone. Well, to me and Madison. I don't know how he'll react to you—I thought I'd wait until after the wedding to introduce the two of you."

"So you like him?"

"He's nice," I admitted. "We're going out on Friday, as a matter of fact. Now, do you want to talk about my love life or your past life?"

"I don't have anything else to say about my past life— maybe Dr. Kirkland does. I want to see her again."

"Sid, assuming that we could arrange that in such a way that does not give the good professor a heart attack, what then? 'Excuse me, but do you recognize my skeletal friend here?' 'Are you missing a skeleton?' 'Did you kill somebody and skeletonize the body?'"

"That's not funny," Sid snapped.

I couldn't remember the last time Sid had snapped at me.

"I'm sorry," he said quickly. "I know I used to be human

and therefore somehow went from living human to what I am now, but I don't like to think about the process."

"I'm sorry. As for what you are now, you're my friend. Okay?"

"Okay," he said. "So what now?"

"Shall we see what else we can dig up on the Web?"

The answer to that was "Not a lot." There were listings of a career's worth of scholarly papers and awards, mentions of her three grown kids and her dead husband, and notes from appearances at conferences in her field.

Sid looked at every scrap of information and every picture we could find, and still felt nothing other than that same sense of fear and guilt.

It was getting late and Madison was going to be coming up to bed soon, so I needed to get Sid back to his attic. "Tell you what," I said, "tomorrow I'll work the adjunct network and see if I can find out more about Kirkland, maybe figure out what she was doing on campus Saturday. Okay?"

"Okay," he said grudgingly. "Or maybe we could snoop around her house—there might be something there that would spark a memory."

"And we would get in how?" Before he could answer, I said, "Sid, we are not breaking into that woman's house."

"You wouldn't have to break anything—Deborah could show you how to pick her lock."

"Even if that were so—and you know Deborah wouldn't help—it would still count as breaking and entering. The 'breaking' part is metaphorical, as in 'I'm going to break your head if you don't get into the clothes basket so I can get you to the attic.'"

"If I had a tongue I'd be sticking it out at you!"

"That would be fine as long as you did so from inside the basket."

Twenty-three hours later, we were back in my room with Sid sitting in the clothes basket.

I'd spent every spare moment that day talking to other

adjuncts, starting with Charles because he was always on campus, and eventually found out why Dr. Kirkland was on campus. "Here's the scoop," I said. "Kirkland was there to meet with a computer science grad student she's hired to do some statistical analysis."

"Wow, that's really boring."

"The only thing more boring was the story about one of the computer science adjunct's cats I had to listen to before I could ask him about Kirkland. I'd share it with you, but since I dozed off midway through, I'm missing details."

"Thanks for that. So, what next?"

"I was hoping you'd come up with something while I was following the trail of boredom."

"I've tried remembering, and there's just nothing else there."

"Trauma has a way of messing with memory, and dying is usually pretty traumatic."

"Maybe I could find a therapist," Sid said. "A blind one."

For a moment, that almost made sense.

He went on. "I'm still not remembering anything but Kirkland. You have to go talk to her."

"And say what? 'You don't know me, but somebody who used to be alive recognized you, and . . .' I can't even come up with a hypothetical question, Sid."

"Maybe I could get to know her." Before I could point out the obvious, he held up one hand and said, "Not in person, but online."

"You two could trade funny cat pictures and Harry Potter GIFs all day long, and it wouldn't help. It was the guy you used to be who had a connection with Kirkland, and we don't know anything about him. If you were a him—for all we know, you were a woman."

"Hey!"

"Well, I don't know the difference between a boy skeleton and a girl skeleton." Despite the many hours I'd spent with a skeleton, I was hardly an expert on bones.

"The guys on *CSI* can tell as soon as they see a skeleton."

"That's because they're trained forensic scientists. Even if we have any forensics people in the Pennycross Police Department, I don't really want to explain to them why I have an unidentified skeleton."

"Who said anything about the police? There's a physical anthropology department at McQuaid, isn't there?" Of course he knew the school's departments—he'd been reading my parents' school bulletins for years.

"That's not a bad idea."

"Don't sound so surprised. I'm a brainy guy, even without the brain."

"Of course, if I take you to McQuaid, you know how you're going to have to travel."

"Coccyx! Fine, bring on the ossifying suitcase."

13

Part of the joy of working in colleges and universities is the vast number of knowledgeable people dying for someone to take an interest in their specialty—surely bone experts would be as eager as anybody to show off.

After my morning class the next day, I checked around the adjunct office to see if anybody in there had skeletal skills, but Charles was fairly sure the only one who might was Sara, and as I'd already learned, Sara didn't play well with others. Sid and I were going to have to look elsewhere.

The Anthropology Department seemed like our best bet, so I got the suitcase out of my van to wheel to Easton Hall, easily the largest building on campus. There was a persistent squeak but I knew full well that Sid himself was making the noise, not the wheels of the bag. He really hated riding in the suitcase.

The Anthropology Department was on the third floor, and since I didn't want to lug Sid up the stairs, I was searching through the maze of hallways and doors for the elevator when I saw an office door start to open. Hoping it was nobody I knew so I wouldn't have to explain the bacon bag, I hurried past but heard somebody say, "Georgia?"

I tried to come up with an excuse as I turned, but when I saw who it was, I relaxed. "Hi, Charles. What are you doing—?" I stopped, realizing what he was probably doing, and switched tracks. "How is your week going?"

"Splendidly, and I hope yours is the same."

"I don't suppose you know where the elevator is."

"I would be happy to show you." He took me down a narrow hall and waved me to the left. "Your carriage awaits."

"Thanks, Charles. See you later."

He courteously waited until I was in the elevator before giving his usual half bow.

"Who was that?" Sid said from inside the suitcase once the elevator door had slid shut.

"Charles Peyton. Don't worry. He's the one person on campus who will never be nosy about what I'm doing." I suspect Charles would have been equally discreet about anybody, but he seemed to feel he owed me particular service. He had a secret of his own, one I'd discovered by accident and had never even told Sid, and Charles had never forgotten that.

McQuaid wasn't known for anthropology, and the department was small: only four professors were listed in the directory. The door to the main office was open, and either a secretary or a student was tapping away at a laptop covered with a skeleton-pattern decorative skin. I knew it was either a secretary or a grad student because she didn't look up when I stepped inside—an undergrad would have.

"Excuse me," I said.

"Yeah?" the girl said, still not looking up.

"I've got a skeleton, and I was wondering if I could get somebody to take a look at it. It's nothing crime-related or anything, it's just that—"

"Fill out a form." She pointed at a messy stack of badly photocopied pages on top of a bookshelf along one wall.

"Thanks." I sorted through them before I found one with the heading Skeletal Examination Request. Naturally there were no pens in sight, so I pulled one out of my satchel and filled in the blanks: Date, Name, Number of Bones, Condition of Find, and so on. I hesitated over Location Found—I couldn't fit my overly elaborate cover story onto one line—and finally wrote "parents' attic." Then I started to hand it to the girl.

"Put it in Dr. Ayers's mailbox."

I would have, but when I looked at the row of mail cubbies, I saw that the one labeled *Ayers* was already stuffed full. Moreover, the papers toward the bottom were curling—they'd been in there awhile.

"Is Dr. Ayers not in residence this semester?" I asked

"Nope. He's in Belize. Along with most of the department."

"When will he be back?"

"As if he'd tell me anything."

"Is there anybody else who can work with human bones?"

"Anybody who *can*? Yes. Anybody who *will*? I sincerely doubt it."

I took a closer look at the girl. Mid to late twenties. Hair died Crayola red, but not recently, so there was an inch-wide line of brown down the part. She was so pale she probably hadn't been out of the basement during daylight hours for the past six months, and her college sweatshirt and plaid pajama pants gave the impression that it was two weeks past laundry day. Her desk was covered in photocopied journal articles, and there was a battered notebook with carefully written numbers in front of her. She still hadn't stopped typing.

"Let me guess," I said. "You're Dr. Ayers's student, but you didn't get to go out into the field with him because you're approaching the deadline for your dissertation, and you don't have time to waste messing with a skeleton when you've already done your research."

She finally looked at me. "Now, let *me* guess. New hire, but not in my department or even in this building, or I'd have seen you before. Not tenured, or a formal announcement would have gone out. So unless there's something you can do to help me finish my dissertation, you can leave the form in the prof's mailbox."

Before she could go back to ignoring me, I said, "One question: How long does it take to examine a skeleton?"

"Depends on what you want to know. A full examination could take a couple of days, plus another two days to write a decent report."

I knew that wasn't going to happen—I'd never tear her away from her dissertation that long. "What about a quick and dirty exam? Just the basics, and you wouldn't have to write a report about him."

"Him?"

"If it's male," I said, ignoring the muffled raspberry from inside the suitcase.

"An hour or two, which is still more time than I care to spend."

"One more question. How long did it take you to find a parking place this morning?"

"Half a freaking hour," she snarled, "and that was all the way across campus."

Parking was the number-one complaint of McQuaid students, and the expensive parking permits were sold in far greater quantities than the actual number of places available. They were derisively referred to as hunting licenses. To add insult to injury, the parking police were ever vigilant and tickets were outrageously high.

"So you lost an hour of work time just today. Whereas even a part-time instructor gets a hang tag for the faculty lots." Since the university was working hard to attract name professors, faculty lots were plentiful and closer to the school buildings than the student lots—I'd passed several empty faculty spots on the way to Easton. "I even have spares. My parents teach here, too, and admin automatically sent them theirs for the year even though they're on sabbatical." Knowing the power of a good bribe, I'd tucked one of the tags into my satchel, and I pulled it out to twirl around on my finger. The grad student stared at it like . . . well, like a grad student seeing a convenient parking place. "Still too busy to look at my skeleton?"

"How long do I get to keep the hang tag?"

I probably could have offered a month and settled for the rest of the fall semester, but I was willing to be generous. "When is your dissertation due?"

"May."

"You give me a good consult on the skeleton, and you can keep it until it expires in August."

"For that you get two hours. I guarantee gender and approximate age, and will take a stab at race. Plus anything else I can find out in that length of time. Nothing written, no liability if I'm wrong."

"Deal."

The girl reached for the tag, but I put it back into my satchel and handed her the form I'd filled out instead. "After you look at my skeleton."

"Have you got the bones with you?"

"In the suitcase."

"Then let's do this." She got up, put a battered sign that said *Back soon* on the door and locked it. "Bring it out to the workroom." There was an open hallway behind the desk, and the student led the way down it. "FYI, if your bones turn out not to be human, you still owe me the hang tag."

"I'm pretty sure he's human," I said, ignoring a kick through the side of the suitcase from Sid. "I'm Georgia Thackery, by the way."

"Yo."

I tried to keep conversant with high school slang in order to communicate with Madison and college slang for communicating with my students, but I wasn't sure I'd encountered that particular usage before. "Pardon?"

"I'm Yo. Short for Yolanda."

The door to the workroom was festooned with an articulated Halloween skeleton with its middle finger bones pointed up defiantly. Yo unlocked the door to reveal a room that would have been kind of creepy to anybody who wasn't a physical anthropologist or a woman who'd grown up with a skeleton for a best pal.

A wide variety of bones and skulls filled translucent plastic bins on the metal shelves that lined the walls. Any walls that weren't filled with shelves were decorated—if *decorated* was the right word—with enlarged photos of skeletons, with and without flesh, and anatomical charts. There was also a selection of scales, measuring equipment, and tools I hoped Yo knew how to use. In the middle of the room were two worktables topped with the black, inert laminate typically used in labs.

"Do I have to denude the bones?" Yo asked. "If I do, I'm going to have to leave them soaking overnight. We don't have a beetle colony."

"Nope, he's clean." Sid gave himself regular wipes with hydrogen peroxide to make sure he looked his best, which was a lot more pleasant to think about than beetles. I slid down the handle of the rolling bag, then hefted it onto the table.

"A suitcase?"

"It's what he always rides in."

Yo gave me a look.

"Just kidding," I said with a fake grin. "I didn't have anything else big enough to carry it in." I unzipped the bag and reached in to pull out Sid's right hand.

"Okay, it's human," Yo said. "You'd be surprised how many people bring in bear paws."

"Are they that similar?"

"Sure, to an amateur," she said dismissively. "How do you come to have a human skeleton, anyway?"

"It's been in my parents' attic for years," I said, which was true enough. "They used to use it for inspiration for writing exercises." That was made up, but it would have been a good idea if Sid hadn't been the skeleton in question. "My sister and I found it while cleaning and got into an argument about it." Again, there was a grain of truth. Deborah and I had been arguing about Sid for years. "She watches all those crime shows and claimed she could figure out all kinds of things about the skeleton. I bet her that she couldn't."

I looked at Yo to see if she was buying it, but given the bored look on her face, I could probably have just shrugged.

That's what she did, and with practiced indifference muttered, "Whatever."

I started to hand her Sid's hand when she said, "How is it articulated?"

"What?" Of course, most "whole" skeletons are in fact wired together—I vaguely remembered that Sid had had wires and hinges when we'd first gotten him, and there were still holes where the wires and screws had been—but since he had his own methods of cohesion, we'd never bothered to replace the fittings as they broke or rusted, which meant that he really shouldn't be holding together.

Sid must have realized the same thing because the bones of his hand suddenly fell apart, with most of them landing back in the suitcase. I tried to look innocent.

Yo shook her head. "Never mind. Let's lay him out. I mean, it."

I was impressed by the grad student's skills—she placed the bones into their proper locations as fast as I could hand them to her, as if she were putting together a familiar jigsaw puzzle. Not bad, given that Sid had two hundred bones, more or less.

Once the bones were in their relative positions, Yo said, "Okay, it looks mostly complete."

"Mostly?"

"A couple of the minor toe bones are missing, but that shouldn't affect the analysis. Let's see what we've got. He looks robust, so that means probably male." Then she picked up Sid's pelvic bone, and stuck her thumb in it. It was a tight fit. "Yep. Male."

"Told you so," Sid whispered without moving his jaw.

"Excuse me?" Yo said.

"I said, 'Is that so?'"

Yo looked suspicious, but even a sleep-deprived graduate student wasn't going to think it had been the skeleton talking. She picked up his skull, opened the jaw, and ran her finger over his teeth. "Twenty-eight. He's missing his wisdom teeth—not sure if they fell out or they were extracted before death." She pulled over a magnifying lamp, and peered at the teeth more closely. "Huh."

"What?"

"He has fillings."

"So?"

"Do you know where most skeletons come from?"

"When a mommy skeleton loves a daddy skeleton very much . . ."

She gave me her best withering glare, but it wasn't nearly as good as Madison's, so I was unfazed. She said, "Most skeletons come from India, but they're from poor areas and they sure don't have dental work like this. These fillings mean that he—that *it* probably came from somewhere in the US."

Sid had spoken with an American accent from the first, so it had never occurred to me that he could have been from elsewhere.

Yo kept looking at the skull. "I'd be worried that your parents had gotten rid of an annoying student if it weren't for the ID marks."

"The what?"

"Here, inside the skull." She held Sid's skull upside down so I could look inside, which seemed oddly rude. There was a series of letters and numbers written in there: P-A-F-60-1573. "Those markings tell me that, at some point, this bad boy was part of some sort of collection."

"What do they mean?"

"No idea. There's no standard system for marking bones— every school and museum has its own conventions. All I can say for sure is that he's not from McQuaid." She reached into one of the storage boxes, pulled out a skull, and turned it upside down so I could look inside to see its series of numbers and letters. "We mark our GRAIDs with Sharpies."

"Grades?"

"G-R-A-ID. Gender dash race dash age dash file ID." She went back to Sid's skull. "This looks like India ink, but I don't know what the code means."

"What about JTU? Could this have been one of their skeletons?" After all, Kirkland had taught at JTU, though I didn't know what a zooarchaeologist would be doing with a human skeleton.

But Yo said, "Can't be. I worked with some loaner specimens from them last year, and though I don't remember all their codes offhand, I do know the third one was for gender. F for female, M for male, X for undetermined. Your guy is definitely a guy—even Ayers admits I rock at sexing skeletons."

Sid snickered, and I coughed to cover it up. "Maybe it came from a school that was throwing it away."

"The term is deaccessioned," Yo said, "and nobody just throws a skeleton away. Especially not a relatively rare specimen like this."

"Why is it rare? Because of the dental work?"

"Because with that particular kind of dental work it's almost certainly American, and we don't get many American skeletons. There's no established bone trade in this country, and donated bodies usually end up as dissection material. So this is definitely unusual."

"What else can you tell me?"

"Hang on. Sexing is easy—it gets harder from here."

Sid snickered again, I coughed again, and Yo ignored us both while she went to work.

After thirty minutes of her looking at, weighing, and measuring bones—with the odd excitement of consulting charts, making cryptic notes, and entering numbers into a computer—I realized that there was more to the process than was typically shown on TV. I wandered off to look at the other bones in the room, wondering if Sid could communicate with any of them. When I got bored with that, I found a stool and pulled out my phone to check e-mail and play Angry Birds. I was trying to get that third star on level twenty-three when Yo said, "I'm done."

"Excellent!" I said. "What did you find out?"

"The palate shape says Caucasoid—as opposed to Negroid or Asian. Six foot tall, plus or minus an inch. No sign of being overly heavy or overly thin. Adequate nutrition. Teeth in good shape and, as I mentioned before, he had fillings. Four, in fact."

"If he had dental work, maybe I could identify him."

"You'd have to have the right dental records to compare the teeth to. It's not like there's a database."

"Right," I said, deflated.

"Anyway, from looking at the teeth, he was in his mid-twenties."

I'd have guessed younger, given Sid's sense of humor, but then again, I laughed at most of his jokes and I was a whole lot older. "Anything else?"

"There are two fractures. The right wrist was broken antemortem but completely healed long before he died, and one rib was broken postmortem and glued back together."

I'd cracked that rib myself when tackling Sid, and had felt horrible about it, but he'd insisted that it hadn't hurt.

Yo went on. "There are also two perimortem injuries."

"*Postmortem* is after death, and *antemortem* would be before death. What's *perimortem*?"

"At the time of death." She held up Sid's skull again. "See this dent? Something hit him hard enough to make that mark while the bone was still living."

"Is that what killed him?" I said, oddly upset by the idea. Of course Sid had to have died at some point, but like Sid, I'd never liked thinking about the process. It was like hot dogs—I didn't want to know how they came to be in the form with which I was most familiar.

"Possibly," Yo said. "Dr. Ayers would know for sure, but I'd put my money on this." She picked up a piece of the rib cage. "See this groove here? That's the mark from some kind of sharp instrument, like a knife. And this is right over the heart."

"You're saying he was stabbed?"

"That's what it looks like to me. You've got yourself a murdered skeleton."

14

Yo showed me a few other marks on Sid, but she thought they were from when the meat had been removed from the bones or something like that. I wasn't paying strict attention because I was pretty much fixated on the "murder" thing. Even though Sid had been dead since before I'd known him, finding out that he was a murder victim was disturbing.

"That's the express service," Yo concluded. "Any questions?"

"Is there any way to tell what he looked like? I've heard about facial reconstruction."

"There's software to do computer imaging, and some people are trained to sculpt or sketch based on the skull, but nobody here can do it. You'd need a place that's more about the forensics than the anthropology, and you sure couldn't get anybody to do a job like that for a hang tag."

"Just a thought." If need be, maybe I could finagle some connections from my parents. In the meantime, at least I had more information to work with.

I reached for Sid's suitcase, but Yo said, "Have you

thought about selling this thing? You could get a few grand for it."

"Seriously?"

"Easy. You know how I said skeletons come from India? I should have said they used to. They changed the laws over there back in the eighties, and now it's a lot harder to get them. Last week a guy called from a school that's starting up a new anthro department wanting to know if we had any spares, which we don't. You want his number?"

Sid's skull shifted, probably in indignation that he could no longer restrain, and I reached for it before Yo noticed. "No, thank you."

"Whatever," she said, and helped me pack Sid back into his suitcase. As soon as I had the bag zipped up, she stuck out her hand.

"One faculty hang tag, expiration date August thirty-first," I said, pulling it out. "Once in a blue moon security will call to verify that it's actually me using it, so what kind of car should I tell them I drive?"

"A black Toyota Corolla."

"Good enough. Thanks for your help."

"Thanks for the tag."

I headed for the parking lot, noticing that Sid didn't squeak on the way. Once in the van, I put the suitcase on the floor of the front seat, then unzipped it to allow conversation.

"You okay?" I asked him.

"Kind of weirded out."

"Me, too."

"I mean, that girl's hands were *cold*."

"Silly me. I thought you meant about the other stuff."

"Yeah, that, too. Mid-twenties . . . So I'm younger than you are."

"Sid, you were in your mid-twenties when I was six. That makes you fifteen to twenty years older than I am."

"But I haven't aged."

"You certainly haven't matured."

"Hey, I stayed still all the time Yo was pawing at me. I think that shows that I've grown as a person."

"Might I remind you of the snickering?"

"Two snickers, and I couldn't help it. I haven't been sexed in a *long* time."

"Mid-twenties? You may never have been sexed."

"Please. I was a stud."

"Is that a memory or wishful thinking?"

"A logical deduction from my manly skeletal structure and irresistible personality."

"Uh-huh."

"She said I'm robust—that's a scientific fact. Of course, my charm goes without saying."

"Nothing about you goes without saying. So shall we talk about the elephant in the room now?"

"She had an elephant skeleton in there? I thought only Tufts had one of those."

"Sid."

There was a long pause. "So I was murdered."

"So it seems. Are you okay?"

"I don't know what to feel. How about you?"

"I'm mad. No, I'm beyond mad. I'm furious."

"Patella, I'm sorry, Georgia. If I hadn't made you take me to the con—"

"Don't be an idiot. I'm not mad at you—I'm mad at the person who hurt you. Some bastard murdered my best friend!"

"I wasn't your best friend when—"

"I don't care!" I took a deep breath. "I don't think I ever told you this, but do you remember Jean Shannon?"

"Your college roommate? I thought you two lost touch."

"We did, and I wish it had stayed that way. A while back she got religion and decided she needed to confess to the sins committed during her heathen past, so she started hunting people down on Facebook. When she found me, she asked for my phone number, and I figured it would be nice to talk to her."

"Not so nice?"

"Very not nice. We spent a few minutes comparing notes, and then she started with the confessions."

"Plural?"

"She had a hefty list. First off, she used to help herself to my change jar to do her laundry. Plus, she took money from my wallet that she 'forgot' to replace—more than once, mind you. And there was this one guy we met at a party who told me he'd call, but never did. It turns out he did call—she told him I had a boyfriend, thinking she could get him for herself. Except he wasn't interested in her anyway!"

"Serves her right."

"But here's the biggie: You remember the sapphire earrings Mom and Phil gave me for high school graduation, the ones that had been Grandmother's? Jean 'borrowed' them for a date and dropped one somewhere. So she threw out the other one and let me think I'd been the one to lose them."

"That ossifying piece of sacrum! I remember how pissed your parents were when you told them."

"So do I! Even worse—they were *disappointed* in me. God, I hate it when they're disappointed in me. Anyway, after all that, Jean had the nerve to ask me to forgive her. She thought we could be friends again. After all, it was so many years ago."

"What did you say?"

"Nothing. I was too busy hanging up. I had to hang up five more times before Jean got the hint that I didn't want to talk to her anymore. Maybe it was old news to her, but it was hot off the presses to me!"

"I don't blame you."

"Then you should understand how I feel now. So what if you were killed thirty years ago, and so what if it was before I met you? As far as my feelings go, I just found your body.

I'm going to find out what happened, Sid. If Yo was right and it was murder, I'm going to find out who it was!"

Of course, I didn't know how I was going to go about solving a thirty-year-plus-old murder, but I didn't see any reason to bring that up. Instead I said, "I take it that Yo's results didn't shake any more memories lose."

"Not a one," Sid said. "I'm not sure I want any more memories, anyway."

"I don't suppose you do. Who wants to remember being hit or stabbed?"

"It's not just that. I mean I don't want to remember being the kind of person who gets murdered."

"Blaming the victim much? Do you think you were dressed in a provocative way and incited your killer?"

"I know perfectly innocent people get murdered every day, but we both read the papers enough to know that most murder victims put themselves in harm's way. Think about it: a young guy with a stab wound. What if I was a gang member or a dope dealer? A carjacker or a bank robber?"

"What if you were a nice guy stabbed while trying to save a basket of puppies? Which, I might add, fits your personality a whole lot better than grand theft auto."

"Come on, Georgia, we don't have any clue as to what my personality was like before."

We were discussing topics we'd spent years avoiding, but it was obvious that we couldn't avoid them any longer. "What's the first thing you remember?"

"You know that."

"Tell me again."

"I heard a little girl crying."

"And what did you do?"

"I got myself loose and went

mean."

"What kind of carjacker'

would be to help a crying

"You think?"

"I *know.* If we ever find out who you were, I don't think it'll be anything to be ashamed of."

"Thanks, Georgia, but . . . I'm still worried."

I took a deep breath. This was Sid's story—not mine. I couldn't barrel through if he didn't want me to. "If you'd rather stop, we will."

There was an extra-long pause, ending only when I parked in the driveway at home. That's when he said, "I want to know who I am."

"Then we'll keep going. We'll just be careful."

"*You* be careful. I don't really have anything to lose. Except you."

15

We didn't have any time to discuss the next steps. I got Sid's suitcase inside the house and opened it so he could get himself up to the attic, and grabbed an apple on my way back out the door. It wasn't much of a lunch, but I had an afternoon class to teach. I made it back to McQuaid with minutes to spare and thought I was doing a good job forgetting about skeletons until I referred to *The Nightmare Before Christmas* twice during class.

My darling daughter was already home, and if she'd been as hungry as she claimed to be, would have had a figure similar to Sid's. Since I had plans for the evening, I made her a veggie pizza and, in a burst of optimism, put some salad into a bowl for her. She could handle dessert herself—hunting for my Oreo stash was one of her favorite games. While she was digging in, I went to shower and primp for my date.

Since Fletcher had said dinner and a movie, I thought jeans would be appropriate as long as they weren't mom jeans, and fortunately the one pair I had that fit that description was clean. The peacock blue sweater I wore with them was cut just low enough to look hot without being slutty—or so Madison informed me—and I wore short boots instead of my teacher sneakers. A little jewelry, a little makeup, and a lot of second-guessing, and I was good to go.

As I came through the living room, I had a suspicion. I tapped on the armoire, and there was an answering tap from inside. Sid was either hoping to get a peek at Fletcher or planning to keep an eye socket on Madison while I was gone. More likely, both.

I didn't mind. When it came to men, Sid's snooping had saved me a world of hurt in the past, and though my daughter was perfectly able to stay by herself, I didn't mind having somebody around in case of emergency.

Madison was planted on the couch, clearly intending to inspect Fletcher. When she was four, she'd decided that if it was okay for me to vet her friends, it should be acceptable for her to do the same to mine. Her logic was impeccable, so I allowed it. Though I didn't promise not to go out with a guy she didn't like, I did take her feelings into account. Introducing Madison to my dates also gave me a chance to see how they acted with her—I had zero interest in going out with a guy who didn't like her.

Fletcher's initial scores were solid. He arrived right on time, and his outfit was a masculine counterpart to mine, though he lost half a point for the sneakers. Then he got massive extra credit for sitting down next to Madison when I introduced them rather than rushing us out the door.

They made polite small talk for a minute, then Fletcher said, "Do you have any questions for me?"

"Excuse me?" Madison said.

"My sister is a single mother, and my niece and nephews always have questions for the men she goes out with. I'll see if I can remember what they usually want to know." He ticked them off on his fingers. "I've never been married. I have a steady job, even if it doesn't pay as much as I'd like it to. I don't drink to excess often, but if I do get overly festive I know not to drive. I don't do recreational drugs. And I've liked all pets I've been introduced to except a tarantula." He smiled as if sure he'd covered all the bases, but if he'd thought he'd taken Madison by surprise, he was mistaken.

She said, "Political leanings? Religious affiliation?"

He blinked, but went with it. "Liberal and Democrat, though I have voted for one Republican because I knew her personally. Raised Episcopalian, but not a regular church-goer since high school."

Before she could ask "Boxers or briefs?" I said, "Now it's your turn, Madison."

She grinned. "Never married, full-time student, don't drink other than one half glass of champagne on New Year's Eve, don't drive, and I'm a dog person. I intend to vote Demo-crat as soon as I can, and I'm nominally Christian in that I celebrate Christmas and Easter, but I'm not a churchgoer."

"Are you both satisfied?" I asked.

They nodded, and Madison added, "You kids have a good time. Don't stay out too late."

"Oh, that's a new one," I said drily. "I haven't heard it since the last time I went out. Do you need me to write down the number for 911?"

She sighed, which was hardly fair since she'd started it, and Fletcher and I left. The door clicked behind us, too, so she'd remembered to lock up. My maternal instincts satis-fied, I was ready to turn my attention to my date.

I know a lot of people detest first dates, but I rather enjoy them. The guys are usually on their best behavior, there are no simmering disagreements, and the expectations of all involved are low, which makes it all the more special if things go well. If things don't go well, it's easy to bow out of the relationship without acrimony.

The night with Fletcher was definitely in the top ten. We had dinner at a cozy Italian place I'd never been to, and having had the ice broken by Madison's interrogation, conversation was relaxed. While we were enjoying our lasagna, the subject of single motherhood came up, but I'd expected that—I like to know if my dates have ties to other women, so I can't blame them for wondering about me. Besides, I find a man's reaction to be an excellent litmus test of his character.

I explained, "Reggie and I started dating in grad school—I think we spent half of our so-called dates working on our dissertations. We were just starting to plan out which universities we could both get jobs at when I got pregnant. I was all for adding a baby to the plan, but Reggie freaked. He never actually asked me to pick him or the baby, but he might as well have, so we went our separate ways." It was an overly simplified version, but it was plenty enough information for a first date.

At that point in the conversation, I'd had previous escorts ask me why I hadn't aborted or, almost as infuriatingly, wax poetic about my nobility in keeping my daughter. None of those had made it to a second date. Fletcher simply said, "His loss," which shot his score way up.

After that, we talked about being adjuncts, but it was more shop talk than interview, so I didn't feel that he was multitasking in order to write off our dinner bill on his taxes.

As it turned out, I was the one multitasking. Though I was trying to keep Sid's murder out of my mind, when Fletcher told me about some of the more interesting stories he'd covered, I asked, "Have you ever done anything with a murder? Like a cold-case murder?"

"Only a piece about Charles Manson's effect on society back in college. Why do you ask?"

"Just morbid curiosity. Somebody I know had a friend who was murdered years ago, but the murderer was never caught. She'd always wanted to find out what really happened, and I wondered how one would go about investigating something like that."

He swirled the wine around in his glass. "First off, I'd

check the police files. Then I'd research the victim—his friends and family, his job and coworkers."

"That makes sense," I said, though I couldn't quite see how to apply it to Sid. Since I didn't want him to ask more about my cold case than I was willing to answer, I changed the subject to the choice of a movie. By the time the check came, we'd agreed on a spy thriller. I don't like romance movies on a first date. There's no better way to scare a guy off than have him think you're eager for a happily-ever-after.

We enjoyed our selection, though Fletcher had some critiques of the way the reporter love interest covered a story. Apparently wild sex with the subject of an investigation was frowned upon in journalistic circles.

At the end of the evening, Fletcher walked me to the door but turned down my invitation to come inside. It wasn't because he wasn't interested in more dates—he just had to be up early the next morning to supervise his students at the soccer tournament.

Madison pounced as soon as I came in. First she quizzed me on the date, and when I'd told her as much as I intended to, she asked if she could spend the afternoon at Samantha's the next day for an anime marathon. After making sure she'd already done her homework for the weekend, I agreed.

I checked out the armoire while Madison was on her way up to bed, but apparently Sid had managed to sneak upstairs at some point during the evening. He hadn't even left a note in my room, which should have alerted me that he had a plan swirling around his empty skull.

16

Saturday afternoon, Sid came clattering down the stairs as soon as I got back from taking Madison to Samantha's house. "I've got a plan!" he said cheerfully.

"Movie, game, or dance party?"

"Murder investigation!"

"Did you remember something?"

"No, but I realized we have a suspect: Dr. Kirkland!"

"Okay, that would explain why you felt scared when seeing her, but she doesn't seem the murderous type. That whole noted-academic thing."

"Shall I remind you of the Parkman-Webster case?" Sid replied. "Where one Harvard academic killed another?"

"Oh, right," I said, wondering which book my parents had left lying around for Sid to get ahold of. "Whether or not she's a killer, she probably is the first person we should talk to. Fletcher says if he doesn't have police records, he starts by researching the victim."

"You told Fletcher about me?" Sid said, eye sockets seeming to widen in alarm.

"Never on a first date."

"Not funny!"

"No, Sid, I did not tell Fletcher about you." I'd never told anybody about Sid, not even Madison's father. I'd intended to, but I never got around to it before I broke up with him. "I merely asked, in a general way, how somebody would go about investigating a cold murder case."

"Did he have any good advice?"

"Just the bare bones," I said, waiting for an appreciative laugh, but Sid didn't take the bait. "Fletcher said he'd start with police files, but that's no good for us. Then he'd talk to the victim's friends and family and coworkers—anybody the victim had known. In your case, that means Dr. Kirkland."

"Then you haven't changed your mind?"

"Nope. I'm just as mad as I was yesterday."

He grinned. "Then here's my idea."

A couple of hours later, we were parked on the street in front of Dr. Kirkland's house. She'd moved into a fairly isolated neighborhood, where the houses had lots of room between them. Her ranch-style home screamed nineteen-seventies to me and looked completely out of place in an old Yankee town like Pennycross, but it was freshly painted and the yard was well maintained.

I'd put Sid into the hated suitcase, but just to get him into the van unobserved. Then I'd opened it again so we could talk. Fortunately, with the advent of hands-free cell phones, nobody looks askance at people who seem to be talking to themselves.

Though he wasn't visible unless somebody was standing right next to the van, and I had a blanket handy to cover him if need be, I was still having terrifying daydreams about being pulled over by cops and having to explain why I had a skeleton. Then I'd end up as the subject of Fletcher's next article.

"Is she here?" Sid wanted to know. "Do you see her?"

"Her car is in the driveway."

"Have you got your cover story memorized?"

"Of course." Not that it was that great a story. I was going to claim that my parents had heard that Dr. Kirkland had moved to town, and since they knew her from academic circles, they wanted me to welcome her. For all I knew, they might actually have met her at some point, but they had no idea Kirkland had moved to town, and even if they had, they certainly wouldn't have insisted I go see her.

Still, it sounded semi-reasonable, and if I let it slip that I was an adjunct, it would sound even more plausible. Adjunct faculty members have a reputation for trying to suck up to get jobs. I admit that it's not unwarranted.

"Are you sure I can't go in with you?" Sid said.

"How? She'd either faint or call the cops. Maybe both."

"You could stick my skull in your purse and—"

"No." Before he could come up with some other crazy scheme, I got out of the van with the fruit basket from the "markdown" shelf at the grocery store. In my defense, all the items in it still looked fresh.

I put on my brightest smile, went to the front door, and rang the bell. A minute passed. Two. Well, Dr. Kirkland was old and might not have good hearing. I rang the bell again, for slightly longer than before. Three minutes later, I knocked on the door loudly. I waited a few more minutes, then knocked again. Then I went back to the van and climbed in.

"I guess she's not here."

"But her car is here!" Sid said indignantly.

"Maybe she doesn't want to come to the door. Maybe she's got two cars. Maybe somebody picked her up. Maybe she's out jogging."

"So, now what?"

"We go home."

"But . . ." He didn't say anything else, but two finger bones dropped to the floor of the van.

I sighed. "Tell you what. Madison is out for the day anyway. We'll kill some time, then come back."

Sid's finger bones snapped back into place.

I was so being played.

We started with a trip to the nearest McDonald's drive-through, followed it with a sumptuous meal in the front seat of the van, and rounded off the festivities with a stop at a gas station.

Since Sid was getting what he wanted, he was good as gold. He hid and made sure not to talk to me when he could be overheard, and he didn't steal any of my fries, which Madison always does.

An hour and a half later, we were back at Dr. Kirkland's house. Even though it was dark by then, there were no lights on in the house, so I wasn't optimistic when the fruit basket and I went back to the front door. Ring. Wait. Repeat. Back to the van.

"She's still not home." Before I could start the engine, I heard the thud of bones hitting the floor. "Dude, you've played the 'I'm falling apart' card one time too many. If you've got a suggestion, I'm happy to listen, but otherwise I'm going to go home and eat one of these apples."

"Maybe she's in the back of the house and can't hear the bell. You could go look back there."

It wasn't completely ridiculous, so I got back out of the van. Sid, against all instructions to the contrary, was getting out, too. "Where do you think you're going?"

"Come on, Georgia. It's not safe for you to be wandering around alone in a strange place. It's dark, and there are trees in the way, so nobody is going to see me."

"What if Dr. Kirkland shows up?"

"I'll duck."

It didn't seem worth the argument, especially since I didn't have any idea that Dr. Kirkland was there, so I let it go.

We started around to the back of the house, trying to look in windows as we went. Unfortunately Dr. Kirkland kept all her blinds down and her curtains firmly closed—we couldn't even get a peek. There was a window in the back door, but even that had a blackout blind on it. The woman liked her privacy.

I gestured for Sid to step back a bit and knocked loudly. Nothing. I knocked again.

Finally, I heard noise from inside the house.

"Somebody is home!" Sid said triumphantly.

A second later, he was proven absolutely correct, though not in the way he'd hoped. A dog came barreling out of the dog flap in the door, which we hadn't noticed in the darkness.

I jumped back, thinking he might attack, but the dog barely noticed me. Because there in front of him was a canine dream come true—not just a single bone, but a whole skeleton, all for him.

17

The dog ran toward Sid with a bark that had to be one of pure joy. Sid backed away, tripped, and fell flat on his back. The dog was on him in an instant, going for a leg bone. Sid was doing his best to push it off when I got to them.

Later, I noticed that the dog was red, with a lighter belly and a tail that curled up onto its back, and later still, I found out it was an Akita. At the time, however, it just looked like a mass of fur and teeth. Especially teeth. Sid was trying to shake the dog off, but it had a good grip on Sid's left femur.

I'd always been told not to stick my hand anywhere near a dog's mouth during an attack, but when I tried for the tail, I got nothing but fluff. With an awful scraping sound, Sid finally pulled his leg bone from the dog's mouth, but it instantly turned his attention to his arm. Then I heard a kind of popping sound as one of the bones came free. The dog ran back to the door with the bone in its mouth, slipping back through the doggie flap before I could stop it.

"That ossifying hound has my ulna!" Sid yelped.

"It went into the house." I bent over so I could peer

through the flap and into the house, but there was no light and I couldn't see the dog. Or Sid's ulna. I thought I heard ominous noises that could have been the dog gnawing. "Here, boy!" I called out hopefully.

"What if it's a girl?"

"Here, doggie!" I corrected. "Come on out—there are more bones waiting for you."

"Hey!"

"How else are we going to lure it out?"

"Forget luring. It'll just leave my ulna in there and come back for more."

I tried the doorknob, but of course it was locked.

"Can you pick the lock?"

"Wrong sister."

"Can we call Deborah?"

"One, she wouldn't come. Two, it would take too long." Not only was Dr. Kirkland likely to show up at any moment, all the commotion might have convinced the neighbors to call the police. Worst of all was what that mutt could be doing to Sid's bone—we'd learned long ago that Sid didn't heal. We could glue him back together if need be, but any tooth marks would be permanent.

"You could break a window so we can open it and crawl in."

"I could," I said, reluctant to cause damage to the house or get myself into more trouble. "Look, she's got an alarm system." I pointed to the telltale sticker on the door. "The doggie flap must be left off the system, but I bet any windows opening would set it off."

I stared at the house, hoping for the dog to feel guilty and return Sid's bone.

Then Sid snapped his fingers—which is a much sharper sound with no flesh in the way. "The doggie door!"

"I don't think I'll fit."

"Not you, me. Slide me in a bone at a time, and then I'll pull myself together on the other side."

"That's actually kind of brilliant."

"Don't sound so surprised."

Sid let himself fall apart just in front of the doggie flap, and I knelt down and picked up his skull. "In you go!" I said, and slid him inside the house.

"I'm in!" he said triumphantly, if needlessly.

I kept stuffing in bones until the stoop was clear. A moment after the last handful of foot bones went in, I heard the familiar clattering of metatarsals against the floor. Then the door opened and a skeletal hand reached out to drag me inside.

"Hey! The alarm!"

"It's not on," Sid said, pointing to a number pad right by the door. The status screen said *Ready to Arm* in blinking green letters.

"Do you think it's safe to turn on a light?" I asked.

"Probably safer than fumbling around in the dark." Sid did fumble a little before finding the switch, and after he flipped it, waited to make sure there was no hue or cry. "Let's go find my bone."

Sid led the way, turning on lights as we went. I followed more reluctantly, feeling exceedingly uneasy about being in a stranger's house or, technically, being the stranger in the house. Besides, though the place looked clean enough, it smelled funny—a combination of chemical scents, old lady smell, and something kind of stinky.

The back door opened into a mudroom, and from there we went into the kitchen. I noticed that the dog's food dish was empty, which might explain the attraction of Sid's ulna. The kitchen led to the dining room, but I doubted Dr. Kirkland ate in there. The table was covered with specimen jars and nothing inside them looked appetizing. Academics do have a tendency to bring their work home—I was lucky my parents were in literature.

Next was a fairly generic living room with a TV that was small by the day's standards of big-as-a-movie-theater screens. The wall was hung with maps and animal photos, not family keepsakes.

A hall led to a bathroom, then a small bedroom with a rumpled bed, which was probably where Dr. Kirkland slept. The larger of the two bedrooms was outfitted as an office, but it clearly wasn't large enough. The biggest testament to that was that I saw the piles of books and papers first, then the dog chewing on Sid's ulna, which I retrieved and tried to give back to him.

The last thing I got around to noticing was the body of Dr. Kirkland. Well, next to last. The very last thing was her blood pooling on the floor.

18

If I'd ever given thought to how I would react upon finding an apparently dead body, I would have guessed that I would either scream or immediately rush over to try to help the stricken person, but I did neither. I didn't scream, because it was more of a slow realization than a sudden shock, and I didn't rush over because I didn't want to make it real. I just stood and wished that I were just about anywhere else in the world.

"Is she dead?" Sid asked.

"I think so. Go look." He didn't move, and I decided that if she was still breathing, having a skeleton examining her might not help her any. So I stepped closer and made myself reach out to touch her with one finger. She felt cold and stiff, and if that weren't enough, when I got closer I could see blood and tissue and other stuff that should have been in one of the creepy bottles in the dining room. "Yeah, she's dead."

"What do we do?"

"Shouldn't we call the cops?"

"And explain us being here, how?"

He was right of course. I couldn't let the cops find out about Sid, and I couldn't explain how I'd gotten into the house without him. "Okay, then we've got to get out of here."

I hesitated just a second to try to decide if I could have left fingerprints anywhere, then backed out of the room. "Turn out the lights as we go." Since he didn't have to worry about fingerprints, it made sense for him to take care of anything that needed touching. We made it back to the mud-room and peered out the curtain before going back outside, leaving the door locked behind us. I thought about latching the dog flap so Dr. Kirkland's pet couldn't come back out, but decided it was best to leave the place just as we'd found it.

I really wanted to run back to the van, but I knew it was better to take my time and make sure I didn't trip and leave some trace that forensics experts would recognize as evidence of a thirtyish single mother with sedentary habits who'd just eaten a medium order of French fries.

When we got to the van, Sid hid on the floor of the front seat without being asked, even pulling the blanket over his head. I wouldn't have minded hiding myself, but somebody had to start the van.

A few minutes later, Sid said, "Georgia, are you okay to drive?"

"Why wouldn't I be?"

"Your hands are shaking."

I looked down and saw he was right. "Maybe I'd better pull over." I was close to that same McDonald's, so I parked at the back of the lot, put my head down on the steering wheel, and tried some of those deep-breathing tricks I hadn't needed since going into labor with Madison.

Sid patted me on the leg. "It's okay, it's okay."

"I've never touched a dead person. Other than you. Could you have, you know . . . talked to her?"

"What am I, the skeleton whisperer?"

"I don't know!"

"No, I cannot talk to dead people. Or other skeletons. Your parents checked years ago."

"Really?"

"They snuck me into the med school to visit corpses, and then to the Anthropology Department to commune with my fellow flesh-deprived. Nothing."

"Maybe that's better." Just the thought of Sid talking to the dead woman started me shivering again.

"I'm so sorry," Sid said.

"It's not your fault. I wanted to talk to her, too. I don't know how we're going to find out about you now, but—"

"It doesn't matter anymore. That poor woman is dead."

"We've got to call the cops. We can't just leave her like that."

"And that dog needs real food." He rubbed the tooth marks on his arm.

"I guess we should find a pay phone." Of course, I hadn't used one in years, and didn't even know where to look for one.

"Crime Stoppers," Sid said. "You can call them from any phone and it's completely anonymous. They advertise on late-night TV."

"Are you sure?"

"Cross my ribcage," he said with a trace of his usual humor. "But just in case, let me do the talking."

I dialed the number for him—touch screens don't react to bare bone—and handed him the phone.

"I want to report a disturbance," he said, and gave Kirkland's address. "The dog never runs loose, but he's been in the yard barking, and I haven't seen the lady who lives there all day. She's old and I'm worried something might have happened." Then he gave the phone back to me so I could hang up. "That should do it."

"I just hope nobody saw us. Or got my license plate.

Or—" I shook my head. There was nothing else we could do. "Let's go home." I started to back up, then stopped and put the van back in Park. "Wait a minute." I got out, grabbed the fruit basket out of the backseat, walked to the nearest trash can, and chucked it in. Back in the van I said, "There's no way I could ever eat that."

19

As soon as we got home, I sent Sid to the attic and heard his door shut just as Madison was dropped off. Somehow I managed to pay attention as she told me about the awesome anime videos she and Samantha had watched, the awesome manga collection her friend had, and the awesome chicken dish Samantha's mother had made for dinner. Apparently she'd had an awesome day.

We watched something on TV that wasn't awesome enough to make me remember what it was five minutes after the credits, then headed for our respective bedrooms. I took a quick spin around the Internet to see if anything about Kirkland had shown up or if an APB had been issued for me, but there was nothing.

I did sleep that night, but I'd probably have been better off if I hadn't. Every time I drifted off, I found myself in another nightmare. Twice I was arrested for breaking into Kirkland's house, once I was arrested for killing her myself, and in the horror-movie version, Dr. Kirkland came knocking at my door, much as Sid had all those years ago, but instead of being a nice, clean skeleton, she was decayed and awful.

The worst was the dream in which Kirkland was still breathing when I found her, and I was able to get her to the hospital in time to save her. I cried when I woke from that one because I so wished that had really happened.

As soon as I was out of bed the next morning, I got back on the Web and checked the site for the TV station in Springfield, which was the closest city. All I found was a tiny paragraph about a woman being found dead in her Pennycross home. The police were investigating, but details were being withheld until the family was notified. I printed a copy of the report and slid it under the attic door for Sid.

For the rest of the day, I alternated between my usual weekend chores of laundry/bills/housework, going online to gather more and more details about Dr. Kirkland, and waiting for the police to come knocking at my door. Fortunately Madison was busy with a social studies project and didn't notice that I was distracted.

The TV station in Springfield gave the story a fair amount of play—Kirkland was moderately well known, albeit in a specialized field, and murders were fortunately rare in Pennycross. Early accounts said that she'd been found dead, with the hint that the circumstances were suspicious. Our anonymous tip wasn't mentioned. The dog, which I learned was an Akita, got the credit for alerting the authorities with his barking.

It was later announced that the death was murder, and it was tentatively linked to the rash of break-ins that had been keeping Deborah so busy. They thought the burglars had broken in thinking that nobody was home, but things got out of hand when they found Dr. Kirkland there. One of Kirkland's adult sons confirmed in an interview that his mother had a tendency to concentrate so thoroughly on her work that she could easily have missed it if the burglar had rung the doorbell or knocked before breaking in, even if the dog had barked.

There was no mention of a second break-in by a single mother with a really skinny cohort. By dinnertime I was ready to believe that I hadn't been seen at Dr. Kirkland's house, or if I had been, I hadn't been identified.

Once I was sure Madison was asleep that night, I snuck up to the attic to catch Sid up on the news, finishing with, "It looks like we dodged the bullet. Can you imagine what would have happened if we'd been caught?" The loss of my job, jail time for the break-in, possibly suspicion of murder. That was just for being in the same room as Dr. Kirkland's body. Once Sid was brought into the picture . . . it would have been a real-life nightmare to rival mine from the previous night.

"Now I feel guilty for suspecting her of murdering me," Sid said.

"She's not necessarily in the clear for your murder. Her murder was just a break-in gone wrong—it had nothing to do with you."

"Do you really think that's what happened?" he said skeptically.

"I guess. Honestly, I've been pretty much focused on 'Please, please, please don't let the cops catch us.'"

"I get that. It just didn't seem as if anything was stolen."

"We didn't look at her bedroom that closely—they could have taken jewelry from there. And I didn't see a purse."

"Her computer was still in the office."

"I saw drops of blood on the keyboard. I don't think anybody would be able to fence it. If they had sold it and the police found it, blood evidence would make it easy to track back to the killers." I was proud of myself for that line of reasoning. All those hours watching various incarnations of *CSI* and *Law & Order* had not gone to waste.

"I guess that makes sense," Sid said. "And I guess that's it for trying to find out about me. About what happened to me, I mean. We've hit a—"

"Sid, please don't say dead end."

"Yeah, too soon. We've run out of gas."

I could have nodded, clapped him on the scapula, and gone to bed, but if I had I wouldn't have been able to sleep. I'd been furious when I first found out Sid had been murdered, and that was just with murder as a theoretical construct. Now I'd seen a woman just after she'd been murdered, and it wasn't theoretical anymore. Moreover, Dr. Kirkland would have the police hunting for her killer, with her family and the press watching them to make sure they did their job. All Sid had was me. I couldn't let him down.

I said, "Not on your life. So to speak."

"I won't think any less of you if you want to stop."

"Well, I'd think a lot less of myself. So, next steps . . . Our only link is still Dr. Kirkland."

"I don't want you being linked to a murder victim."

"I'm not—we're not. Your interaction with the woman, whatever it was, predates her death by three decades."

"I don't know. . . ."

I didn't know, either, but I was willing to pretend I did. "Anyway, we were kind of distracted at her house, but did anything there spark more memories?"

He shook his head.

"There's going to be more coverage of the case, and probably more stuff about her life and career. We'll keep following the stories online—maybe something else will catch your attention."

"Like what?"

"Maybe you'll recognize one of her children. Or an associate. I bet there will be coverage of the funeral."

"Maybe," Sid said, clearly not convinced.

"Come on, we'll think of something. What's the rush? You're not getting any older!"

That got me a quick grin, but just as I was about to head downstairs, he said, "Georgia, don't you think it's kind of funny that she was killed now? I mean, I recognize the first person from my past in thirty years, and less than a week later she's dead."

It had been in the back of my mind, too, but I hadn't wanted to say so. "The police think it was part of the break-ins."

"If I were going to kill somebody around now, I'd make it look like a break-in, too. Not that I would."

"Sid, I never even thought that. You have a warped sense of humor, but you're not a killer."

"Maybe I was," he said sadly.

"Cut that out!"

I got him settled with a stack of manga and hoped it would cheer him up, but I knew from that moment on that I couldn't give up until I found out who Sid had been in life. I was sure he'd been a good guy, but if not, we'd deal with it. Whoever he'd been in life—whatever he'd been—he deserved to know the truth.

20

As soon as I finished with my first class Monday morn-ing, I went to the adjunct office to scour the Web for information on Kirkland's murder. As far as I could tell, there had been nothing of importance found since the last coverage I'd read, but that didn't stop me from reading as carefully as if I were proofing my doctoral dissertation.

I was still at it when a shadow fell on my screen and I noticed Fletcher standing behind me, looking at what I was reading.

I closed my laptop with a snap. "Excuse me," I said stiffly. "It is considered impolite to read over another adjunct's shoulder."

"Sorry. Old reporter habits. We stick our noses in every-where." He grinned, and it was a great grin, but I could tell he thought it would be enough to win me over.

It wasn't.

I deliberately turned away from him, reopened my laptop, and angled it so he'd really have to get into my personal space to see what I was looking at.

He must have realized I was pointedly ignoring him. "I really am sorry, Georgia."

I looked at him, and decided that he was looking appropriately sincere. No grin. So I relented. "It's okay this once, but it's hard enough to share space with this many people without having to think about somebody looming behind me."

"No more looming, I promise."

He sat down at his desk and turned to face me. "Obviously you heard about that professor being killed."

Since I'd expressed a fair amount of interest in Dr. Kirkland just the other day, I figured it wasn't a violation of shared-office protocol for him to ask. "I did. Kind of a bizarre coincidence. I ask about her, and then she ends up dead."

"You also asked if I'd ever covered a murder, and now I'm doing just that."

"Also bizarre, which means I've probably used up my store of bizarre coincidences. I wish I'd asked you if you'd ever interviewed an English instructor who'd won a multimillion-dollar sweepstakes."

He laughed.

"Is it creepy for you, covering a murder, asking the kinds of questions you have to ask?"

"The old pros at the paper say I'm lucky it was a relatively clean crime—and not a child. Anecdotes ensued. So I shouldn't complain. I have to admit that I was worried about talking to the dead woman's family, but the son I interviewed was very reserved, so it wasn't too terrible."

"Old New England reserved?"

"More like cold-fish reserved. But people react to death in very different ways."

"The stories I read said that it was connected to the break-ins around town."

"That's what the cops think."

"Good. I mean, I'm sorry it happened, but glad it had nothing to do with—with her being here at McQuaid the other day."

He looked at me curiously, but let it go, probably not wanting me to slap him down again. "I tracked down the person she was here to meet, thinking there might be a human-interest angle, but it wasn't that interesting."

"Don't tell me—meeting the chancellor to discuss a guest lecture: 'Zooarchaeology for Dummies.'"

"Not even close. She was supposed to be meeting a grad student in the computer science building but got lost. Apparently she had some old data from the stone ages—literally and figuratively. He said she had pages of measurements and numbers and hired him to put it into a database. But get this: part of her data was on an eight-and-a-half-inch disk!"

"Seriously? Is there even a machine on campus that would read it?"

"Apparently there is."

"I suppose it could have been worse. It could have been punch cards."

"Wow, those are before my time."

"Mine, too, I'll have you know, but we used to have a Christmas wreath my mother made out of old punch cards and spray-painted silver. It was surprisingly pretty."

After that, the conversation wandered toward odd uses for obsolete computer equipment, and I didn't even try to bring it back to Dr. Kirkland. For one, I didn't think he had anything else useful to tell me, and for another, I didn't want him to wonder why I was so curious. The conversation continued over lunch at Hamburger Haven, and though we bought our own meals, I was fairly sure that counted as a second date. Though my week had been so hectic, what with finding dead bodies and such, I had been wondering if he liked me as much as I liked him. Evidence suggested that he did.

The rest of the day was nothing special. I assigned the week's essay to my class, trying not to think of the stack of comparison-contrast papers I'd be dealing with over the weekend, and met a few students after class to help them clarify their ideas without writing the paper for them. By the time I got home, I was happy to go fast and simple for dinner: cheese omelets with fresh fruit on the side.

Madison was as tired as I was—the amount of homework was starting to weigh on her. So after watching a couple of episodes of *The Big Bang Theory* my parents had recorded, we were both more than ready to go to bed.

Unfortunately for me, there was a note waiting on my pillow:

Do you have time to talk?

I sighed, but after my emphatic declaration of the night before, I couldn't very well blow him off. Sid was so glad to see me that, if he'd been a dog, his tail would have been wagging.

"Are we okay?" he asked. "The police didn't show up today, which I assume is good news."

"As far as I can tell, we're in the clear. I read everything on the Web and even talked to my source in the press, and the police are still saying it was just another break-in. The burglars stole the professor's jewelry box and took the money out of her wallet, which was dropped on the floor next to her pocketbook." Though I was still sorry the woman was dead, I couldn't help but be relieved that it had nothing to do with Sid.

"What about her being at Mangachusetts?"

"She was meeting with a computer science grad student she'd hired to do some data translation for her. The timing was actually pretty lucky for us—if you hadn't seen her, you wouldn't have started to remember your past life and we wouldn't be as far along as we are."

"And we wouldn't have found a dead body."

"Okay, not my favorite moment, but maybe somebody wants us to find out the truth after all these years."

"Like a higher-power kind of somebody?"

I nodded.

"Call me a skeptic, but I'd rather believe in random chance than anything supernatural."

"Sid, you're an ambulatory skeleton. I'm pretty sure that counts as supernatural."

"I get that, but it's just that I've never encountered anything else supernatural. I'm not even sure what I am exactly. I suppose I could be a very skinny zombie."

"Also supernatural. And in that case, wouldn't you be trying to eat my brains?"

"That's profiling!"

"I've always thought you were a ghost haunting your own skeleton."

"Don't ghosts normally have a reason to exist? Like a problem to solve or a job to finish? My schedule has been pretty open for the past thirty years."

"But now it's not. So, next steps?" I looked at him expectantly.

Unfortunately he was looking at me just as expectantly.

Somebody had to blink, and since I was the only one with eyelids, it was me.

"Let's think about this," I said. "You're a skeleton."

"I am? OMG!"

I ignored the interruption. "You're a skeleton, and Dr. Kirkland had all kinds of specimens in her house. Maybe you were one of her specimens."

"Wrong time period and wrong concentration. Zooarchaeology deals with prehistoric animals, not modern man. Besides which, I remember the good doctor from when I was still among the living."

"Maybe you were one of her students. She would have been in her forties around the time you were in your twenties, so she'd have been teaching already, and you did know what zooarchaeology is."

"That's common knowledge."

"Maybe, maybe not. Do you have any more factoids about zooarchaeology floating around in your deceptively empty skull?"

He thought for a minute, then shook his head. "All I'm

getting is the word, and that it involves dealing with poop and statistics."

"Then probably you weren't one of her students, but you could still have been a student at JTU. Or a neighbor, or a friend of the family—"

"This isn't helping."

"Too many choices."

"Besides, the fact that Kirkland was the first person I've recognized in thirty years indicates that she was important to me."

"Maybe you two had a thing."

"What kind of thing?"

"You know, a *thing*. A bit of Mrs. Robinson."

"Oh. That would explain the guilt when I saw her. According to her obituary, her husband had only been dead twenty years. Maybe he killed me to get rid of the competition."

"The obituary said Mr. Kirkland was an actuary. I don't think skeletonizing remains is part of their skill set."

"Maybe I had a relationship with the actuary, and the professor was the killer. She would have known how to denude a skeleton."

"Better, but if a student handed in an essay with no more reason for making a conclusion than that, he'd be looking at an F. It's all just speculation without evidence about who you are. Or were."

"We're short on evidence, Georgia. All we've got is the stuff Yo told us."

"And the fact that you knew Dr. Kirkland."

He hesitated. "I know my last plan didn't work out so well—"

"That's putting it mildly."

"But here's a thought. If I recognized Kirkland, I might recognize somebody else from her circle—family, friends, or coworkers."

"Yeah?" I said warily.

"Aren't those the kind of people who go to a funeral?"

"The paper said her funeral is going to be private—family only."

"I saw that, but there's also going to be a memorial service at JTU. Anybody can go to that. Well, anybody but me. And your phone takes pretty good pictures."

21

Luckily for me, Dr. Kirkland's memorial service was set for Thursday afternoon at three o'clock, which meant I had plenty of time to get there after class. After much discussion, we decided that my walking around Kirkland's memorial service taking photos might cause a stir, so I made other plans.

I arrived an hour early in order to score a parking place right in front of the door to the JTU chapel, then I put a webcam on the dashboard and aimed it at the door, disguising it with a partially folded map. The plan was for me to record people arriving at and leaving the service and then show the results to Sid so he could see if anybody looked familiar. Meanwhile, I'd put on my interview suit again so I could attend the service and, with luck, get names for anybody Sid recognized.

Though I was there early, I didn't want to actually go inside the chapel until a crowd formed, so I walked around the campus to kill time. JTU was a stereotypical New England college. There was a grassy quad in the middle with aged trees and a fountain that probably hadn't worked properly since the trees were planted; a mixture of stately older buildings and brick monstrosities that probably had superior wiring; and fliers posted everywhere to advertise the weekend movie, available tutors, and pizza delivery joints.

At about twenty minutes before the service was to start, I went back to the chapel—one of the stately structures—so I could mingle with the real mourners.

Fortunately for my goal of finding Dr. Kirkland's family, the university had provided name tags, and I hunted for family members as discreetly as I could.

I spotted two almost stereotypical professorial types who I suspected were Dr. Kirkland's children, and quite likely twins. They both had glasses, tweedy jackets with suede patches on the elbows, and black shoes that were either timeless or hopelessly dated, depending on your point of view. They had the same build, too: slightly sunken chest, skinny arms and legs, and just a hint of potbelly. At first I thought the only real difference in their appearances was that the man was wearing black slacks while the woman was wearing a black skirt, but then I noticed that the man's dirty blond hair was longer.

The next family name tag I spotted was on a man who was the polar opposite. He was tan, fit, and had a full head of artfully dyed chestnut locks. His pinstripe suit was reflected in his gleaming Italian loafers, and the price of his Rolex could have funded a small research project.

There were assorted younger relatives who I guessed were grandchildren, middle-aged ones I thought were nieces and nephews, and one who was elderly enough to be a brother or cousin.

Unfortunately, the vast majority of attendees had last names other than Kirkland, and it was hard to know if they were former students, colleagues, or just friends. And of course I had no way to find out which they were.

I was trying to get the right angle to read the name tag on a carefully coiffed woman who clearly believed in the power of Spanx, when she turned suddenly to look right at me. On the plus side, I could read the name on her tag. On the minus side, I had to pretend I'd meant to speak to her.

"I'm so sorry for the loss of your mother," I said when I saw her name was Corrina Kirkland.

"She was my mother-in-law, not my mother." Though she didn't say *thank goodness for that*, the message was clear. She brushed by me, saying, "I think the service is starting." I wasn't surprised when she went to sit next to the man in pinstripes. They both had that same air of *Get me the hell out of here*.

I took a place near the back of the chapel, which felt marginally less awkward than being up front, and made sure to pick up one of the printed programs to use as a reference. Then I tried not to doze off during the service.

It wasn't just that I hadn't actually known Dr. Kirkland, it was more the fact that I'd attended countless university memorial services and they all blended together after a while. Born scholar and/or researcher, endured hardship to finish degrees, invaluable contributions to science starting with a doctoral dissertation project that set the field on its ear, even greater contributions of teaching and mentoring, incalculable loss to the field and great personal loss to colleagues. An amusing anecdote ended the service.

In Dr. Kirkland's case, her anecdote was about being so caught up in a project that she forgot to eat and had to raid a grad student's stash of granola bars to get through work one night. The academics, including me, chuckled, but I noticed that Italian loafers and the Spanx queen just exchanged disgusted looks.

The only notable thing was that all of the stories and words of admiration were for Dr. Kirkland's professional life. Even the twins–Dr. Donald Kirkland and Dr. Mary

Kirkland, who both taught at JTU—paid homage only to her work as a scientist. Either she hadn't had much of a personal life, or it wasn't worth talking about.

I started to feel sorry for the deceased. My parents were pretty eminent in their fields, but when their time came, I was certain there'd be as many stories about their personal lives and family as about their publications.

Once the service ended, Jim Michaels, the chair of JTU's anthropology department, invited everyone to join him out on the chapel green, where refreshments would be served. I was glad for the invite, and not just because I was hungry. The happy-making part was that the buffet table was set up right in front of my van, and therefore in a perfect location for the webcam.

Of course, that meant I was going to have to stay until the bitter end to give Sid the best possible chance to recognize people, so I thought maybe I'd take advantage of the opportunity for some snooping of my own.

My first target was Professor Morgan from the English Department who'd read a poem in Dr. Kirkland's honor. I made eye contact with him over the punch bowl, and said, "That was a lovely choice for a eulogy. I think so many people associate Robert Louis Stevenson with *Treasure Island* and *Dr. Jekyll and Mr. Hyde* that they forget his other work."

Morgan smiled. "I've always enjoyed his poetry, particularly the ballads."

We got our punch and I casually made sure to walk in the same direction that he did.

"Were you one of Dr. Kirkland's students?" he asked me.

"To tell you the truth, I never met her." Finding her body didn't really count. "I'm here on behalf of my father. He taught at Salem State when she was there. I'm not even in Dr. Kirkland's field—I'm in the English Department at McQuaid."

"Really? I thought I knew all the professors there."

"I'm new."

"An adjunct?" he asked sympathetically, the way one might say, *Have you been reduced to digging ditches for a living*? "Teaching composition?"

"I'm afraid so. My real field is—"

He looked over my shoulder. "I'm sorry, but I really must pay my respects to Dr. Kirkland's family. It was a pleasure meeting you."

"You, too," I said to his quickly retreating back.

I finished my punch and went back for a refill and a fresh conversation. This time it was an archaeologist, but before I could ask if he'd known Dr. Kirkland well, he asked what I did. As soon as I uttered the word *adjunct*, he excused himself and walked away.

Were people afraid my adjunct status would rub off on them, or did they think I was trolling for work at a memorial service? The fact that I *was* trolling, only for information, did nothing to cool my indignation.

I thought about trying to speak to JTU's chancellor, but he really was paying his respects to Dr. Kirkland's family, so it didn't seem the thing to do. Besides, I was afraid that if he found out I was an adjunct, he would instruct the caterers to take my punch cup away. Even now, the maintenance people might be preparing nets to capture me before the presence of an adjunct besmirched the ivy-covered walls.

Maybe I was getting a tad sensitive.

It wasn't like I'd planned to spend my career as an adjunct, but when I'd finished up my degree, Madison had still been a toddler and I'd needed my parents and sister to help care for her. That meant that I had to stay in Pennycross. Since there'd been no available tenure-track positions in the area, I'd taken a succession of adjunct jobs, thinking that I'd use them as stepping stones. Instead they became more like millstones tied tightly around my neck.

My parents had never worked as adjuncts and had never realized how pervasive the stigma attached to the position was. By the time Madison was old enough that I felt ready to move out of the area for a more ambitious job, I was no longer considered qualified for anything but adjunct work. Most other adjuncts had similar stories, other than the few like Fletcher who were only working part-time.

Since nobody wanted to talk to me, I decided to exact my petty revenge by blowing through as much of the catering budget as possible. I filled my punch cup again and piled half a dozen cookies and a bunch of grapes onto my plate. I was going to slice some cheese when a hand reached in front of me and grabbed the entire chunk and deposited it onto a paper napkin.

"Excuse me," a grubby-looking guy said. Then he got most of the grapes, and even more cookies than I'd taken. I stepped back before he could forage from my plate. He was piling on crackers when he saw Michaels, chairman of the Anthropology Department, and scurried away.

Michaels surveyed the wreckage, then signaled to a caterer. "They'll have more refreshments out in a minute," he told me.

"I've got plenty," I said. "I'm guessing that was one of your grad students."

"A very promising one, too, despite appearances. I believe he's scheduled to take his quals in a week."

"I wish him luck." I hadn't slept or eaten much in the week before my doctoral qualifying exam, either, though I had taken time for regular bathing.

"Oh those halcyon days of yore." He offered a hand. "I'm Jim Michaels, chair of Anthropology." Michaels looked like what I would have imagined a department chairman would look like if I hadn't encountered so many examples to the contrary. He was tall with a face that was attractively craggy, and he had salt-and-pepper hair and a strong nose. His hand was free of calluses, but I was willing to bet that, before he'd hit his fifties, he'd put in his time out in the field.

"Georgia Thackery," I said. "That was a very nice eulogy you gave for Dr. Kirkland."

"It was the least I could do. She guided me through my own quals and beyond. Of course, I hated her with a passion when she was my thesis advisor, but afterward I realized how much she'd done for me."

"After you caught up on sleep, you mean."

"Exactly. I take it you've been through the academic mill yourself."

"Yes, but in English. I'm adjunct faculty at McQuaid." I waited for him to make a break for it.

Instead he said, "How did you know Dr. Kirkland?"

"Actually, I never had the pleasure. I'm here representing my parents—they're on sabbatical." Before he asked how they'd known her, I said, "From what people were saying, I can tell she was very well respected."

"Enormously so. I don't think I ever met a more conscientious researcher, and her work was her life. She only retired because we have a mandatory age limit. After this, I really think we should revisit the issue. It would have been better if she'd stayed in harness. Of course, if we did that, we'd run into the problem of not being able to afford to hire new blood."

"No solution works for everybody." Goodness knows I was sensitive to the issue of new blood finding positions.

A trio of earnestly talking people approached the table and looked nonplused at the lack of sustenance.

"Excuse me," Michaels said, "I better go nudge catering. It was a pleasure meeting you."

"Likewise." I was pathetically grateful that he hadn't shouted, *Unclean!* when learning I was an adjunct. I was about to start up a conversation with the newcomers at the table when I saw them glaring at the overabundance of food on my plate, and realized that they thought the ravaged refreshment table was my doing. So I smiled vaguely and found a concrete bench off to the side of the chapel where I could sit to gorge on my ill-gotten goods.

I was still at it when Dr. Kirkland's daughter-in-law walked in my direction, talking on a cell phone.

She looked at me suspiciously before sitting down at a bench a few feet farther down the sidewalk, her back turned deliberately to me. Her snub might have meant more if she hadn't been talking loudly enough that I could hear every word she said.

"I'm sorry I haven't called back, but we had a death in the family. . . . No, it was just my mother-in-law. I'm at a memorial service at the college where she used to work right now. . . . No, he's fine. It's not like they were close. I mean, my father was in the Navy and was off on deployment for months, and I think I saw more of him than Rich did of his mother. . . . Devoted? Try obsessed! I've got nothing against education or science, but a woman with kids has no business going out into the field for months at a time. . . . That's it exactly. Rich decided a long time ago to stay as far out of that world as possible. . . . No, the twins are just as bad as she was, though at least they had enough sense not to get married or have kids. Not that there's anything wrong with a working mother, as long as she leaves the work at the office. Mother Kirkland never did—her house was like an auxiliary lab. I honestly don't think she minded when her husband died. It gave her more room for her experiments. . . . It was terrible. The kids could never have friends over. And the summers were worse! Did she put the work away and spend time with her children? No, she kept on working, and while other kids were going to Disney or summer camp, Rich and the twins got to be lab assistants. It was practically child abuse. . . . Didn't you hear? It was really awful. She'd just retired to Pennycross, and they've been having a crime wave down there. You'd think it was New York! Some thugs broke in to rob the house and killed her! Of course, anybody else in the world would have heard the crooks breaking in, but Mother

Kirkland was working. So much for being retired . . . She never called anybody unless work was involved, so nobody was expecting to hear from her anytime soon. If it hadn't been for the dog, she probably wouldn't have been found as soon as she was. It just makes me sick to think of it."

Actually, I thought she sounded kind of gleeful in a stare-at-the-car-wreck kind of way, but since I was just as gleefully eavesdropping, I had no high moral ground on which to stand.

"Oh, don't get me started on that damned dog," Corrina said. "I do—you know I have two of my own. But here's the thing. When Rich was growing up, he wanted a dog in the worst way, but Mother Kirkland wouldn't let him have one. . . . No, no cat either. Not even a hamster! She said a pet might mess up her experiments and that she didn't have time to deal with one, anyway. Then, when she retired, the first thing she did was get a dog, which she paid more attention to than she ever did her grandchildren. . . . Well, we certainly weren't going to take it, and the twins wouldn't, so Rich dropped it off at a shelter. . . . Lunch next week would be great. Pick somewhere with a good bar. Having to deal with these academic types makes me crazy!"

Corrina's husband, Rich, came striding our way, and I pulled my own phone out of my purse so I could pretend to read e-mail or tweet or watch Justin Bieber videos— anything that would make my nosiness less obvious.

Corrina ended her call, and after she spoke to her husband for a few moments at a much lower volume, they went back toward the chapel. I saw that the lawn was nearly empty of people and the caterers were cleaning up the buffet table, so it was time to go. I took my empty plate and cup back and headed for my van.

I just hoped Sid would see something on the video I'd taken that would help him remember something useful.

22

He didn't.

"Are you sure you don't recognize anybody?" I asked after showing him every bit of footage I'd filmed. It was late, and we were in the attic again. I was spending more time up there than I was in my bed.

I pointed to people I'd thought were key players, saying, "These two are of Kirkland's kids. This guy is their little brother. The woman is her not-so-devoted daughter-in-law. Michaels there is head of the anthro department. He said he'd known her for years. This other guy gave a eulogy, too." I showed him everybody whose identity I'd found out, but he kept shaking his head. "Don't any of these people look familiar?

"Not a one," he said. "It's like the red carpet for the most boring awards show in the world."

"Coccyx!"

Sid patted me on the shoulder. "I'm sorry, Georgia. I'm just causing trouble. Let's forget I ever saw that woman. I don't care that much."

I might have believed him if I hadn't noticed one of his smaller bones lying on the floor under the table. "I'm not giving up!" I kicked a box of books, which didn't help but did make me feel better for the millisecond before the pain kicked in.

"Stop that and go to bed. You can leave me the computer and I'll go through the video again. Maybe I'll see something."

It was a better plan than anything I had to offer, and I was beat. So I told him to sneak the laptop back down to my bedroom before I got Madison up in the morning.

I was too tired to stay up worrying, but in the morning, I really was hoping he would have found something. Instead, I found a note on top of my computer bag:

I'm sorry. Nothing.

"Damn it!" I said.

Of course Madison picked that moment to come out of her bedroom. "What's wrong?"

"I stubbed my toe." I noticed she was rubbing her eyes more than usual. "What about you? You're not looking too chipper this morning."

"I didn't sleep well. I kept hearing noises from the attic. Did you get a squirrel trap yet? I think he's having squirrel raves up there."

I'd forgotten that particular lie. "I'll take care of it today." Another lie. I really hated lying to her, but I didn't feel I could break Sid's confidence, either. Bouncing back and forth between the two of them was starting to make me feel like a philandering wife, but instead of getting twice the sex, I was just getting screwed.

The two of us stumbled through our morning routines, and since Madison was running late, I went the few blocks out of my way to drop off her and her bike at school so she wouldn't be late. Of course that made me late for my first class, which provided a new dose of guilt.

After class, I bought myself the biggest cup of coffee offered on campus and stumbled toward the adjunct office.

I would have gone to my parents' office instead, since it was bound to be quieter, but if I had, I'd have fallen asleep and missed my afternoon classes. I didn't need any more reasons to feel bad about myself.

In a desperate attempt to impersonate a useful member of society, I got caught up with all the e-mailed questions and requests for deadline extensions. Next I whipped through some early essays that had shown up in my mailbox. It was a better-than-average showing—a few papers showed some nice turns of phrase, and none were utter disasters. Most cheering of all, Fletcher called and asked if I had time to meet him for lunch, which I definitely did.

It wasn't fancy—we went to Jasper's, the diner just outside McQuaid's front entrance—but I was happy to count it as a third date, especially when he expressed regret that he had to cover a story that night, so we couldn't go out. Instead he suggested we go out on Sunday. I accepted, and got back on campus early for my next class.

I'd thought I could spend some quality time with Madison that night, but she had other ideas. After she wolfed down a grilled cheese sandwich and tomato soup, a friend picked her up for a movie. A less-fortunate woman might have felt glum at the prospect of a Friday evening alone, but I had an ace in the hole. Or rather, a skeleton in the attic. I made sure all the blinds were down, put the chain on the door so Madison wouldn't come in unexpectedly, and went up to knock on Sid's door.

"Who is it?"

"Who do you think? Want to come down and watch a movie?"

"I don't know. I just started a book and it's really good."

"Uh-huh. You've been eavesdropping and you know I'm alone, so now you're playing hard to get."

"I'm made of bone. You don't get much harder than that."

"Suit yourself. I thought you might want to watch *The Nightmare Before Christmas* in Blu-ray, and—"

Before I could finish, he came clattering down the stairs.

Since Jack Skellington was one of the few positive role models in media for ambulatory skeletons, the movie was a favorite for both of us, so we didn't talk until it was over. Only then did I say, "I guess you still don't recognize anybody from the memorial service."

"Maybe I shouldn't have expected to. People can change a lot in thirty years."

"You recognized Dr. Kirkland."

"She's an exception—from the stuff you found on the Web, she looked and dressed the exact same way for the last forty years."

"I suppose we could try to find pictures of people from thirty years ago. . . ." I said, but we both knew I was grasping at straws. Which people would I look up? Kirkland's family? Colleagues? Students? "Have you come up with anything else?"

"There's still my tattoo."

"Your what?"

"My tattoo. In my skull."

"That's not a tattoo."

"Sure it is. All the cool kids have tattoos."

"If you say so. Anyway, I don't know what to do about the 'tattoo.' Yo said there's no standards for IDs, so how can we track down the collection you came from?"

"Put it up on the Web, see if anybody recognizes the markings? Or check around with other adjuncts?"

"What if word gets back to the curator of whatever collection you came from and he or she wants you back? Yo said you were worth a lot of money—"

"I'd say I'm priceless."

"Without a doubt, but it's not like we have a bill of sale for you—the carnival you were in probably thought somebody stole you."

"I escaped," Sid said haughtily. "Speaking of the carnival, maybe the people there killed me."

"Sure, traveling carnivals kill patrons and then use them

to decorate their haunted houses all the time. They probably caught you in the tunnel of love making out with the carnival owner's voluptuous daughter and took umbrage. Didn't Wes Craven use that story? Or was it George Romero?"

"I'd totally watch that movie."

"But not as a documentary. Anyway, back to the tattoo. An ID number says *scientist* to me, not *carnival*. So what connection would Dr. Kirkland have with a carnival?"

"I don't know, but the carnival is the first place I remember. Maybe somebody there could tell us more."

"Sid, I don't even remember which carnival it was. Do you?"

"No," he admitted. "Would your parents know?"

"We're only supposed to call if there's an emergency."

"Yeah. Not an emergency."

I heard a bone hit the floor and knew he was letting pieces of himself fall off on purpose. Not that it mattered—it worked every time. "Deborah might remember."

"Good idea! Only you better do the asking. She's still on her 'Sid doesn't exist' kick."

He looked at me, and I realized he was expecting me to call right away. I didn't know if Deborah was even home, but I did know he'd keep looking at me with those big, black eye sockets until I tried, so I got the phone.

Apparently her social life was as lively as mine—she answered on the first ring.

"Deborah? Georgia."

"What do you need?"

"Glad to hear your voice, too."

"Uh-huh. What do you need?"

"Just your memory. What was the name of the carnival where we got Sid?"

"Why do you want to know?"

"I know this is going to sound crazy—"

"Everything involving that bag of bones sounds crazy, because everything involving him *is* crazy."

"I'm trying to find out who he is."

"What's that supposed to mean?"

"He wasn't born a skeleton. Okay, he was born *with* a skeleton, but it's a safe assumption that there were also skin, organs, and such included with the original package. And a name. It's the name I want."

"Why?"

"Haven't you ever wondered what his real name is?"

"Not once. I've wondered about how to get him out of our lives, but not how he got into it."

"Look, if you don't remember the name of the carnival—"

"Oh, I remember, but I'm not going to tell you unless you tell me what caused the sudden interest."

I sighed. Deborah could give mules lessons in stubborn and was impervious to any bribe I could afford to offer. "Sid saw somebody he remembered from when he was still conventionally alive."

"What? Where?"

"At that anime convention. He saw a woman he recognized."

"Did she recognize him?"

I didn't bother to answer.

"Please forget that I asked that."

"It's forgotten. Anyway, we found out her name and a lot about her, but he hasn't remembered anything else.

"He's not planning to approach her, is he?"

"No, of course not." That was a safe bet. "But now that he's remembered something from his past, he wants to know more. I thought we could track him back to where we got him."

"Meaning the carnival." There was a pause. "It seems to me that you're just opening a can of worms. What if I don't tell you?"

"Then I'll get in touch with Mom and Phil. If they don't remember, I'll go to the library and find any ads for carnivals in that period. Or maybe there was a newspaper article about the fire that night. It might take me a while, but you know I'll find it."

"If you'd devote some of that energy to researching a paper or two—"

"You don't want to finish that sentence."

"Okay, fine. The carnival was Fenton's. Fenton's Family Fiesta, Fenton's Fun Festival, something like that, but it was definitely Fenton's."

"Thank you."

"What are you going to do now?"

"I'm going to say good night and hang up the phone. Good night." I hung up the phone.

The next step was to get my laptop out and Google "Fenton" and "carnival" and hope for the best. Much to my surprise, it turned out that carnivals had entered the Internet age. Not only did Fenton's Family Festival have a Web site, but it was on Facebook and Twitter as well. I thought about trying to send an e-mail or make a phone call to ask for information, but it's much harder to turn down a request for information in person.

According to the site, the show stuck with the New England area, so I checked the route, hoping it wasn't too late in the year for them to be touring. I lucked out. They were going to be about an hour's drive away in Westfield for Oktoberfest. We could even go the next day, since Madison had already planned to hang with Samantha for anime-related shenanigans.

That cleared the way for Sid to come with me, or so he informed me when I told him I was carnival bound. "And I am not riding in that suitcase."

"Let me guess. You want to sit in the front seat with me and give heart attacks to all the other drivers. I think that would snarl traffic a bit."

"You've got more degrees than a thermometer, and I'm brilliant. I'm sure we can come up with something."

23

We came up with something, but it would have been a stretch to call it brilliant. I took Madison to Samantha's house first thing in the morning, teenager time, which was just before noon. Then I drove back to the house, where Sid was waiting for me, already in disguise.

He was wearing a hooded sweatshirt that was a souvenir from one of my previous jobs, hood up, and he had a Red Sox cap over that. A pair of oversize sunglasses, left over from when oversize sunglasses were fashionable, covered most of his face. For his legs, he'd cinched a pair of sweatpants as tight as they would go, but was still in danger of losing them if he wasn't careful. When we added a pair of tan stretchy gloves and my father's snow boots, he was mostly concealed. I figured that as long as I didn't let any other cars get overly close, we should be okay.

Getting him to the van unseen took a little maneuvering, but we got it done and were soon on the highway to Westfield.

"This is great," Sid said. "I haven't ridden shotgun since that Halloween back when you were in high school."

"I remember that," I said. "We crashed Rinda Patterson's Halloween party."

"*I* crashed the party," Sid corrected me. "You just drove the getaway car."

"I was still close enough to see." I grinned. "And hear." Sid had rung the doorbell, and Rinda answered, expecting either a trick-or-treater or a tardy party guest, not a skeleton moaning at her. She'd screamed and fled, leaving the door wide open for Sid to go inside. Which he'd done with enthusiasm, zipping into the living room, through the kitchen and dining room, and then back out the front door to dive into our car, which I'd parked behind a bush in case anybody was watching. Nobody was—they were too busy screaming and running to notice as I drove away, laughing my ass off. "I suppose I should feel guilty about that, but I don't. Not inviting me to the party was one thing, but inviting every girl in our class except me was just mean." It had been worth being grounded for two weeks when my parents heard about it through the school-yard grapevine and deduced the identity of the monster.

We reminisced about other Halloween pranks for the rest of the drive and even laid some possible plans for the upcoming holiday. At the very least, we could put Sid in the front yard and pretend he was one of those animated skeletons I'd seen in the stores.

Once we got closer to the Oktoberfest, traffic slowed and Sid obediently scooted down in the seat so he wasn't visible. But when I parked, he balked about being left behind.

"Sid, I am not taking you with me. If it were dark, maybe, but it's broad daylight. You're going to stay here until I get back."

"What if you get into trouble? At least take my skull in a bag so the rest of me can come running if you need me."

"The rest of you wouldn't be able to see where it was

going! Besides which, if a headless skeleton ran through that crowd, people would probably panic. At the very least, they'd spill their beer and take pictures with their phones. Either promise to stay behind, or I'm turning this van right around and taking you home."

"I'm developing claustrophobia thanks to you," he muttered, but he collapsed himself onto the floor of the van and let me cover him with a blanket.

I double-checked to make sure the door was locked behind me, not wanting to scare any sneak thieves to death, then headed for the festivities. After paying the two bucks admission, I headed for the midway, resisting the tantalizing aroma of bratwurst.

None of the rides looked particularly familiar. Of course, I assumed that everything had been repaired, repainted, and brought up to current safety codes any number of times in thirty years. I found a haunted house, but the one from my memory had a house-of-wax theme, with grotesque scenes of melting faces and buxom girls in fringed vests running from shambling mad scientist types. This one was a zombie beach party, with grotesque scenes of rotting faces and buxom girls in bikinis running from shambling undead types. Apparently, buxom, running girls and shambling villains were key to haunted-house decor.

It could have been the same ride with an extreme makeover, but I couldn't be sure, and one important thing was missing: a gibbet, with a skeleton inside. There had been some sort of mechanism to wriggle the cage and make the skeleton rattle. Ironically, I'd barely noticed the skeleton—the skeleton hadn't scared me—but I'd been fascinated by the gory paintings in that way that kids can't help staring even when they know it's going to give them nightmares. In my case, however, the nightmares had come while I was awake.

I couldn't really remember all the details of what had happened that night—I'd only been six—but over the years, I've filled in the gaps with my family's memories.

It had been early spring when we'd come to the carnival and was already dark when we arrived. My parents had promptly herded Deborah and me past the haunted house and thrill rides to get to the kiddie stuff. That had been fine with me, but ten-year-old Deborah quickly grew bored with the little boats, little motorcycles, little racing cars, and other miniature modes of transportation going around in circles. She wanted to go on big-kid rides like the Tilt-A-Whirl and the Scrambler.

After consultation, Mom had agreed to go ride with Deborah while Phil escorted me to the little helicopters and the little stagecoaches. I'd been so proud to be riding without a parent or my big sister for the first time.

Then the power went out.

I learned later that it wasn't the city power but the carnival's own generator that had been the problem, but at the time, all I knew was that the ride stopped, and it was suddenly dark as far as I could see. Immediately people started screaming. Kids screamed for their parents, parents screamed for their kids, people trapped on unmoving rides screamed to be rescued, and carnies screamed for people to stop screaming.

Deborah and my mother were stuck several feet off the ground on the Octopus, but Mom kept Deborah from getting overly anxious, and in fact got all the people on the ride to sing along to "Octopus's Garden."

Meanwhile, Phil was trying to get to me, but so were the parents of all the other kids riding on the little stagecoaches. He shouted for me, but again, so were all the parents, and I didn't hear him.

I wasn't really scared at first. Once I was sure the ride had come to a complete stop, I carefully unbuckled my seatbelt, climbed out of the stagecoach, and made my way to the exit, but I couldn't find Phil. He'd forced his way onto the ride by that point and was looking through each of the stagecoaches to find me.

The commotion started to bother, though not really scare,

me, and I decided I wanted to go home. I started retracing my family's earlier path back toward the exit, getting jostled like crazy as people panicked. Some folks claimed to smell smoke, and others said they'd seen people falling from the Ferris wheel. Neither turned out to be true, but it added to the confusion.

Somehow I found myself in front of the haunted house, and if those paintings had been creepy before, now they were downright terrifying. A few of the carnies had pulled out flashlights and were trying to herd people to safety, but the flickering lights made it look as if the mad scientists were moving, reaching for me.

I began to cry, too scared to move.

A big hand landed on my shoulder and a stranger put his face right up to mine. His breath smelled bad. "Hey, little girl. Calm down, it's okay."

I was nearly as frightened of the man as I was of the monsters. When I tried to jerk away, his grip tightened, and I whimpered.

"Come along with me, I'll take care of you." He started pulling me toward the one place I didn't want to go—the entrance to the haunted house.

Now I started screaming, but with so many other screams, nobody even noticed.

We were right under the gibbet when the skeleton started rattling. Which made no sense. The power was still off.

"What the hell?" the man said.

A creaky voice said, "Leave the kid alone!"

"Who said that?" He looked around wildly.

I tried to wriggle free again, but he clamped down on the back of my neck, pulling my hair in the process.

"Let her go!" came a voice from above, and both my captor and I looked up.

The skeleton was looking down at us, and while we watched, he reached above his skull to unhook himself from the chain that was keeping him suspended. The gibbet wasn't particularly authentic, so there was plenty of space between the bars for him to get out, and he dropped to the ground in front of us. "Let her go," the skeleton said.

The man's grip loosened, and I smelled pee. He stumbled away and ran, knocking through people in the crowd as he went.

If I'd been older or younger, I'd have wet my panties, too, but there was something about being six that kept me from being afraid. Besides, compared to the smelly man and the gruesome pictures, the skeleton looked downright friendly.

He knelt down in front of me. "Are you okay?"

"I want to go home."

"Okay. Where do you live?"

I gave him my address.

"Is that far?"

I rolled my eyes. "You have to drive."

"I don't think I know how to drive, and I don't have a car."

"We have a station wagon. You can take me to the parking lot and Phil will drive us home."

"Who's Phil?"

"My father."

"Why do you call him Phil?"

"Because that's what Mom calls him. Sometimes Mom drives, too, but mostly Phil."

"Do you know where your car is?"

"I may need you to help me look. It's blue, with a white top."

"Okay." He offered his hand, and I took it without hesitation and started leading him toward the exit.

I don't know why nobody noticed that there was a skeleton walking around with a little girl—either they were too busy going berserk or assumed it was somebody in costume from the haunted house or just didn't believe their eyes. At any rate, nobody stopped us on the way to the parking lot.

It was an absolute zoo in that lot, with people driving like idiots in their efforts to escape the carnival. I probably would have been hit a dozen times if I'd been out there alone, just because it was so dark and I was so small, but the skeleton lifted me up for a piggyback ride.

Again, nobody seemed to notice us, but of course nobody would expect a monster to be giving a child a piggyback ride. From the vantage point of those bony shoulders, I managed to spot our station wagon, and we made our way over there. The doors were locked, but my new friend plopped me onto the hood before climbing up himself.

"My parents will be here soon," I said with complete assurance.

"I'll wait with you."

"Okay. Then you can come home with us."

But the skeleton was looking at his hand as if he'd never seen it.

"What's the matter?"

"I think I'm having a really strange dream. I'd ask you to pinch me, but I don't seem to have anything to pinch."

"You can't pinch a skeleton."

"I guess not." He looked at his hand, then his feet, and then reached up to feel his skull.

At about that point, I decided it was time to attend to the social niceties. "My name is Georgia Thackery. What's yours?"

"I don't know."

"How can you not know your own name?"

"Maybe skeletons don't have names."

"I think your name is Sid."

"Why Sid?"

"You look like a Sid."

"Okay. Sid sounds good to me."

I asked Sid about living in the carnival and who that smelly man was, but he didn't have any answers for me. I later found out that he only became completely aware at the moment he saw that guy grab me. He had some very vague impressions of seeing things happening around him before that, but said it was as if he'd been watching the world through a wall of water.

Then he asked me about myself, but I don't remember what I said. Now that I was safe, I was getting sleepy, and before too much longer, I dozed off. The next thing I knew, I was being hugged awake by my mother.

The carnival's lights were back on and she and Deborah had been rescued from the Octopus only to find my father frantically searching for me. They got the carnies involved, and Mom had come out to get a jacket for Deborah because it was getting chilly. She'd found me sound asleep on the hood of the car.

Sid was nowhere to be seen.

Mom grabbed me up and ran back to the carnival, yelling at the top of her lungs that she'd found me. Phil heard her and started running, too, and an orgy of hugging and crying commenced. Even Deborah, not the most demonstrative of people even as a child, socked me in the arm and said, "About time you showed up."

The carnies were mightily relieved, and the owner gave Deborah and me stuffed Scooby-Doos that we kept for years, even after we realized they were knockoffs. My parents let us accept the toys but turned down the offers of a wall clock and matching watches that were prizes from the dart game.

Nobody thought to ask me how I'd ended up at the car. They just assumed I'd found my way there alone. Between the hugging and my being half asleep, I didn't think to explain. I did see Sid back in his gibbet when we walked by the haunted house, and I waved, but he didn't wave back.

It wasn't until the next morning that anybody asked for details about the previous night—characteristically, it was Deborah who demanded an explanation. I think it was because she was jealous of the attention I was continuing to get. Mom and Phil had made my favorite breakfast: cheese and eggs with extra-crispy bacon. Plus Deborah's

Scooby-Doo wasn't as nice as mine, and she didn't even like Scooby-Doo that much.

When I told her about Sid, she accused me of making it up. An argument broke out, and when the volume reached the lower end of the Richter scale, my parents intervened.

I told them my story, and they just smiled indulgently, figuring that my skeleton was nothing more than a skinny carny. When they called Fenton's to let them know that one of their employees had gone above and beyond the call of duty, Fenton denied having anybody named Sid working for him. Since my parents couldn't offer a better description than my insistence that Sid was incredibly pale and really, really skinny, they let it drop.

Two weeks later, Sid showed up at our back door.

24

I was so caught up in remembering my previous trip to the carnival that I didn't notice the man speaking to me until he repeated himself.

"It's really not that scary," he said again.

"What?" I responded brilliantly.

"I'm just saying that the ride isn't that bad. Or were you admiring the artwork?"

Standing beside me was a man with reddish brown hair, deep blue eyes, and just the hint of a cleft in his chin. He was wearing jeans and a purple polo shirt with *Fenton's Family Festival* embroidered on it. He looked a few years older than I was, and was much less taken aback.

"I was wondering how often you changed the theme on a haunted house," I said. "It looks like some of the zombies on this one snuck in from *The Walking Dead*."

"We try to stay current," he said. "This particular ride has had incarnations ranging from atomic horrors to witch's dungeon to werewolf's lair. I think there was a wax-museum thing when I was younger."

"Interesting." So it probably was the same ride I remembered, and this guy had been with the carnival for a long time, which might be helpful.

"It was a vampire's castle most recently, but then vampires got sexy, so we switched to zombies. Nobody has tried to make movie zombies sexy yet."

"Thank goodness for that. How about skeletons? Have they ever made an appearance?"

"Usually in more of a supporting role. There are none inside, if that's what you're afraid of. Just zombies, rats, and some mild dismemberment."

"I'm not scared of going in," I said indignantly.

He was grinning at me mockingly, or perhaps mocking me with a grin. In either case, I was pretty sure I'd lost control of the conversation.

"Let me start over," I said. "My name is Dr. Georgia Thackery, and I'm from McQuaid University." Okay, I was hardly there in an official capacity, but it sounded impressive. "I'm trying to establish the provenance of a human skeleton that was recently donated to our collection."

"Huh. I've been on the show since I was born, and I would have bet that there was no townie story I hadn't heard before, but you have indeed come up with a new one."

"Here's the situation," I said, starting my lie. "A man in Pennycross recently passed away, and in cleaning his house, his family found a human skeleton. They said he used it to decorate for Halloween, and they'd assumed it was fake, but one of the man's grandchildren realized that it was real. Since nobody in the family wanted an actual skeleton around, they donated it to the university."

"How does that get you here?"

"When the skeleton was examined, they found identifying marks on him . . . on *it*. The kind of markings that would have been on a skeleton in a museum or university collection, but they aren't from McQuaid."

"So? Finders keepers, right? Just put your own marks on it and nobody will know the difference."

Had the scenario I was describing actually taken place, that's probably what would have happened, especially after what Yo had told me about skeleton prices, but for the sake of my fiction, I pretended we had more integrity. "The chancellor is a real stickler for establishing rightful ownership. She insists that we find out where the skeleton came from and if it was obtained legally."

"Still wondering where we come in."

"The man who had it told his kids he bought it from a haunted house operator at a carnival. This carnival."

"We sell many things, but we do draw the line at human remains."

"This would have been about thirty years ago."

"Who would care after thirty years?"

"The chancellor is a Roman historian. To her, thirty years is recent."

"Wow." He scratched his head, showing a small tattoo of a carousel horse on his forearm. "Okay, that makes it about what, nineteen eighty-three?"

"Plus or minus a couple of years." I knew the exact date, of course, but that would be too much detail to explain away.

"I would have been eleven or twelve, so if anybody was selling skeletons, I wouldn't have known. We better talk to the boss."

"Is he around?"

"She's always around. Come with me." Then, almost as an afterthought, he added, "I'm Brownie Mannix, by the way."

"Pleased to meet you," I said. He led me across the midway, cutting between the merry-go-round and the giant slide. A trailer marked OFFICE was parked behind the rides, where the wires were exposed and the engines cranking. Brownie knocked on the door before opening it, then waved me inside.

An older couple—man and woman—were sitting at matching desks. The man was counting money while the woman worked at a laptop computer.

"Hey, boss," Brownie said to the woman. "I got a new one. This towner—"

"Brownie!" the woman snapped. "You know better than that."

"Excuse me, this patron wants to know about a skeleton."

The woman gave me the kind of searching look that made me glad I'd worn clean underwear and brushed my teeth that morning. "I'm Dana Fenton, and this is my show. What's this about a skeleton?"

I repeated my story, hoping it sounded more plausible to her than it did to me. If she could tell I was lying through my teeth, she was at least polite enough to hide it until I'd finished.

Then she said, "I'm sorry, ma'am, but I don't know anything about any skeletons being sold from this show. My father was still in charge then, but I'm sure I would have known."

"That just goes to show that your father didn't tell you everything," the man counting money said. "Don't you remember that chester who used to run the dark show? He had a skeleton hanging outside that was rigged to move to scare the townies."

Ms. Fenton sighed, but didn't bother to correct him. "This is my husband—"

"Call me Treasure Hunt," he said.

"Dad is big on nicknames," Brownie explained.

"What good is a carny without a nickname?" Treasure Hunt asked. He put a rubber band around a stack of twenty-dollar bills and made a note on a piece of paper before going on. "It was back in eighty-two. The dark ride was a wax show then, plenty creepy, and the ride operator had himself a skeleton to hang out in a cage outside. There was a motor to make it wriggle and build up a tip."

I nodded. I could only understand about two thirds of his words, but he was talking about Sid, all right.

"I was working as outside man for him that week—his usual guy got DQed for being overly friendly with a couple of townie girls, and we hadn't found him a new one. So I was there when he hung up the skeleton. Only he said it was a cast, because he knew Brownie—"

"He means my grandfather," the current Brownie said.

"Well, even a clem would know I didn't mean you, college boy."

Brownie rolled his eyes while I tried to figure out if I'd been insulted. Actually, I was sure I had been, I just wasn't sure how badly. I was starting to think that the man was using carny lingo just to bug me, and I was determined not to ask for annotation.

"Anyway, the operator knew Brownie wouldn't have let him put out a real skeleton. It wouldn't have been respectful."

I said, "Excuse me, but didn't carnivals back then have tents with 'alien babies' and 'the missing link' in jars?"

"Sure we did, but the devil babies and pickled punks were all gaffed. Brownie had standards—he always ran a Sunday-school show."

"So it wouldn't have been okay to show the real thing, but it was okay to fake people out?"

He just grinned, and I knew where Brownie—the younger Brownie—had gotten his grin. "I didn't figure out it was genuine until it had been hanging there a couple of weeks. That's when he started to get funny about it."

"Funny?" I said, wondering if this was another instance of carny lingo.

"He acted like he was scared of the thing, said it was going to come after him. We put it down to the drinking of course—we'd known he was a drinker, but he'd started hitting the bottle pretty hard about that time, and Brownie was thinking about DQing him because of it. Then one day I was looking at that skeleton, and damned if it didn't look real to me. So I waited until there wasn't anybody around, and I licked it."

"I beg your pardon?"

"If you lick a bone, your tongue sticks to it."

Yo had neglected to mention that bit of trivia to me, and as much as I adored Sid, I'd never had a reason to lick him. "I didn't know that."

"A carny needs to know the difference between real and gaffed," he said in a superior tone. "I told the operator that he was going to have to get rid of it before Brownie found out, and he said he'd be glad to. He was still acting afraid of it, and said he was going to grind it or beat it with a baseball bat, and a couple of days later, it was gone. Of course, if it ended up in that townie's attic, he must have sold it to him instead. It would have been just like him to do that and then pretend he was short on money."

"So he didn't have it long?"

"Maybe two, three weeks."

"Do you know where he got it?"

"He bought it from some kids. College boys, from the look of 'em."

"Do you know which college?"

He gave me a look that even a non-carny could interpret.

"I don't suppose there would be any records."

"Lady, all I know is three townies with their noses stuck in the air came round one night when I was out front and wanted me to get my manager." He snorted. "The operator went out to the parking lot with them and came back a few minutes later with the skeleton in a sack, laughing because he'd only paid a double for it. I didn't get any names, and I'd be mighty surprised if he did."

"Can you tell me which town you were set up in?"

He threw up his hands. "It was thirty years ago! Ask me who was with the show then, and I'll you, but don't ask me to try to remember which Podunk town it was."

"I can look it up in the route book if you know when it was, Treasure Hunt," Ms. Fenton said.

"It was nineteen eighty-two, like I said. Around the time of the blow-up. You remember, when some damned townies decided it would be funny to mess with the generator? We had to stay in place an extra week waiting for repairs. Don't you remember how much ice and flash we had to give out afterward, and it wasn't even our fault!"

Dana just said, "We were so fortunate nobody was injured." She went to a file cabinet, pulled out an old binder, and flipped through it. "The blow-up happened in Granville. The previous week we were in Great Barrington, and the week afterward, Brimfield. You sure it was in that window, Treasure Hunt?"

"Around that. A man doesn't forget the first time he licks a skeleton."

After that mental image, I couldn't think of any more questions, at least not ones that any of them would be able to answer, so I thanked them for their time. Ms. Fenton said she hoped I'd enjoy the carnival, and I said I was sure I would, but I knew I wouldn't. In fact, after I left the three of them in the trailer, I headed for the exit, even though I was dreading getting back to the van.

I was going to have to tell Sid that we'd hit another dead end.

If a trio of college students had had a skeleton in a sack, chances were that they hadn't come by it legally, but had likely liberated it from their school as a prank. So now we could be fairly sure he'd come from a college, but which one? The carnival had been somewhere in Massachusetts when Sid arrived, and Massachusetts was lousy with colleges. The only two we could eliminate were McQuaid and JTU.

I'd nearly made it back to the neon arch that marked the midway entrance when I heard somebody calling, "Dr. Thackery!" I turned and saw Brownie loping toward me.

"I'm glad I caught you. My father just remembered

something that might help you. I asked him how he knew that the townies were college students, and he said it was because two of them were wearing sweatshirts that said *ox* on them, like a college mascot. He only remembered because he said the one who wasn't should have been, because he was as big as an ox. Anyway, if it had just been one of them wearing a shirt like that, it might have just been somebody who bought a shirt, but two of them? All you've got to do is find a school that has an ox as its mascot."

"That's great!" I said. "Offhand I don't know which school it could be, but I can find out. Thanks so much!"

"Let me know how it goes." He handed me a business card and walked me as far as the arch. Just as I turned to go, he said, "Something else I wanted to tell you. You know Dad was just laying on the carny slang for your benefit, right?"

"I suspected."

"Not that he doesn't use a fair amount, but this was excessive, even for him. He's got this thing against townies."

"But you don't?"

"Depends on the townie." He grinned. "So if you decide to tell me why you're really trying to track down that skeleton, I'd like to know."

Talk about wasting a good cover story! "Brownie, I can almost guarantee that you wouldn't believe me if I told you."

Now I couldn't wait to get back to Sid, and back home to the computer to search for collegiate oxen. Finding Sid's origins was still going to be like finding a needle in a haystack, but the haystack had just shrunk substantially.

25

M y burst of optimism was unfounded.
     Yes, Sid was thrilled by the news, and speculation
kept us happily engaged all the way back home. It was even
better when Madison texted me to ask for more time at
Samantha's. With her gone, we could get onto the computer
right away. That's when we hit another dead end. As far as
I could tell, there was no college in New England whose
mascot was an ox.

In fact, I couldn't find a single college in the country that
used an ox. The closest was a high school team—the Blue
Oxen. Going further afield, there was the Minnesota Blue
Ox roller hockey team, but it hadn't been founded until 1995,
which left them out of the picture.

"Still, college boys and Dr. Kirkland," Sid said. "That's
got to be the link."

"Except that, at that point, she was already at JTU. Their
mascot is a Wildcat."

"So maybe the guys who sold me weren't wearing college
sweatshirts."

"Or maybe they weren't college kids at all, and the link with Dr. Kirkland has nothing to do with a college."

That only stopped him for a second. "No, from everything you've heard, Dr. Kirkland's work was her life, and we know I was college age, so that's the most likely place for me to have known her."

"I guess that's logical. Maybe you'd recognize the JTU campus."

"Another road trip?"

"How about looking at pictures on the Web?"

"Boy, you know how to suck the fun out of things."

"Hey, at least I have lips with which to suck."

"Cheap shot!" He nudged me to one side. "Let me drive. I'm faster."

"You're noisier, anyway." I moved to another chair so he could take over the keyboard. He was getting awfully fast. I only wished I'd known that when I was typing all those essays and papers during my grad-school days.

As I watched, he Googled up the JTU Web site and started looking at the pictures posted to attract students— sunny days with smiling students studying on the grass, brightly lit classrooms filled with smiling students, smiling students conferring with distinguished faculty members, suspiciously clean dorm rooms peopled by smiling students. . . . After twenty minutes of viewing a parade of smiling students, I said, "Anything?"

"Maybe. I'm not sure." He paused. "No, not really."

"You know, these are current shots. It seems to me that I ran across a site that has uploaded digital files of old college yearbooks. Maybe we could find one from the right era."

"Good idea!" Sid's finger bones flew across the keyboard to find the site I'd mentioned, then to track down a 1982 JTU yearbook. He started flipping through the pages.

There had been smiling students back then, too, but their hairstyles and clothes were different, and more important, the buildings they inhabited were different. At some point, JTU must have had as busy a building program as McQuaid.

"You know, this does kind of . . . Maybe . . . Yeah, I think this could be something," Sid said.

"Really?"

"It doesn't look familiar, exactly, but it doesn't look strange either."

"You're not filling me with confidence, Sid."

"I'm trying!"

"I know, I know, but—" He flipped past a virtual page. "Wait! Go back!"

"What?" He pressed the back button and went back to a montage of pictures labeled *Greek Life.* "More like *geek* life if you ask me."

"Look at that guy in the picture in the middle of the page."

"Hey! His shirt says *ox.*"

"Not it doesn't," I said. "That's not an *O*. It's a theta. That's a shirt from a fraternity. Theta Chi! Of course Treasure Hunt would have read Theta Chi as *OX.*"

"Because it was all Greek to him!"

I thumped him on the top of his skull, which would have hurt my finger if I hadn't had years of practice doing it. It didn't hurt him, either, but it made such a satisfying sound.

I directed Sid to make a quick search to confirm that there was a Theta Chi chapter at JTU. Moreover, it was the only chapter of Theta Chi in the area. Just to be extra paranoid, I also checked for the sorority Omicron Theta—which really was spelled *OX*—but there were no chapters nearby.

"So what were three frat boys doing with a skeleton from somebody else's collection?" I wondered.

"Either they took hazing their pledges a bit too far, which would make another great movie, or judging by fraternity stereotypes formed by watching too much TV, they stole it."

"Do you suppose we can scope out which of the fraternity brothers was as big as an ox?"

Sid got us to the yearbook page for the fraternity. There was a photo of what looked like all the guys in the frat, but it was hard to tell because the original photo was pretty fuzzy, and the scan wasn't exactly high quality. "What about him?" I asked, pointing to a big guy in the back row with a mop of curly hair.

"He looks oxlike to me," Sid said. "What are you thinking? That we find him and ask him if he ever stole a skeleton?"

"It sounds nutty when you say it out loud." I showed him how to enlarge the photo, but the low resolution on the picture meant that the pictures got blurrier as we enlarged. "Can we figure out what his name was?" There was a list of names under the photo, and since our ox was the eleventh guy in the third row, I started counting off. "Sid, look at the ninth name on the list for the second row."

"One, two, three . . . oh. That's interesting."

The name was Rich Kirkland. Dr. Kirkland's son.

"That doesn't make any sense," I said. "Rich and his large friend—who we assume sold you to the carnival—were at JTU, but you didn't come from JTU. Where on earth did you come from?"

Sid drummed his fingers on the table, which made a horrendous noise. "I bet Rich could tell us."

"I bet you're right."

By the time I had to leave to pick up Madison from Samantha's house, Sid and I had found out what Rich did for a living and decided how I was going to get to him.

26

On Sunday, I finally got the quiet time with Madison I'd been craving. We slept in, went to a used bookstore and the comic book store, cooked Mexican food, and did only the chores necessary for the coming week. Sid stayed quietly upstairs, which I appreciated. I returned the favor by leaving a stack of my purchases from the used bookstore where he could find them.

Monday was fairly normal—school and work. The only thing out of the ordinary was my call to Rich Kirkland's office. It turned out that he was a financial planner who offered free consultations to new clients. I made an appointment with him for Tuesday afternoon.

Kirkland had an office with several other financial consultants in a small brick building with awnings that were the dark green of a dollar bill. I was right on time, and the receptionist smilingly led the way to Kirkland's office.

"Ms. Thackery?" he said. "I'm Rich Kirkland." He stood up from behind a well-polished wooden desk and offered his hand for a firm "trust me with your money" handshake.

"A pleasure to meet you." He didn't show any sign of recognizing me, which was all to the good.

As I remembered from the memorial service, he was a tall man, well built, with dark hair, a good tan, and a snazzy suit. He looked prosperous but not showy: frayed cuffs wouldn't speak well of his financial acumen, and too much bling would make it look as if he was gouging his clients.

"Nice to meet you, too," I replied. We both sat.

"What can I do for you?"

"I'm trying to look ahead toward retirement. I'm a single mother, I have next to nothing saved, and a daughter starting college in a few years, so it may be too late."

"It's never too late to improve your financial position," he said confidently. "It is better to start sooner, but I'm sure there's a lot we can do. Before we go any further, let me tell you a bit about my qualifications. I've been in financial planning for eighteen years, and I also act as consultant to a number of charitable organizations, including my college fraternity."

"Theta Chi, right?"

"That's right. Joshua Tay University chapter."

"I recognized your tie tack," I said, grateful he'd worn it to give me an excuse to bring up the frat.

"Very observant. I was wondering if you'd seen me listed on the frat Web site."

"Actually, I saw you at your mother's funeral and somebody mentioned to me that you're a financial planner. I figured that you'd understand the academic lifestyle better than the average guy in your field."

"Ah. I should warn you that I'm not an academic myself."

"Thank goodness for that. I never met an academic yet who could handle money." I smiled. He smiled back. We were united in our opinion of academics.

"I take it that you're in academia yourself?"

"I teach at McQuaid."

"Tenured?"

"Adjunct."

"Ah."

The tone was unmistakable. Even he knew enough to diss me, though it was probably more for my income level than for my lack of academic stature. His smile started to fade as he mentally tallied how much money I was likely to bring him, so I decided to sweeten the pot. "As a matter of fact, I'm part of a group of adjuncts."

"A union?"

"Oh, don't say the U-word—colleges don't like it when adjuncts go in for collective bargaining. We're just trying to pool resources."

"How many are in your group?"

"About thirty. No one has a decent retirement plan, and we're looking to change that. The idea is for me to be the guinea pig."

"I'll try to make the experiment as painless as possible," he said, looking more cheerful. Maybe I could only bring him a pittance in fees, but thirty pittances might add up to a car payment or three.

Rich started asking questions about my finances, and entered my answers into his computer. I gave him points for not sneering at my income or paltry savings, and even my credit card debt only prompted him to say, "That's probably the first thing I'd like to look at—I bet we can get you a better interest rate than you're paying now."

When I'd answered all his questions, he said, "Let me look at some current offerings, and I should be able to suggest some things to consider." He started scrolling through windows on his screen.

I figured that I'd better get to the real reason I'd come before he presented me with something to sign or buy. "You know, I think I knew a Theta Chi from JTU who used to date my aunt. I can't remember his name for the life of me, but he was a big guy."

"Moose?"

"That's it." It had to be.

"I pledged with Moose—great guy, but I haven't heard from him in years."

I was relieved—though I'd purposely kept the relationship vague, I had been worried he'd offer to reconnect me with my old pal Moose. "He used to tell our family the funniest stories about you guys. Did you really pull all those pranks?" I tried to make it sound as admiring as possible.

"We may have played a few jokes," he said with what was surely intended to be a boyish grin.

"So the story about the professor's car?"

"No, it was the football coach's van. And it was completely filled—it took us days to blow up all those balloons!"

That had been a shot in the dark, but vehicles are a popular target for collegiate pranksters. "But the office . . . ?"

"That was a professor. We wrapped every book, every pen, every piece of paper. Even wrapped her can of Sprite—an open can."

We laughed merrily, and I thought I'd bonded with him enough to get to the question I wanted to ask. "Did you really run off with a skeleton?"

He barely chuckled. "Did Moose tell you about that? That one was supposed to be a secret."

"Oh, sorry." Feeling bad for Moose and not wanting to get him into trouble, I added, "He'd had a lot of my grandmother's eggnog at the time. I doubt he even remembers saying anything."

He looked somewhat mollified. "I don't suppose it makes any difference now. But it was just gathering dust in that classroom, and I doubt anybody at JTU even noticed it was missing." He looked back at his screen. "Of course, we took it back after the party."

I didn't have to be a parent or a teacher to know that was a lie, but I was too distracted to call him on it, and it wasn't by his recommendations for investment opportunities I should look into. I was stymied by a seeming impossibility.

I did try to look interested as I took the hefty sheaf of materials he printed out for me, and I really was planning to look the stuff over—just because he was a skeleton-napper didn't mean he wasn't a good financial planner. But I wasn't thinking about money market accounts as I drove back to Pennycross.

It just didn't make sense! Unless some other Theta Chi students had stolen some other skeleton from some other collection which then ended up in Fenton's carnival, Rich's story meant that Sid had come from JTU. Which was impossible—he didn't have JTU markings.

Unless . . . What if Yo had simply misread the ID number? She'd been tired and not all that invested in the result. It was such a simple explanation that I convinced myself that it had to be true. Madison was already home when I got there, so I had to save my brainstorm about Sid's brainpan until she went to bed. Then I hotfooted it up to the attic and told Sid what I'd found out.

"Can I look inside your skull to check those numbers?"

"Mi cranium es su cranium." He popped his skull off of his spinal column and handed it to me.

I peered inside but couldn't get a good angle in the dim attic light. "Have you got a flashlight?"

"Sure." His headless body walked in the direction of an old dresser Sid used for storage, and banged his patella against a table. "Aim my head this way, would you? I can't see what I'm doing."

"Sorry." I carried him to where he could look inside the drawer his body had opened.

"Found it," he said, and handed me a pink-and-white plastic flashlight.

"Hello Kitty?" I said. "Oh, man, was this Deborah's?"

"I grabbed it from the Goodwill box when she moved out. It still works fine."

If the evening produced nothing else, at least I knew what

to get Sid for Christmas. Maybe by December I'd even figure out why a creature with no eyes needed light in the first place.

"Hold Kitty for me, would you?" I pushed his hand into place so I could see the numbers more clearly.

"Coccyx. P-A-F-60-1573."

"That's what Yo said," Sid said, his voice echoing oddly from his upside-down skull.

I wrote the numbers down on a pad of paper on Sid's table, noticing that the pen was from a Holiday Inn and the pad was from Toys for Tots. Had we always stuck Sid with cast-offs, or was it a habit the family had fallen into? If his head hadn't been right there, I'd have started a Christmas list for him that very minute.

"Now what?" Sid wanted to know after I'd given him back his skull.

"I'm not sure. I want to know what this ID number means, but if I ask somebody at JTU, they might lay claim to you. Since Rich and his frat brothers stole you, legally you do belong to them."

"Not unless they grant me tenure!" Sid said indignantly.

"Granted, but I still think we might get in trouble."

"Is there perhaps somebody who used to be at JTU who might help? Somebody who is not necessarily completely loyal to that institution?"

I hit myself on the head when I realized what he was implying. "Like an adjunct, you mean? Of course. I bet we either have somebody at McQuaid who knows that system, or we have somebody who knows somebody who knows that system, or we have—"

"Stop now. Please."

"Anyway, I'll see what I can find out tomorrow and cross my fingers that word doesn't get back to JTU."

"Hey, if they come get me, I'll just steal myself this time. No cage can hold me!"

"Truly you are the Houdini of skeletons. Though I guess,

at this point, Houdini is the Houdini of skeletons. Anyway, now that we have a plan, I'm off to bed."

"Sleep well," he said a little wistfully. Sid didn't sleep as far as we could tell. I wasn't sure if that led more credence to the skinny-zombie theory or the bone-bound-ghost idea.

"I'll get started on this first thing tomorrow!" I said, and he looked happier.

The way things worked out the next day, I wished I'd just promised him a new flashlight.

27

On Wednesdays, I had a long gap between my morning class and my afternoon stints, which meant I had time to work the adjunct network.

The first step was to check the JTU faculty list. I saw some familiar names, including Charles's, but unfortunately I didn't know anybody in the right departments. Still, I had access to a room full of people who might, so I started making my way around the office.

I started with Kazmi. She was in chemistry, which didn't have anything to do with skeletons, but she knew more of the other adjuncts than I did and gave me the name of somebody else to talk to, who referred me to yet somebody else. Eventually I heard tell of a biologist who'd worked at JTU for two years and, even better, it was thought that she'd cataloged specimens while there. Unfortunately, the biologist in question was Sara.

Since she already didn't like me, I was reluctant to devise a new cover story. Most of mine didn't even fool people who trusted me, let alone somebody like Sara. But I wasn't going to tell her about Sid, either. Instead I was going to try to finesse the situation with a subset of the truth.

Though Sara seemed to be working at her desk, I knew her eagle eyes hadn't missed a step of my information-gathering trek through the room, so I didn't bother to act casual. "Hey, Sara. Have you got a minute?"

"Not really," she grumbled, but turned my way.

"I hear you worked at JTU for a while."

"Yeah?"

"I've got a skeleton that might have come from their collection, and I'm trying to figure out the markings it's got on it."

"And?"

"I thought you might know what they mean."

"It's been a few years—I don't have their system memorized."

"Do you know anybody—?"

"I might, but who's got the time to find out? You know how many classes I'm teaching?"

She was teaching five, the same as most of the rest of us, but I knew what she was really saying. "Okay, what do you want in return?"

"I heard that you've got a key to your parents' office. I've got a bunch of one-on-ones with students this week, and I'd rather not have to find an available classroom or try to squeeze them in here."

I thought about it. My parents had locked all their file cabinets and desk drawers, and had taken their computers with them, so there wasn't anything Sara could snoop into, if snooping were part of her plan. Still I didn't trust her enough to just hand over a key. "I've got some meetings scheduled, too," I hedged, "but my parents have adjoining offices. We can set it up so that you can use one while I'm using the other."

"Deal. Give me the ID number, and I'll check with a friend of mine at JTU."

Wow. She had friends? "It's P-A-F-60-1573."

She wrote it down. "I'll call my friend after we get the appointment times worked out."

I was impressed. She didn't trust me any more than I did her. Maybe that mutual distrust could be the basis for a new and meaningful relationship. But after a half an hour of schedule wrangling, I discarded the notion. We just didn't like each other.

After all that, her contact wasn't available until the next morning, which was coincidentally just before her appointment in my parents' office. She wasn't taking any chances on my changing my mind. I'd have found that level of attention to detail admirable in most people—in Sara, it was just a pain in the coccyx.

The rest of the day was refreshingly normal for a change. I was afraid Sid would be disappointed when I didn't have any news for him that night, but he was philosophical about it. It didn't hurt that I'd brought him a bribe: a paperback copy of an archaeology mystery that was written by one of the few academics who didn't make adjuncts feel like the lowest of the low. I thought the subject matter might appeal, given our current project.

The next day, Sara was impatiently waiting for me when I got to my father's office.

"You're late," she said.

"Your watch must be fast. Did you find out what the ID number means?"

"You mean you're not letting me in until I tell you?"

I just looked at her.

"Fine." She reached into her purse for a pad, which just happened to be opened to the right page. "P-A-F-60-1573 does appear to be a JTU file number. The structure matches, at least. The 1573 at the end is a file number—somewhere in the computers at JTU there's a record with details about the specimen, but I couldn't get access to it."

"Okay," I said, jotting the info onto my own pad.

"The P means it was a purchased specimen as opposed to being excavated on site or donated. The A is for Asian."

"Really?" Hadn't Yo said Sid was Caucasoid? "I mean, it's possible to tell that from the skeleton?"

Sara shrugged. "That's the best guess. People of mixed races can skew that."

"What about the F?"

She gave me a disdainful look. "Female, obviously."

"Obviously."

"The 60 is the estimated age, plus or minus a few years. The detailed analysis will be in the file."

Could Yo have been that far off the mark? Wrong race, wrong gender, wrong age? "How reliable is this kind of information? Or rather, how hard is it to determine? My parents had a grad student look at it once, and she said it was a man's skeleton, and a young man at that."

"Grad student in what? Art history? Trust me, JTU is a stickler for vetting their specimens. They wouldn't have put anything down that hadn't been verified by at least two scientists—the kind who've got their degrees."

"What if the skeleton wasn't from JTU after all? Couldn't another school use a format that looks like this, but in which the F means something else. Like . . . French?"

"Anything's possible," she said in a tone that showed what an idiot she thought I was to ask such a question. "But I did get the info you asked for, so you still owe me use of the office." A nervous-looking student turned onto the corridor. "That's my first appointment, so if you don't mind—?"

"A deal's a deal. I'll be next door—let me know when you're done." I opened the door to Mom's office to let her in, then I went into Phil's office. The door between the offices was closed so Sara could have sufficient privacy, and while she met with students, I sat at Phil's desk and stared at my notepad.

I came up with four possibilities: One, Yo had completely botched her analysis of Sid's skeleton, either from ineptitude or lack of sleep. Two, Yo had misled me for a cheap joke. Three, Sid hadn't come from JTU after all. And four . . . I didn't want to think about number four.

Neither of the first two was too bad—I could rectify either situation by finding a more expert expert to take a look at Sid. That could even be good news if Yo had misread all the evidence—maybe Sid hadn't been murdered after all.

The third was more problematic, because I'd have to swallow a triple dose of coincidence: Dr. Kirkland being at JTU, her son stealing a different skeleton during the same time period, and a code inside Sid's skull that only looked like JTU's identification conventions. That wouldn't just blunt Occam's razor—it would shatter it.

It was the fourth possibility that really worried me. What if somebody had purposely mismarked Sid's skull? The only reason to do that would be to hide him, and there aren't that many reasons to hide a dead body. Of course, we already knew that Sid was murdered, but now it looked like he was murdered at JTU. A thirty-year-old murder, even of some-body I'd known, wouldn't have scared me, but when I tied it to Dr. Kirkland's more recent death . . . That was scary.

Yet it wasn't as scary as what Sid came up with after I shared my speculations.

28

"Please tell me you're kidding."

"Seriously, Georgia, this will work. We need to get a look at the files at JTU to research my ID number, your pal Charles has access there, and you yourself dubbed me the Houdini of skeletons. You practically suggested this plan yourself!"

"No, Sid, I did not suggest that we get Charles to leave you at JTU so you can prowl around all night."

"Why didn't you? It's so obvious!"

"It's obvious that you're insane." Since it was Wednesday night, Madison was at her Yu-Gi-Oh! tournament and Sid and I were in my bedroom. I'd worried he'd be upset, freaked, even frightened by the news that something was off about his ID markings. Instead, he popped out with this crazy scheme.

"What could go wrong?"

"Charles could open the suitcase and see you."

"You said he was trustworthy."

"He is, but . . . Okay, you're right. Charles won't do that

if I ask him not to." Even though Sid had never met Charles face-to-face, or face-to-skull, he'd grasped that we could trust him to take Sid's suitcase, leave it outside the door to Dr. Kirkland's office, and never look back to see what was going on. "Okay, then. The office is bound to be locked."

"I'll either slip enough of myself under the door to open it from the inside, or find a chair to stand on so I can drop pieces of myself through the transom. I've spent hours looking at photos of that campus—just about all of the offices have transoms over the doors."

"What if the transom isn't open?"

"I can get it open. And if all else fails, I'll break the door lock. I'm sure I can get in, but if I can't, I'll crawl back into the suitcase and wait for Charles to get me in the morning."

"What if somebody steals your suitcase?"

"I'll escape as soon as possible and either get home on my own or call you to come pick me up."

"What if a security guard sees the suitcase and takes it to the security office?"

"You're going to put Charles's name on it, so he'll call Charles to come get it. Otherwise I'll escape as soon as possible and either get home on my own or call you to come pick me up."

"What if—?

"I'll escape as soon as possible and either get home on my own or call you to come pick me up. Look, Georgia, I am eternally grateful for all the work you've done to help me find myself, but this is something I can do. Please let me do it."

I didn't like it, but I didn't see how I could refuse. It was Sid's life. More or less. "All right, I'll ask Charles to help, but if he says no, we're giving up the idea."

Of course Charles agreed without hesitation.

I caught him in the adjunct office after teaching my Thursday classes, and since I didn't want anyone overhearing—particularly Sara—I asked him to join me at the McQuaid Coffee Corner.

First we wrangled over who was paying for the coffee, which resulted in him agreeing to let me treat him to coffee and pastries as long as he got to pick up the next check. Then I said, "Charles, you're teaching two classes at JTU this semester, aren't you?"

"I am."

"Then I need a favor."

"Anything, dear lady."

"It's kind of odd, and maybe technically illegal—"

"I said anything. Illegality does not concern me, and I know you would never ask me to do anything immoral or dangerous. So of course I am happy agree to whatever you need."

"Charles, you are a pearl without price." The plan was simple: I'd meet him in the parking lot after he was done at McQuaid for the day and give him Sid's suitcase, which he would take to JTU and leave outside Dr. Kirkland's office. Then, just before people started arriving the next morning, he'd retrieve the suitcase. I'd meet him at Jasper's Diner, buy him breakfast, and take the suitcase back.

His only objection was to my paying for breakfast. He maintained that since I'd just bought coffee, the next day would be his turn. I finally conceded. Getting a free breakfast was little enough to endure.

All that was left was to arrange a time for us to meet that afternoon. Sid was already ensconced in his suitcase in my van. At the appointed time, the transfer was made. I was supposed to be off the hook for the rest of the evening, but it didn't work out that way.

Madison probably slept great with no "squirrels" moving around in the attic, but I tossed and turned most of the night, worrying about Sid.

29

I finally dozed off at four in the morning and ended up sleeping through my alarm. If Madison hadn't set hers, I never would have gotten up, and as it was, I was running so late that I missed the rendezvous with Charles. When I didn't see his car at Jasper's, I checked for text messages and found one saying he was sorry he'd missed me. He promised to leave the suitcase at my desk.

After that, I just barely made it to class on time. As soon as that was over, I had to trot to my parents' office to meet half a dozen students who'd asked for critiques before handing in the week's essay. So it was nearly noon before I got to the adjunct office.

As soon as I walked in the door, I could tell something was off. Nobody was looking at me. More than that, they were pointedly *not* looking at me, and the room was unnaturally quiet. Every experienced teacher or instructor knows that situation. The last time it had happened to me was when I was in the middle of a class and had to take an emergency call from Madison's school. I excused myself, made sure that Madison was in no immediate danger, then came back to discover that I urgently needed password protection on my laptop.

I hadn't left my laptop unattended this time, but Charles had left Sid's suitcase at my desk. Knowing his penchant for tidiness, I couldn't imagine he'd left it stuck out into the aisle, and there was no reason for it to be partially unzipped. I opened the bag just enough to see that Sid was still in there. Then I cleared my throat, and one finger bone moved just enough to point at the desk in front of me. Toward Sara.

Neither Charles nor Fletcher were in the room, which meant that I was without my closest allies, so I pushed Sid under the desk, sat down, and pulled out some random papers while I thought it through. Then, in a calm voice that was intended to carry throughout the room, I said, "Sara, if you'd wanted to know what was in my suitcase, you could have just asked."

"I don't know what you're talking about," she said, looking around for an informant.

"I'm talking about you opening my bag. You know we adjuncts have little enough privacy as it is. We have to share this office, and our desks don't lock. We have nowhere to store anything, or meet with students, or even make a confidential phone call. It always seemed to me that the only way we keep from killing each other is by respecting each other's space. So I would appreciate it if you'd respect mine from here on out. Okay?"

Without waiting for an answer, I pretended to read my random papers, but out of the corner of my eye I could see other adjuncts glaring at Sara. They were realizing that if she was that open about snooping in my things, she wouldn't hesitate to do the same to them.

"You can't prove I opened that bag!" she sputtered.

I tried to look surprised that the conversation was ongoing. "I don't intend to press charges, if that's what you're worried about."

"If anybody should press charges, it's JTU. You stole that skeleton from them! I know how much that thing is worth on the black market—you only wanted to see if it could be traced."

Now every adjunct in the room knew I had a skeleton, and in very short order, every adjunct in the college would know, too. Word might even spread to the regular faculty, and it would certainly spread to adjuncts on other campuses. It was time to redirect the conversation.

I sighed in exasperation—that was easy, because I really was pretty damned exasperated. "Number one, I found this skeleton in my parents' attic, where it has been for over thirty years. My sister is a locksmith, and I thought it might make a good display for her front window for Halloween. Skeletons, keys, skeleton keys?" I looked at her as if making sure she was keeping up with me.

"Then why did you ask about the identification number?"

"Because I realized the skeleton is real, and not a reproduction. I knew my parents had obtained it legally, but I didn't know about the place they bought it, so I thought it wouldn't hurt to check. Which I trusted you to help me with." I paused, letting the silence imply how sadly my trust had been misplaced. "At any rate, this skeleton can't be from JTU—as you pointed out, they only mark female skeletons with an F. This one is male. So I don't know where it came from. At any rate, my sister doesn't want a real skeleton in her shop window, so I'm going to put this one back in the attic. It is legal to keep a skeleton, by the way."

"Not if it's stolen! Where did your parents get it?"

"It followed them home, okay? Look, Sara, I've been trying to be polite, but I have no intention of discussing my skeleton with you anymore. I'm also not going to discuss the papers in my satchel, the candy hidden in my desk, or the tampons I've got in my pocketbook. Because none of them are any of your business!"

I turned back to my bogus paperwork, and pretended to

work while I tried to get a feel for the reaction of the other adjuncts. Did they think Sara was in the right? Did they think I was a freak for carrying around a skeleton? Were they hoping for more fireworks?

A few minutes later, a drama instructor I'd barely spoken to came by, and said, "If you want help tracking ID marks, a friend of mine teaches at a med school at BU." I thanked her, and I noticed that she gave Sara a dismissive look before leaving. Then my old boyfriend stopped at my desk long enough to tell me about a book he'd read that he thought I'd like, and a physicist asked me for my sister's phone number because he needed a new lock put on his house.

Nobody spoke to Sara.

I stayed in the office about an hour after that, killing time in order to make the point that I had no reason to be embarrassed, then went to teach my next class.

I took Sid's suitcase with me.

30

As soon as class was over, I headed for the van and put Sid up front so we could talk as I drove home.

"Are you okay?" I asked him.

"I'm sorry, Georgia. That woman opened the suit-case and—"

"But are you okay? Are all of your pieces intact?"

"I'm fine."

I let out a deep breath. "Thank goodness—I wouldn't have put it past her to steal a bone as a souvenir. And don't apologize for what that ossifying piece of sacrum did. If I'd met Charles when I was supposed to, this never would have happened. It's my fault for sleeping late."

"But now people know about me. I mean, they don't know I'm alive—sort of alive. Moving, anyway. But they know you've got a skeleton."

"So what?" I scoffed. "Academics are supposed to be weird. I went to a party at a stats teacher's house once, and he had three stuffed cats on his mantel. Not plush toys—taxidermy stuffed. They were all his former pets. Now that caused talk."

"But—"

"It's done, it's over. Just tell me you found out something in Dr. Kirkland's office."

He hung his head.

"They've cleaned the place out already?"

"No, but—"

"Could you not get out of the suitcase?" As part of our prep work, we'd rigged it so he could open the case from the inside, but the bag was old, and the zipper could have gotten stuck.

"It worked fine, but—"

"Were the file cabinets locked? I knew I should have dug up a skeleton key for you. No offense. Or—"

"Can I get a word in edgewise? Somebody else broke into the office."

"Somebody did what?"

"I'm starting at the beginning now. Charles left me at the door, as planned, and I waited for half an hour to make sure he was gone." I'd lent him a watch with a glow-in-the-dark face for the occasion. "Then I got out and used the over-the-transom method to get into the office."

"You didn't chip a bone, did you?"

"Nope. There was a rug, and that kept things quiet, too. Once I got enough of myself inside, I opened the door, pulled myself together, and got the suitcase inside. I was about to start looking around when I heard somebody coming down the hall. Of course, I didn't know if he was coming into that office, but just in case, I got back into the suitcase and zipped it shut. I was just in time, too. The guy came in."

"Did he have a key?"

"It sounded like he did."

"Who was it?"

"Do you see X-ray-vision eyes?" Sid asked, and stuck his fingers into his sockets.

"Stop that. It looks painful."

If Sid had had eyes of any description, I suspect he'd have rolled them. "I don't know who it was. I was afraid it was somebody coming to pack up the office and was worried that I'd end up in storage, but as far as I could tell, all the guy did for the next hour was fiddle with Dr. Kirkland's computer."

"How do you know it was a he if you didn't see him?"

"I don't," he admitted, "but it sounded like a man mumbling under his breath while he fiddled."

"Then what?"

"He walked around, opened drawers, flipped through papers. I think he was looking for something."

"Did he open your suitcase?"

"He tried to, but I held on to the zipper from my side." Sid was fairly strong, given his lack of muscles. "I was afraid he was going to try to force it, but he gave up pretty quickly. Whatever it was he was looking for, he didn't expect it to be in a suitcase. Then he rummaged around some more and left."

"I suppose it could have been perfectly innocent," I said.

"Yeah. In the middle of the night, somebody sneaks into the office of a dead professor and messes with her computer. He was probably just playing Minecraft."

"Okay, not innocent. Sacrum, I wish I knew who it was."

"Maybe we should put a peephole in the suitcase before I go undercover next time."

"There's not going to be a next time! What if that guy had opened the suitcase and found you? Or just wheeled you away? I just hate that we risked you like that and then didn't learn anything."

"It wasn't like I didn't try."

"Don't tell me you left the suitcase after all that."

"Well . . ."

"Sid!"

"I waited for an hour to make sure he was gone, and the first thing I did was wedge a chair under the door to make sure nobody else could come strolling in."

I was torn between wanting to smack him for taking the chance, and wanting to smack him for teasing me. So I smacked him. "What did you find out?"

He looked disgusted. "Zilch. I went through all the files, but there was nothing about the school's skeleton collections. Nothing useful on her computer, either."

"There was no password protection on it?"

"Dr. Kirkland used one of those 'remember me' features, so I didn't have to enter it, so I'd have found anything if there was anything to find."

"Coccyx!" I thought I heard a bone drop. "Don't you fall apart on me now, Sid. We aren't through, not by a long shot."

"Then what next?"

"I don't know, but we'll come up with something. Okay?"

"I just wish I had a 'remember me' feature for myself," he said sadly.

31

Madison was doing homework while listening to music when we got back to the house, so I was able to sneak Sid into the house and up to the attic without her noticing. Only when he was out of sight did I let her know I was on the premises.

I wandered to the kitchen to see what was available for dinner and was weighing the ease of ordering pizza against the impact on my budget when my cell phone rang. It was Fletcher.

"Did you really take a skeleton to class?" he asked.

"It took you this long to hear? The grapevine is running slow."

"I wasn't on campus today, so it took a while for the news to get to me. So, did you?"

"Yes, actually. My parents had one in the attic and I was trying to check on the provenance. No biggie. What is a biggie is that Sara had the nerve to open my suitcase! Why aren't people talking about that?"

"Because nosy coworkers are a dime a dozen, whereas

skeletons in suitcases are far more gossip-worthy. If it makes
you feel any better, I hear that the way in which you dressed
her down was masterful."

"I like the sound of that. I know it's probably not very
mature, but there's something cleansing about righteous
anger."

"I live for righteous anger. Why do you think I became
a reporter?" He went on to tell about the first really big scam
he'd revealed in print, which I appreciated both because it
was interesting and because it distracted him from the skeleton in the suitcase.

Unfortunately, he eventually got back to Sid. "You know,
I bet my boss would get a kick out of a feature about strange
things people keep in their attics. Do you think your parents
would mind if I used them as an example? Maybe take a
picture of the skeleton?"

"No. I mean, yes, they'd mind. They're really private
people."

"Oh," he said, surprised by my refusal. "I wouldn't have
to use their names."

"Fletcher, there are people all over campus who know I
was lugging a skeleton around. I think they'd figure out who
you were writing about."

"Since everybody already knows, what difference would
it make if it was in the paper?"

"There's a difference between everybody on campus
knowing and everybody in town knowing. Not to mention
the fact that the paper goes online, too."

"There's already a picture of it online."

"Excuse me?"

"Sara posted a picture of the skeleton on Facebook."

"Are you serious? Please tell me she didn't use my name."

"She did misspell Thackery."

"That ossifying piece of sacrum!"

"Um . . . what?"

"You realize that colleges Google people before hiring

them, right? Which means that any time I try to get a job, somebody could bring up Sid."

"Sid?"

"The skeleton." I took a deep breath. "I'm sorry, I'm too enraged to make any sense. But if I miss out on any jobs because of that woman, I am going to cram *her* into that suitcase!"

"I could ask her to delete it, maybe sweet-talk her a little, take her out to dinner. Well, coffee. I don't think I could stand her for a whole dinner."

"Thanks, but as soon as she realized you were just trying to get her to take it down, she'd plaster it all over the Web. No, this is going to require a special effort on my part."

"That sounds ominous."

"Don't worry—I can virtually guarantee that there will be no loss of life."

"Now you're scaring me. But I like it."

"You go for a badass, do you?"

"Oh yeah. I know this is incredibly late notice, but are you free for dinner tonight?"

"I might be. Let me check something and call you back." In other words, I wanted to see if Madison minded being on her own for the evening. It turned out Deborah had invited both of us to go out with her, but was happy to settle for a one-on-one with her favorite niece. In fact, she was willing to have Madison sleep over so I could make it a late night. I could almost see the wink when Deborah said that.

I called Fletcher back to set a time, then scooted upstairs for a quick shower and change. I was finishing up my makeup when I saw Deborah coming up the stairs.

"I didn't hear the bell," I said suspiciously.

She just smirked and patted the pocket that presumably held her lock picks. "So you've got a hot prospect."

"A prospect? You make it sound as if I'm actively hunting for a husband."

"It would be a good thing, wouldn't it?"

"I haven't noticed you saying yes to the dress, or ordering pastel-colored padlocks to use as wedding favors."

"I may not be married, but I'm settled. I have a business and a home of my own. You, on the other hand, are living moment to moment."

"How can one live other than moment to moment? Should I be skipping moments, or going back for moment do-overs?"

"You also have a daughter who deserves a home and a father."

"Stop right there," I said, no longer willing to play. "I have always given Madison everything she needs, and that is not going to change."

She must have realized she'd gone too far, because I got one of her rare apologies. "Sorry." Deborah's apologies were always brief, perhaps because she had so little practice. Then she went back for a do-over. "So I hear you're seeing a new guy. Is he hot?"

"Do you want it in Fahrenheit or centigrade?"

"How about in English? Which I believe you're supposed to know something about."

"Touché. He is pretty hot. Dark hair, dark eyes, nice butt."

"Madison mentioned the butt."

"He writes for the *Gazette* full-time and teaches at McQuaid part-time."

"He's not afraid of work. I like that."

I ran down the other specs I knew she'd be interested in: family, hobbies, pets, political leanings, and romantic history as far as I knew it. "It's early days yet, but I like him. He's funny, and he treats Madison well."

"He'd better," she said firmly.

"Damn straight."

"So have you . . . ? Are you going to . . . ? Have you planned how to . . . ?"

"Deborah, are you trying to ask me if I've had sex with Fletcher?"

"God, no! I just wanted to know what you're going to do about your friend in the attic."

"Of course I haven't told him about Sid! I've never told anybody about Sid."

"Then what are you planning to do about him? Not necessarily with this guy, but say you do meet the right guy and want to get married. Then what?"

"If I meet Mr. Right, I'll tell him. Not on the first date, but eventually. When it's a good time."

"When is a good time to tell a man about a walking, talking skeleton?"

"I don't know. I haven't met the right guy yet."

"You never told Reggie."

"A good thing, too." I shuddered to think what my former fiancé would have done with that knowledge. In retrospect, my reluctance to share the secret of Sid should have been a clue that some part of me knew the relationship wasn't healthy. "Anyway, I don't want a guy I wouldn't be willing to introduce to Sid."

"Meanwhile, while you're looking for this guy of your dreams, you stick Mom and Phil with the job of taking care of the skeleton."

"One, they don't mind. Two, this is Sid's home, too—he's part of the family."

"He's not part of the family, Georgia. He's a freak of nature."

"As long as we're all happy with the status quo, why do you care?"

"Because I care about my parents. They've kept this big house years longer than they intended to just to make sure that they can keep that thing hidden."

"They never said anything to me about wanting to sell the house."

"You're not around as much as I am. Besides, they aren't getting any younger. What happens to the skeleton when they're gone? Don't expect me to take it."

"Sid will always have a home with me."

"You say that now, but you sure didn't mind dumping him when you moved away."

"As if I could have taken him to a one-bedroom apartment with a toddler he didn't want seeing him."

"And what about Madison? We don't know if it will ever die. You want Madison to be an old lady with a skeleton in her armoire, not ever being able to get married for fear of him being found out?"

"Jesus, Deborah, having Sid around has never affected Madison! Why do you hate him so much, anyway?"

"I don't hate him. I just don't want him holding you back."

That was when Madison yelled up the stairs. "Are you guys fighting? Am I going to have to separate you two?"

"We aren't fighting," I lied. "Your aunt just doesn't approve of my friends."

"It's not a friend," Deborah said. "I don't know what it is, but it's not a friend."

I ignored her and went downstairs to wait for Fletcher. If I hadn't been so mad at my sister, I might have noticed the slight sounds from the attic. By the time I realized that Sid had heard every word we'd said, it was almost too late.

32

All in all, the date went very well. The dinner was good, the banter light and a touch suggestive without being vulgar, and in between bouts of banter had come some real conversation. Had I been asked to provide a score, I'd have given it an 8.5 out of 10. Whether or not I raised the rating would depend on the quality of the necking that took place once we got back to the house. That was assuming that necking was part of Fletcher's lesson plan. It was definitely part of mine.

Unfortunately my cell phone rang when we were halfway to the house.

"Sorry," I said. "I'd better see who that is."

"No problem—it might be your daughter." That got him up to 9.0.

Only when I looked at the caller ID, it wasn't Madison—it was Charles Peyton. Since I couldn't imagine Charles calling at that time of night without it being important, I took the call. "Charles?"

"Georgia?" he said in a weak voice that didn't sound like

him at all. "I find myself in need of assistance, and fear there is nobody else I can call."

"What's wrong?"

"I've been injured. If you could come by my abode . . ." His voice faded away.

"Charles? Charles!" There was no response, though I thought I could hear him breathing.

"What's the matter?" Fletcher asked.

"That was Charles. He's been hurt. I've got to get out to McQuaid."

"Do you want me to come with you?"

"Yes, please," I said. The last thing I wanted to do was roam around campus alone at night, plus I was afraid of what we'd find. I'd encountered one dead body in the recent past, and my stomach clenched at the thought of a repeat. "Do you have a first aid kit?"

"Always. Standard reporter training."

Reporter training must also have included driving lessons—Fletcher got us to the main entrance of the campus in half the time I'd have taken.

The guard on duty spotted the faculty hang tag and waved us through, but Fletcher started to slow down.

"Don't stop!" I said.

"Shouldn't we tell him about Charles?"

"Not yet."

"Do you think Charles was playing some sort of trick?"

"I'll explain later."

"Which building?"

For a moment I was at a loss, but then remembered seeing Charles coming out of an office the day I'd taken Sid to be examined by Yo.

"Easton Hall."

I had my ID card out before the car stopped, and hopped out to run for the front entrance. I swiped the card in the lock, opened the door, and waited impatiently while Fletcher found his first aid kit. As he caught up, I took off down the hall. The door to the office where I expected to find Charles was open, and I called out to my friend as I went. There was no reply.

When I finally got to the doorway, I saw Charles with his face down on the desk. There was a dark mat of blood on the back of his head. I froze for a moment, remembering the sight of Dr. Kirkland's body, and Fletcher pushed past me, clearly better than I was in a crisis

"Talk to me, Charles," he said. "How bad are you hurt?"

The older man stirred, and I suddenly remembered that it had been too long since I'd taken a breath.

"Oh, it's all bad, I assure you," Charles said. "I never consider any form of hurt to be good."

A giggle slipped out of me, though it was definitely the wrong time for it.

Charles looked up, and while his face was much too pale, his voice sounded better than it had on the phone. "I see that I must humbly apologize for interrupting your tête-à-tête."

I said, "What you must do is tell me what happened. Did you fall?"

"Assuredly, but only after I was struck."

"What? By who?"

"By whom," he corrected me. "I'm afraid I don't know. I was taking an evening constitutional when I saw someone moving around in the adjunct's office. My first thought was that some poor soul had an onerous assignment that had to be completed, so I intended to offer my assistance. The intruder undoubtedly heard me coming, because I was whistling so as not to startle anyone. As I went in the room, the light went out and I felt a blow to my head—he must have concealed himself behind the door to lie in wait."

"And you didn't see who it was?"

He shook his head, then winced, apparently regretting the motion. "I heard running footsteps, and that was all. When I could walk again, I made my way back here."

"Why didn't you call security?" Fletcher wanted to know. "Or pull the alarm?"

Charles hesitated, then said, "Do you suppose I could trouble you for a drink of water? I have some in the refrigerator over there."

"Of course." I found a bottle, opened it, and handed it to him.

He drank thirstily.

"Georgia?" Fletcher said, looking mystified.

"Charles," I said, "will you be all right for a moment? I need to talk to Fletcher."

Charles looked anxious, but nodded.

I took Fletcher by the arm and pulled him out into the hall. "Okay, here's the situation. Charles didn't call security because he was afraid it would come out why he was on campus at this time of night."

"So why was he here?"

"Because he lives here. In that office."

"What?"

"Charles is a squatter. He doesn't make enough money to live on, at least not the way he wants to live, so he finds places he can stay on campus. That office belongs to a guy who's in the field for the semester—when he comes back, Charles will find another place to live."

"What about the clothes and—"

"At some point he realized he had to make a choice between living in some dump, wearing clothing he'd be ashamed to be seen in, or squatting and dressing like a gentleman. He likes the clothes."

"How long has he been doing this?"

"Ever since I've known him."

"But—how does he—?"

"Fletcher, I don't know every detail, and it doesn't matter right now anyway. What matters is getting him medical attention."

"I don't think that will be necessary," said Charles, who'd managed to stagger to the doorway. "Fletcher, I must apologize again, this time for making you a party to my deception. I only hope you can find it in your heart to help me maintain my illusions."

I would never have guessed that Charles would be capable of making puppy-dog eyes, but he did an excellent job of it right then. Fletcher didn't have a chance, especially not when I added my own look of entreaty.

"Hey, it's none of my business," he said. "You're not hurting anybody as far as I can see."

"Your discretion is a great gift," Charles said, "as were your efforts in aiding me. I thank you both for your assistance, but I'm feeling quite well now."

"Oh, no you don't. You're going to see a doctor," I said.

"I have no physician I can trust, and certainly none I can afford."

That was enough to stop me, too. I couldn't afford to pay for him to go to the emergency room.

"Let me take another look at that head," Fletcher said. "I rode in an ambulance one summer and got pretty good at patching up minor injuries."

"I would be in your debt," Charles said with his customary bow.

Fletcher made Charles stand by the light while he looked at his eyes. Then he carefully examined the older man's scalp. "It's not too bad," he finally said. "A doctor would probably put in a stitch or two, but I think you can get by with a butterfly bandage. It might leave a scar, but nobody's going to see a scar under all this hair anyway."

"I have been blessed with generous locks," Charles agreed.

I was no more a nurse than Fletcher was a doctor, but I'd managed to survive Madison's clumsier periods when I'd had to buy Band-Aids by the crate, so I was able to assist him as he trimmed Charles's hair around the wound, spread on antibiotic cream, and applied a bandage.

Once he was done, Fletcher said, "I bet you've got a hell of a headache, but I don't think you should take anything for it. You don't have any signs of concussion, but—"

"I can endure," Charles said. "A good night's rest is all I need to make myself right, and the sofa in here is surprisingly comfortable."

"The spare bed at my house is even more comfortable," I said in what Madison calls my mother-knows-best voice. "Don't even try to argue with me. You either come home with me, where I can make sure you're okay, or I'm going to call 911. Your choice."

He looked at me for a moment, but knew when he was beaten. "Fletcher, I confess I don't feel up to driving, so could I prevail on you for transportation to Georgia's home?"

Fletcher hesitated, and I flattered myself that it was because he'd been hoping to take advantage of Madison's absence for some physical affection. Or maybe it was just because he was worried about blood on his upholstery. No matter which it was, he said, "No problem." He took one of Charles's arms and I took the other to help the older man along.

Despite his protests, Charles was pretty wobbly on the way to Fletcher's car, and we all breathed a sigh of relief when we got him into the back seat. Conversation was sparse during the drive to my house—Charles was in pain, Fletcher was concentrating on avoiding jostles, and I was all out of banter.

Charles did seem to be moving more easily when we got to my house, and only needed Fletcher to help him out of the car, into the house, and up the stairs to the spare bedroom. At pointed looks from the two men, I stepped out into the hall so Fletcher could help him into bed. I didn't know how fresh the sheets were, but I was sure that the bed would be worlds more comfortable than a sagging couch.

Only when Charles was tucked into bed, the comforter covering every part of him other than his head and a racy bit of shoulder, did Fletcher let me back into the room. While waiting, I'd brought up a glass of ice water to put on the nightstand next to the bed.

"Is there anything else I can get for you?" I asked Charles.

"Dear lady, you have already done far more than I could ever have expected."

"What are friends for? Call if you need me—I'm two doors down on the left."

"Are you quite certain you don't mind my being here? I worry about your reputation if any of our colleagues find out I've spent the night at your home."

"I'll risk it." Besides, we had a chaperone. There'd been enough creaks from the attic to let me know that Sid was on the job. "You get some rest."

Fletcher and I left him alone, and I suspected he was asleep by the time we got to the front hall. I said, "I'd ask you to stay for a nightcap, but under the circumstances—"

"Finding an assault victim tends to kill the mood."

"Yeah, kind of. Thanks for helping me with him."

"No problem. I'm just embarrassed that I'd never figured out his living arrangements. What with being in the observing-and-investigating business and all."

"Charles has had a lot of practice hiding the truth."

"How did you find out?"

"Purely by accident. When I was working at Tufts, an old friend of my parents was on sabbatical and said I could use her office, and I found Charles in residence. We compromised by sharing the office for the rest of the year. You won't tell anybody, will you?"

"Of course not. But don't you think that somebody in security should be told about the assault? What if somebody else is attacked?"

"I didn't even think of that." I rubbed my forehead. "Maybe we can find signs tomorrow that somebody was in the adjunct office and report that?"

"How about an anonymous tip from a student who saw somebody in there?"

"Perfect!"

"I'll call it in on the way home."

I thought that deserved a kiss, so I delivered it. Apparently Fletcher thought something I'd done deserved a kiss, too, and he took care of that. Then we both decided we needed yet another kiss, and attended to the situation. Before either of us could decide on paying bonuses, I stepped back from him and opened the front door. Okay, there was one last kiss, but it was quick.

Once Fletcher was gone, I peeked in on Charles to make sure he was solidly asleep. Then, hearing an insistent *tap-tap-tap* from the attic, I opened the door to find Sid on the other side, tapping his foot.

"What the phalanges is going on out there?"

"Shush!" I whispered an explanation, ending with, "I know it's awkward having a stranger in the house, but I couldn't very well leave Charles at the college alone after that."

"It's just for the night, right?"

"That's the plan. Sorry I couldn't warn you ahead of time."

"That's okay. I'm not crazy about your office being burgled, though."

"It's not *my* office—there are twenty-something other people who use that office."

"Still. Finding dead bodies—"

"One dead body."

"Finding any dead bodies is alarming. Burglars, break-ins . . . Pennycross is getting to be a dangerous place for a woman and a child."

"Fortunately I have you around to keep an eye on us." I patted him on the clavicle. "I'm going to bed. I want to be awake before Charles."

Like so many of my recent plans, that one went awry.

33

Instead of getting up at eight when my alarm went off, I apparently woke up just enough to slap my alarm off and then shove it off the nightstand and into my trash can. When I finally did wake up for real and pulled the power cord to retrieve the clock, I saw it was 10:30.

I told myself that Charles was probably still asleep and Madison wouldn't be returning from her sleepover until noon at the earliest. I continued to think that until I'd gotten out of bed, gone into the hall, and seen that the guest room door was wide open, showing that the bed was both empty and neatly made. From downstairs I heard voices—one was Charles's low rumble and the other was Madison.

I pulled on jeans and a sweater before taking a deep breath and heading for the kitchen.

Charles was wearing his regular suit except for the jacket, had one of my mother's aprons tied around his waist, and was scrambling eggs at my stove. Madison was putting hot bacon onto a platter. The table was set for three. One of them, most likely Charles, had even pulled out cloth napkins. It was a disturbingly domestic scene.

"Good morning all," I said.

"A lovely morning to you, too," Charles said cheerily. "I hope you don't mind my taking over the kitchen to prepare breakfast. I rarely have the opportunity to cook."

"Knock yourself out. It smells wonderful." I turned to my daughter. "How long have you been home?"

"Half an hour? Aunt Deb got an emergency call from McQuaid. Somebody broke into an office or something, so she's got to replace a lock." I'd forgotten, but thanks to our parents' connections, Deborah had contracts for maintaining security systems at several local colleges, including McQuaid.

"Did you two have a good time last night?"

"Yeah, great. You?"

"Very nice."

Madison gave me a look, but I suddenly remembered that I was the grown-up and didn't have to explain myself. "Is there any coffee?" I knew I'd pay for it later, but for the moment, I intended to enjoy the eggs that Charles had nearly finished cooking.

Despite the inauspicious beginning, it was a lovely meal. Charles was a good cook, and kept Madison and me thoroughly entertained with historical trivia about the British royal family of years past. Afterward, he wanted to wash the dishes, but I put my foot down and said that Madison would be delighted to take care of them. She made a face when he wasn't looking, but agreed.

After thanking me for my hospitality, Charles refused my offer of a ride, insisting that he felt perfectly able to walk home. "In fact," he said, "it's past time that I take my leave and tackle an urgent task. My current quarters have proven to be less comfortable than I'd hoped, so I will be devoting my day to securing a new abode."

Even when I walked him to the door, he said nothing

more about the events of the previous night, so I didn't either, other than to say that he should feel free to call me anytime. Once he was gone, I went back to the kitchen to face my daughter.

She raised one eyebrow, which she loves doing because I can't. "I could have sworn you were going out with Fletcher last night."

"I did."

"You went out with Fletcher, and came home with Charles? Yay, Mom!"

"It wasn't . . . It isn't . . ." Then I bowed to the inevitable. "Yay, me!" I left her to finish cleaning the kitchen while I went upstairs to take a nice, long shower. It's good to be the mom.

The rest of the weekend was considerably quieter than the start. I called Deborah to find out about the break-in at McQuaid, though I neglected to mention that Charles had been a witness. She told me that the burglars had gotten into the building by breaking the lock on a door which was usually only used by kitchen staff and janitors. Otherwise, only the adjunct office had been interfered with. That door was undamaged because apparently it had been left unlocked.

Since Deborah believed in locking everything, she was appalled, but it was no surprise to me. Theoretically security was supposed to lock up each evening, but frequently an adjunct or two were still in there working after hours. Since administration didn't want to give the adjuncts keys, it was left open as often as not.

According to Deborah, campus security had three theories: either students had broken in to play a prank, students had broken in to get a peek at an upcoming test, or students had broken in to take revenge on an adjunct. Campus security at McQuaid has a love-hate relationship with students.

No matter which subset of students had been involved, security figured they'd been scared off before doing any major damage.

Sunday evening I got an e-mail from McQuaid's human resources office. Without actually laying blame, the tone was that it was the adjuncts' fault that our office had been broken into because we hadn't been observing basic safety precautions. Despite that, we were assured that we and our belongings were completely safe. I was not particularly comforted, and I intended to check on the contents of my desk as soon as possible.

As soon as my first Monday class was over, I went to the adjunct office where, unsurprisingly, there was a fair amount of hubbub. A copy of the e-mail from human resources was in every mailbox, even those currently unassigned, and another copy had been posted outside the office door. Inside, adjuncts were checking their desks and discussing the situation. As I came in, I heard a statistics teacher proclaim, "People, we all know that correlation does not prove causality." I had no idea what that was in response to, but I nodded just the same, and went to my place.

Somebody had been in my desk.

Though nothing seemed to be missing, and I'm not the the most persnickety person, I could tell that there was something off about the way my folders were hanging in the file drawer and that my pens were scattered in my lap drawer more than they should have been.

I looked suspiciously at Sara, wondering if she'd been snooping again, but it didn't seem likely. Not that I trusted her integrity, but I didn't think she'd have risked being seen after our confrontation on Friday. That meant that the burglar who'd conked Charles over the head had been searching my desk. Of course, I told myself, the burglar had likely searched a number of desks.

I joined in the hubbub, asking who had been robbed, vandalized, or just snooped into. As it turned out, the only one who laid claim to signs of invasion was Sara, and from the eye-rolling I got from Charles, he thought she was just putting it on.

Since nothing was missing, I kept quiet about my own concerns. Still, I was uneasy. Maybe campus security was too eager to blame students. I hadn't had enough time to annoy any students enough to come after me. Of course, nobody knew about the attack on Charles, which would have put a different spin on the incident, but I couldn't tell anybody about that, and I didn't think he would.

It left me feeling unsettled all day, and the feeling hadn't improved when I went back to the office after my last class and found a pink message slip in my mail cubby:

Dr. Kirkland of JTU called—wants you to call back.

34

I'd read ghost stories about messages from the beyond, but those messages weren't usually as prosaic as "while you were out" slips. Eventually I remembered that the late Dr. Kirkland had two children teaching at JTU, both of whom were academics with the same last name.

Then I had a moment of the heebie-jeebies, thinking that I'd been identified as having found the body of the dead Dr. Kirkland, but if that had been the case, it would have been the police who called, not one of the dead woman's children.

Since staring at the slip wasn't helping, I took it and my things and headed for my parents' office, where I could return the call in private. I dialed the number, and a low-pitched voice answered, "Dr. Donald Kirkland."

"Hi, this is Dr. Georgia Thackery. I had a message to call you."

"Yes, Dr. Thackery. I hate to bother you about this, but I'm an archaeologist at JTU, and it's come to my attention that you have a specimen in your possession that may be part of our collection."

"A specimen?"

"A skeleton? A human skeleton?"

"Oh, that specimen." My brain wasn't keeping up with the conversation—all I could think of was that I'd been an idiot to yell at Sara, because she must have been the one to tell on me. "I don't think my skeleton belongs to you."

"The information I have indicates that the numbers correspond with a specimen that's missing from our collection."

"My skeleton is male, and I was told that the ID number is for a female skeleton."

Donald must have put his hand over the phone, but I could still hear him. "She says it's male."

"How would she know? She's an English teacher!" said a woman with obvious disdain. "Tell her to bring it back!"

Back on the phone to me, Donald said, "It can be difficult for a layperson to determine the gender of a skeleton."

"I had an expert sex it."

"Can you tell me who?"

I wasn't going to bring Yo into it—I didn't even want to bring myself into it. "A grad student."

The woman must have been listening in, because she said, "A grad student? Probably wouldn't know the difference between a human hand and a bear paw! Tell her we'll report her to her chancellor!"

Donald said, "I hate to insist, but it would be so much simpler if you'd bring it over so we could examine it for ourselves."

"You know, I'm really not sure I wrote the ID number down correctly. The lighting wasn't very good."

Donald relayed my excuse to his cranky companion. "Who does she think she's fooling? Tell her we'll give her twenty-four hours, and then we're calling the police! We'll get her fired *and* arrested!"

I said, "Why don't I check the number again and call you back tomorrow morning?"

Donald sounded relieved as he said, "I would certainly appreciate that. As I'm sure you realize, it doesn't look good for a specimen to just walk off."

I said something noncommittal before hanging up, but all the while I was thinking about how he'd like it if a specimen just walked in. Of course, I had no intention of taking Sid to JTU. It was too risky, which is what I told Sid that night after Madison was in bed.

"It's too risky. I'll just tell Kirkland Jr. that I wrote the wrong number—he won't be able to prove any differently. Unless Sara looked inside your skull the other day. She didn't, did she?"

"No," Sid said, "but I want to go see Kirkland."

"Are you crazy?"

"I'm not the one talking to a skeleton!"

"Then tell me why you want to risk being kidnapped. Or stolen. Whichever word applies."

"Three reasons," he said, ticking them off on his finger bones. "One, maybe Yo really did mess up my exam. Two, maybe I'll recognize Donald when I see him in person and I'll remember something else. Three, his reaction to seeing me might tell us something."

"What if he decides you belong to JTU after all? He could claim there was a clerical error or some such, and it would be awfully hard for me to argue with him. Let alone the woman who kept wanting him to threaten me."

"Worst-case scenario, I'll sneak out as soon as I can and get back here."

"What if you can't? Maybe they'll lock you in a safe or something."

"No safe can hold me."

"What if you're seen, or caught by dogs, or—"

"And what if you lie to Donald and that woman convinces him to play hardball? It could cost you your job."

"I'd rather lose my job than lose you!"

"I know," he said, patting me on the knee, "but I don't

want you to lose the job or me." Before I could outline more possible disasters, he added, "Georgia, it's been over three weeks since I recognized Dr. Kirkland, two weeks since she died, and we're out of ideas. I need to find out more about myself, and this is my best chance."

I couldn't argue with that—I was out of ideas, too—so the first thing next morning, I called Donald Kirkland and told him that I'd bring Sid to his office that afternoon.

35

Donald Kirkland looked oddly familiar when I met him at his office in JTU's Turner Science Building, and not just because I'd seen him at the funeral. After a minute, I figured it out. His face looked that of fifty-year-old version of Donald O'Connor, the actor. I'd been a big fan of O'Connor's Francis the Talking Mule movies when I was a kid, probably because I'd strongly identified with O'Connor's character. He had a talking mule—I had a talking skeleton. The movies had provided a dandy cautionary tale about what could happen if I ever told anybody about Sid.

He shook my hand. "Dr. Thackery, I really appreciate your coming by so we can straighten this out. You have the specimen?"

"In the suitcase."

"What a practical solution. May I borrow it long enough to transfer the specimen to my lab?"

"I thought I'd come along," I said, not letting go of the handle. "I'm curious about the procedure."

"Certainly." He picked up a folder from his desk and led

the way to the elevator, and on to the basement lab, which was a lot more impressive than McQuaid's facility. It was bigger and brighter, with a bewildering array of equipment that looked like props from the latest version of *Star Trek*. Obviously JTU had put money into their department, and I suspected from what I'd read that the late Dr. Kirkland had been responsible for a lot of that fund-raising. There was nothing like having the leader in a field to help bring in grant money.

I helped Donald remove Sid's bones from the suitcase and place them on a generously sized table, hoping that Sid would behave this time. He seemed to be doing so, other than a tiny twitch of the skull so he could take a better look at Donald, but the archaeologist didn't notice.

Even more quickly than Yo, he put Sid's bones into their proper positions. "Our specimens are typically articulated," he said when he was done.

"This one was, too, but the wires rusted and broke, so we took them out." I was ready to repeat the imaginary tale of how my parents had ended up with a skeleton, but he didn't ask, so I saved it. The less said, the less I could be accused of.

Donald started with the skull, using a magnifying lamp to look inside. "This is the ID number all right," he said, and jotted it down on a pad of paper. Then he looked into the folder, took a look at Sid's pelvis, and frowned. "Hmm . . ." That was all he said for the next half hour as he poked, prodded, measured, and weighed. I found a stool and sat to watch him work, noticing that he was looking more and more concerned.

When he seemed to be done, he said, "If you don't mind, I'd like to call a colleague to verify my findings."

"That's fine."

He pulled out a cell phone, but said, "Reception down here is dreadful, so I'll just step into the hall."

I'd hoped to take a look at that folder of his while he was

gone, but he took both it and his notes with him. After making sure we were alone, I whispered, "You okay, Sid?"

"Fine, but what is it with scientists and cold hands?"

"Probably most of their patients don't notice."

Kirkland stepped back into the room, and said, "She'll just be a minute." It was more like five, and he spent the whole time looking through the papers in his folder as if he expected them to change.

Finally a woman came bustling in, and I recognized yet another Dr. Kirkland: Dr. Mary Kirkland, who I'd also seen at the memorial service. When she spoke, I realized she'd been the one who'd wanted Donald to bully me the previous night. "What do you mean it's not our skeleton?" she demanded.

"See for yourself," Donald said.

Ignoring me, she pushed past her brother and grabbed Sid's pelvis. She went on to repeat Donald's examination from start to finish, only faster and with more slamming of bones. When she was done, she compared her notes with her brother's. "You mismeasured the right femur."

"Or perhaps you did," he said calmly.

She snorted, remeasured, and wrinkled her nose as she erased her original figure. Then she spent a good ten minutes rereading the information in the file folder, which I was dying to see. Finally she turned and acknowledged my existence with a glare. "This isn't our skeleton."

"I suspected as much," I said.

"Our skeleton was a sixty-year-old Asian woman, and she was nearly a foot shorter than this skeleton." She waved at Sid. "This is a Caucasoid man in his twenties. Our skeleton was missing several teeth that are present in this specimen. Ours had a fibula that had been broken postmortem and expertly repaired—this one had a broken rib that was glued together by an amateur and a healed broken wrist. Ours showed signs of poor nutrition and arthritis, but no apparent cause of death—this one had a skull fracture and a knife injury."

"That sounds pretty definitive," I said. So much for her comments about grad students—Yo had hit every nail on the head.

"Then where is our specimen? And why does this skeleton have the same ID number?"

"I have no idea," I said. "We just had the one in our attic." I gave her a shortened version of the fiction—parents bought it at an auction, thought it was fake at first, and so on. "Since this isn't your skeleton, I'll just get it out of your way."

I stepped toward the table, but she got in front of me. "What do you want it for, anyway?"

I could have told her it had sentimental value or explained that it was my parents' and I was honor-bound to protect it, but I just didn't like her. So I told her the truth. "I like to watch movies with him, and sometimes we dance."

She snorted again. "Why don't you donate it to JTU?"

"If I feel like giving a five-thousand-dollar donation, I'll give it to McQuaid." After talking to Yo, I'd done some research—Sid was worth at least that much.

"McQuaid! That idiot Ayers wouldn't know what to do with a decent specimen if he had it. Look, you're an adjunct, right? How would you like something better? I've got pull here—I'll get you a real job."

"Don't you have enough skeletons?" I could see several articulated ones hanging in the storage room next door.

Donald said, "I'm afraid my sister takes the loss of P-A-F-60-1573 personally. She was in charge of inventory when it disappeared." He sounded a bit smug.

"It wasn't my fault the damned thing went missing! It was left hanging in an undergraduate classroom, as if a bunch of undergraduates would know the difference between a real skeleton and a Halloween decoration. Then somebody walked off with it, and I got the blame."

"When did that happen?" I asked.

Donald consulted the file. "It was found to be missing during a routine inventory in early nineteen eighty-two."

"What difference does that make?" Mary said.

"Only that in nineteen eighty-two I was six years old, so I couldn't possibly know what happened to your short Asian woman." I went around her, and started putting Sid's bones back into the suitcase. I could tell from her face that she wanted to stop me, but we both knew she had no legal leg— or femur—to stand on. Still, I think she'd have tried to argue the point if her brother hadn't pulled her aside. They muttered together while I made sure I'd retrieved all of Sid's parts.

Before I left, Donald was polite enough to say, "Thank you for your time, and please let us know if you change your mind." I didn't even get a good-bye snort from Mary.

I managed to keep from running out of the building, but I didn't really breathe easily until I had Sid back in my van with the door locked.

"I'm taking you home right now!" I said to the closed suitcase, and for once, he didn't argue with me.

36

Madison wasn't home from school yet, so Sid and I sat in the living room. He could jump into the armoire if we were suddenly interrupted. I'd skipped lunch to make the trip to JTU, so I was eating an apple while we talked.

"Did you recognize either of them?" I asked Sid.

He hesitated long enough that I knew the answer before he spoke. "No, not really."

"Crap. Then that was another waste of time."

"Not completely. Now we know for sure that I'm definitely not Patty."

"Who?"

"It's easier to say Patty than to say P-A-F-60-1573."

"Are we personifying much?"

"Me, personifying a skeleton? Why would I do that?"

"Good point."

"Anyway, whoever I am—or was—it's not the woman in JTU's records."

"Agreed. So unless we want to postulate the use of that same code-number format in another collection—only meaning something completely different, or some sort of clerical error—then somebody intentionally gave you the same code number as Patty."

"Who is missing."

"Well, yeah. You're here."

"But where's the original Patty?"

"Maybe she came to life, too?"

"Unlikely. And yes, I know I'm the last one in the world who should be talking about unlikely events."

"I didn't say anything," I said, taking another bite of apple. "According to the doctors Kirkland, Patty went missing in nineteen eighty-two, which is around the time you were sold to the carnival."

"So picture this. Fall nineteen eighty-one, and I'm hanging unnoticed in the back of a classroom. Some exuberant Theta Chi members, perhaps led by Rich Kirkland, run off with me to use as a Halloween decoration. I turn out to be the life of the party."

"So to speak."

"In fact, I'm so popular that they decide to keep me. But then the annual inventory takes place, and Rich learns—perhaps through his mother or siblings—that his theft has been detected. He's afraid somebody will find me in the frat house and trace me back to him, so he and his buddies sell me to the carnival."

"But that doesn't answer the question of where Patty went. Let me take a run at that one. I've got a skeleton I want to conceal, and I decide the best way to do that is by hiding it in plain sight."

"The purloined-letter approach."

"Exactly. So I put a fraudulent ID number on my skeleton, and stick it in the back of a classroom where it gathers dust until the frat-boy brigade shows up."

"And the real Patty?"

I shrugged. "Maybe she ended up in a carnival, too. Maybe she was sold to some other collection somewhere or hidden in an attic. Maybe she was destroyed. As long as there is a Patty, there's a good chance nobody will notice it's the wrong Patty."

"Which means that I'm the skeleton that somebody wanted to hide."

"A murdered skeleton," I reminded him. "Whoever it was wasn't just trying to hide a skeleton—he or she was hiding a body."

"Which is creepy."

"No, the creepy part is that it had to have been somebody at JTU who substituted you for Patty."

"And that same person probably killed me?"

I nodded. "I'm starting to think that the only way we're going to figure out who you were is to find out who killed you."

"But how can we find out who killed me without knowing who I was?"

"Catch-twenty-two," I said. "Not to mention the fact that we don't know what to do next either."

"What about the Kirklands?"

"What about them?"

"Isn't it suspicious that they were that intent on keeping me?"

"You think one of them was your killer?"

"Either one would have known how to denude my bones and articulate me. Plus they'd have had the best opportunity to put me in that classroom."

"You're right," I said. "What about their mother? She could have done it, and they could be trying to cover up her crime."

"Don't forget their financial-planning brother. They might have been doing his dirty work."

"Yeah, but he ran off with the skeleton and sold it to a carnival."

"Great way to disassociate it from JTU, wasn't it? Until I woke up, that is. They probably didn't plan for that."

"The problem is, anybody who was at JTU back then

could be involved, or at least the people in the right departments. That doesn't help us figure out who you were." I
rubbed my forehead as if trying to coax some coherent
thought out of it. "Maybe we've been going about this the
wrong way."

"Since we haven't solved anything, I think that's a fair
assessment."

I stuck my tongue out at him because I knew he couldn't
return the favor. "We've been trying to figure out why you
were murdered, right?"

"Right."

"Maybe there's no murder to be found."

"I didn't get this figure from over-dieting."

"No, you got it because somebody went to an awful lot
of trouble to make you into a skeleton. Denuding a skeleton
isn't easy, not to mention articulating you the way you used
to be."

"I like to think that I'm still quite articulate."

"That's true—you do think that." Before he could parse
out the insult, I said, "Given that we're talking about hours
of tough, messy work, the question is: Why would somebody
do that?"

"To hide a body, obviously," Sid said.

"And why would somebody want to hide a body?"

"I get it. The killer made me a skeleton to hide me so that
nobody would know I was dead. It's not a thirty-year-old
murder case we should be trying to solve—it's a thirty-year-
old missing-person case!"

We high-fived—gently, because of past experiences—
and the warm glow of my brilliant epiphany lasted for about
twenty seconds. That's how long it was before Sid said,
"How does that help?"

"I'm not sure," I admitted, "but let's think about it. You
were in your twenties when you died, and Dr. Kirkland was
a college professor. We've been assuming you were a college
student. Shall we stick with that?"

"As a working hypothesis? Sure. I am obviously well educated."

"Obviously. Going a step further, we can assume you were a college student at JTU, since your skeleton was hanging there. So we need to check out students who went missing from JTU in nineteen eighty-one or eighty-two."

"But we don't know how long I'd been hanging around in JTU when I was stolen."

"True. But we know you were modern, and your knowledge of current events didn't seem that far off when you woke up. Let's make the date part of the working hypothesis."

"I just want to make sure the working hypothesis works."

I heard Madison at the door, and Sid headed for his armoire. Homework, dinner prep, and laundry filled up the rest of the evening. Figuring Sid wouldn't want to stay cooped up all night, I made sure to give him plenty of chances to get up to the attic unseen, but he didn't take advantage of them. I had a strong suspicion that he wanted to be around my daughter and me, or at least in the same room, and I didn't blame him. I didn't want to be alone that night, either.

The problem was my training in literary criticism. When you read a novel or short story, you assume that there are links between the various elements of the plot and deeper meanings to every event. So I kept seeing connections in everything that had been going on since Sid had recognized Dr. Kirkland: her murder, the break-in at the adjunct office, the attack on Charles, the intruder snooping around Kirkland's office the same night that Sid had tried to do the same.

But did it really make sense to link Sid's death thirty years ago to Dr. Kirkland's murder, when the police seemed satisfied it was a simple break-in? Did the break-in at McQuaid have anything to do with the person searching Dr. Kirkland's office? We couldn't even be sure that it had been an intruder Sid had dodged—it could have been one of the dead woman's kids or somebody in the Anthropology Department.

How could I know which events were coincidence and which were really related to Sid? The only way to know for sure was to keep going and hope that we wouldn't get into trouble.

It took me a long time to get to sleep because I kept trying to make sense of it all, but even then, I slept better than I would the next night.

Between classes, student meetings, and grading papers, I stayed busy all of Wednesday. I barely got a chance to take a breath until I was driving home. That one breath was about all I got, too. I was about a block from home when I felt my phone vibrate to let me know I had a text waiting—I'd forgotten to turn the ringer back on after class. I figured it could wait another minute.

That's when I saw the police cars in front of my house.

37

There may be something that would panic me more than finding a police car parked in front of my house, but I didn't take time to figure out what. Instead I was out of the van and running for the front door without any memory of actually turning into the driveway, parking, or turning off the engine. I found out later that I'd left the key in the ignition.

The front door was unlocked, and to my indescribable relief, the first thing I saw when I burst in was Madison sitting on the couch with a police officer in the chair next to her. My daughter was up in a second to grab me into a bear hug.

"Are you okay? What happened? Are you okay?"

"I'm fine, Mom," she said, but I could tell from her voice that tears were just below the surface. "Somebody broke into the house."

"What?" I looked over her head at the officer.

"Mrs. Thackery?"

"Ms.," I said automatically.

"I'm Officer Louis Raymond. Your daughter is fine, and

I want you to know that you should be very proud of her. She did the exact right thing. When she realized something was wrong, she left the house immediately, called 911, and went to the convenience store down the street. She was never in any danger. You've got a very smart girl there."

"I texted you, too," Madison said.

"My phone was off," I explained. "Did you catch him? Them? The one who broke in?"

He shook his head. "We suspect the perps heard her arrive and escaped out the back door. We found it ajar, and marks show that it was the point of entry. You'll want to get that lock repaired."

"At least we know a good locksmith," Madison said with a pathetic excuse for a grin.

Officer Raymond said, "Two other officers are canvassing the neighbors to see if they saw anything. In the meantime, do you think you could go through the house to see if anything was taken?"

"Of course." I thought about leaving Madison downstairs, but she grabbed on to my hand, so we all went through the house together. Though I was still mostly concerned about Madison, I couldn't help worrying about what might have been stolen. I was supposed to be keeping an eye on my parents' house, after all. I needn't have worried. We couldn't find anything missing.

The burglar or burglars must have started on the second floor. They'd opened every bedroom closet, the linen closet, and even the cedar chest filled with winter blankets in the hall. But the TV in my parents' room and Madison's computer and stereo were still in place.

"I don't see a jewelry box," Officer Raymond said, and I explained that my mother had left hers with Deborah for safekeeping before she left on sabbatical, while living in sketchy neighborhoods had trained me to keep my few valuable pieces nestled among the towels. Everything was where it was supposed to be.

The door to the attic was still locked, and I used that as an excuse not to take Madison or Officer Raymond up there. My brain was still too frozen to come up with a reasonable explanation for Sid's living arrangements, even if he were hiding. For the first time I wondered if he was okay.

I tapped gently at the attic door, trying to make it look like I was just drumming my fingers nervously, but there was no response.

We moved on to the first floor, but since nothing showed obvious signs of searching, apparently the burglar hadn't had time to do anything down there. The widescreen TV that had been my mother's sixtieth birthday gift to herself hadn't been touched, and that was the most valuable item visible.

"It looks like you were lucky again," Officer Raymond said. "Your daughter must have arrived while they were still scoping out the property."

"Do they usually pick and choose that way?" Madison asked.

He shrugged. "Sometimes it's a quick smash-and-grab, sometimes they're more particular."

We sat down at the kitchen table and Officer Raymond asked about who owned the house and how long Madison and I had been in residence. We'd just finished our explanations when Deborah showed up—a neighbor had alerted her to the police presence—so we repeated the story for her. I could tell how worried she was when she immediately went back out to her truck to get what she needed to install a new lock on the back door, plus an alarmingly large deadbolt.

"When the hell are you going to catch these guys, Louis?" she asked Officer Raymond. "This is, what, the eleventh house they've hit? Not to mention that old lady they killed."

I could have kicked her, because Madison went as white as a sheet.

"You mean the ones who killed that woman were in the house?" she stammered.

"There's no way of knowing it was the same people," Officer Raymond said soothingly.

"Don't give me that crap!" Deborah said. "You really think we have two burglary rings in Pennycross?"

Officer Raymond sighed. "Hold it down, Deb. You're scaring your niece."

"Do your job and she'll have nothing to be scared of!"

Now he was mad. "You could do some work of your own around here."

"What the hell is that supposed to mean?"

"This is your folks' house, right? Why didn't you put an alarm system in here? If your sister hadn't moved in, this house would have been left unoccupied for months, which is like an engraved invitation for lowlifes. In fact, I bet the burglars—who may or may not be responsible for other break-ins in the area—thought it was still vacant. So why no alarm?"

Deborah glared at me as if it were my fault, when we both knew why Mom and Phil had never wanted an alarm. Sid was always around. "My parents didn't want me to go to any trouble," she finally said.

"They might think differently now."

"Fine. I'll install a system tomorrow."

"Good." He turned back to Madison and softened his voice. "Young lady, I don't think you've got anything to worry about. The burglars aren't likely to come back here now that they know the house is occupied, and your aunt is going to have it as safe as Fort Knox by tomorrow."

I know he meant well, but Madison didn't look overly comforted, for which I didn't blame her.

The other police officers knocked at the door, and the three of them conferred while I made hot chocolate for everybody. Hot chocolate always makes Madison feel better, and I had a crazy image of throwing a steaming cup of mocha into the face of anybody who tried to break into the house. Crazy, but satisfying.

I really didn't like the idea of some stranger loose in my

house—despite having lived in some borderline neighborhoods, I'd never been broken into before. It made me want to wash everything the burglars might have touched, or at least spray some Febreze around.

Before he left, Officer Raymond said, "Okay, don't quote me on this, but from what we've found out, the MO here is different from the other break-ins. One of the neighbors saw a single guy running out of the backyard and down the street—the other break-ins were at least two-man jobs, and they had a vehicle. Also, the other jobs were night-time runs, and they moved fast—they weren't the kind to go looking in closets. I think this guy was just taking advantage of what he thought was an empty house."

That he offered that as comfort, and the fact that it really was kind of reassuring, showed how crazy that day had become.

"I'm still putting in an alarm," Deborah said, "and if it goes off, Louis, it's ringing for help at the station and at your place! You just keep that in mind."

He laughed and left.

"I take it that you know Officer Raymond," I said.

"He and I bowl on the same league."

"And you have his home phone number?" Madison asked. "It sounds like a very friendly league."

Deborah sputtered, and Madison poked her some more, which was probably what both of them needed. We all realized we were hungry, so I thawed out some chicken breasts and stuffed them with spinach to roast while Deborah took out her frustrations by mashing potatoes until they were as smooth as silk. Under the circumstances, Madison decided against attending the weekly Yu-Gi-Oh! tournament and instead availed herself of her favorite release valve: she texted all her friends and accepted their sympathy.

After dinner, Deborah asked, "Mad, how did you know somebody was in the house anyway? You guys said nothing was touched down here."

Madison looked embarrassed. "I didn't want to tell the cops, because it sounds crazy, but just as I came in the front door, I heard somebody telling me to run."

"Are you serious?" I asked.

She nodded. "I swear it was just like an actual voice."

"What did you hear?"

"It said, 'Madison! Somebody's in the house! Get out!' So I did. Maybe there's something to all that talk about guardian angels after all."

I looked at Deborah, but she refused to meet my eyes. She knew who Madison's guardian had been as well as I did.

"I'm awfully glad this particular guardian angel was keeping an eye on you," I said in a slightly too-loud voice. I saw the barest of movement from the armoire, and realized where Sid had been hiding during the break-in and subsequent uproar.

38

Deborah stayed at the house until bedtime and, before she left, insisted on inspecting the outside perimeter with a flashlight in one hand and a baseball bat in the other. She didn't find anything but the neighbor's cat.

Madison said she was all right by then, but my maternal instincts said she was putting on a show, so I insisted that she sleep in my room that night so I wouldn't be frightened. Of course, that meant there would be no conferring with Sid about the break-in, but I assumed he'd have found a way to let me know if he'd seen or heard anything that could help.

Even knowing Sid was on guard, I wasn't much more at ease than Madison was. I'd checked to make sure all the doors and windows were locked, and I had that baseball bat on the floor next to me, but I kept thinking of what could have happened if Madison had surprised the burglar. I didn't sleep well.

First thing the next morning, I called my parents—with the time difference, it had been too late to call them the night before. They were understandably concerned about the house, but of course their first priority was for Madison and me. I got their approval for Deborah to put in an alarm system, which was a good thing—she showed up before Madison left for school to take measurements for the equipment she needed.

The sooner the better, as far as I was concerned. While I knew Sid would be extra vigilant from that point on, Madison had no such comfort. Despite sleeping with me, she'd been restless enough to disturb my sleep. Frightened and bleary-eyed was no way for a teenager to face the day.

It wasn't a great way for me to start the day, either—though I trusted Sid to give the alarm should another break-in occur, I was just as worried about what would happen if somebody saw Sid himself.

I thought the day was looking up when I got a text message from Fletcher asking me to meet him for lunch at Hamburger Haven after my classes, but it turned out that the opposite was true.

Fletcher had gotten to the busy campus hangout early enough to grab a table, and as soon as I sat down, he handed me some papers. "I finished this last night, and I'm dying to see what you think."

"What is it?"

"It's my article about being an adjunct. Could you take a look?"

I stifled a sigh. As a composition instructor, I've been asked to proof any number of colleagues' papers, grant proposals, even personal letters. Since even the worst writers seem to think their prose is golden, keeping a friendly relationship after fulfilling a favor like that requires a lot more diplomacy than I had on hand. Then I remembered that Fletcher was a professional writer who was used to being edited. How bad could it be?

While he went to the counter to get our food, I started reading and realized almost immediately how bad it could be.

He had a big grin as he brought back the tray with our burgers and sodas. "Well?"

"I'm appalled."

His grin fled. "What—?"

"Fletcher, you can't blow the whistle on Charles! He'll lose his job."

"I didn't use his name."

"Oh no, you just describe a historian who maintains an impeccable personal appearance while living in college hidey-holes at McQuaid. Nobody will be able to figure that out."

"I don't say it's McQuaid."

"You said it's a Western Massachusetts college. Don't you think somebody might connect that to the Western Massachusetts college where you teach? He'll be fired, and then how long do you think it will take for every school in New England to get word? Who's going to hire him? No administration wants to admit that they don't pay their adjunct faculty enough to live on."

"Making them admit that is the point of the article!"

"And that's a great message to get out, but you don't have to ruin Charles's life in the process."

"But a college teacher squatting that way—it's such a compelling image."

"The adjunct office is full of compelling images—pick somebody else's story. Include a picture of us all crammed into one room, and then compare it with regular faculty offices or even grad-student offices. Or just give the numbers—tell people what you make for teaching a class."

"Numbers aren't sexy, Georgia."

"I can see that, but you're a good enough writer to make it work." I handed him back his manuscript. "The rest of the piece is great, and I really love the way you describe the way tenured professors look down on us. But you can't ruin Charles's career."

"Can I at least mention that I'd heard a rumor of somebody living on campus?"

"Only if you imply really strongly that this rumor came from another part of the country."

He finally agreed, and we ate in relative peace, but I could tell he was sulking. So I told him about the break-in at the house, thinking I'd get a little sympathy, but I got more sulking. He was irritated that I hadn't called him so he could cover the story. The fact that I might be more concerned with my daughter's mental well-being than him writing yet another article about a local break-in apparently didn't occur to him.

I don't think either of us enjoyed lunch very much, and when he left, all I got was a perfunctory kiss on the cheek. As he walked away, all I could think was that his butt wasn't *that* great.

39

"I think I've got it," I said. "Madison, how about you?"

I'd left for home as soon as my last class was over, not wanting Madison to be nervous about being at home by herself, but I needn't have bothered. Deborah was there installing the alarm system when Madison got there, and she'd just shown us how it worked and helped us set our access code. Speaking as a professional, I had to admit my sister did a good job with the instructions: she was clear, concise, patient.

Madison said, "It's a great system, but you know what would make me feel safer?"

"A hunky bodyguard?" I said.

"A dog."

I should have known that was coming. Madison had talked about getting a dog on and off for years, but apartment living and dogs don't mix well.

"Mom, you always said we could have one if we got a big enough place, and this house is plenty big. The backyard is even fenced in."

"Madison, you know living here is only temporary. I can't bring a dog into my parents' house."

"I texted G-mom, and she said that she and G-dad are fine with it."

"Really?"

She nodded. "I was thinking we could get an adult dog from the pound, so it would already be house trained."

"What if we have to move? I don't know how long I'll be at McQuaid, and it's hard enough to find affordable apartments without having to try to find a place that will take a dog. We can't get a dog and then abandon it in a year."

"Aunt Deb says that if anything like that happens, she'll take it. Then we can still come visit."

"How nice of Aunt Deb," I said, glaring at my sister. No wonder she'd been so helpful during the security-system lesson—she'd known this was coming.

"I know it's a lot of work," Madison was saying, "but I'll be responsible for walking him, feeding him, and bathing him. All the day-to-day stuff."

"Sweetie, having a dog isn't cheap."

"I know, but I'll chip in part of my allowance, and Aunt Deb says I can work for her to earn money toward paying for food and shots and stuff."

"You've really thought this through," I said, but I was looking at Deborah, not Madison. My sister knew exactly why I didn't want a dog: Sid. She also knew I couldn't explain that to Madison without breaking Sid's confidence, and that Madison would be really hurt if I just refused without an explanation. If I hadn't wanted to throttle her, I would have applauded her skillful manipulation.

"Well?" Madison said.

"Let me think about it," I said. "Now would you mind going to your room for a minute? I want some alone time with your aunt."

"It was my idea, Mom, not Aunt Deb's. I really do want a dog."

"I know you do, but you caught me by surprise. I need some time to make up my mind, okay?"

"Okay." She looked worried, but she went upstairs.

As soon as I heard Madison's bedroom door close, I said, "Did you put her up to this?"

"No! Get the family Bible, and I will swear on it that I did *not* suggest a dog to Madison, especially not for home security. I'm a locksmith—I don't think there's any substitute for a good lock and an alarm system. Any dog you'd want around a kid would be just as likely to love a burglar, too."

Thinking of Dr. Kirkland's dog, I had to agree. He'd attacked Sid, but only as an extra-special chew toy—he hadn't tried to bite me.

Deborah went on. "I admit that when Mad presented the problems and asked my advice, I did offer to help, but only when I saw how much she wants a dog."

I looked at her, but she wasn't fudging—Madison wanted a dog that much. And hadn't I told Deborah just the other day that I would never let things like job-related moves and a skeleton in the closet prevent me from giving Madison what she needed?

Apparently she needed a dog.

So I called upstairs. "Madison, get your shoes on. We're going to the animal shelter."

She nearly ran down the stairs, and hugged me, then Deborah, then me again. It was very sweet.

I was pretty sure that Sid's reaction wouldn't include quite so much hugging.

For once, I was absolutely right.

40

I'd halfway hoped that there wouldn't be a dog Madison liked at the Pennycross animal shelter, but she picked one out right away. After a little paperwork, she was the proud owner of a one-year-old dog the woman at the shelter assured us was well behaved and house trained. Deborah fronted Madison the adoption fee and money for the alarming amount of supplies we had to pick up on the way home— kibble, a leash, food and water bowls, a brush, a bed, and other accessories. All I had to do was bring it home. And tell Sid.

I snuck up to the attic as soon as Madison and her canine pal went to bed. Sid was slumped down in his old armchair reading, and didn't acknowledge my presence.

"I guess you heard."

He turned a page.

"Madison named him Byron—she'd had the name picked out for years, apparently. He's extremely affectionate, and I can tell he adores Madison already."

Another page.

"Did you know Akitas are Japanese? Madison just loves that. They've got a reputation of being tough for new dog owners to handle, but apparently Byron has a milder temperament than most Akitas. He's handsome, too. Do you want to see a picture?"

I was trying to think of something else perky to say, when he said, "I suppose this means I'm stuck up here from now on."

"Nope. He's going to sleep in Madison's room, and during the day, we'll put him in the big bathroom downstairs in case of accidents."

"Great."

"Or you could let me introduce you to Madison—and her dog—and we could go from there."

"Oh, so this is my fault? You bring a dog into my house—"

"It's not your house, Sid. It's *our* house, and that includes Madison. She's got rights, and one of those rights is to have a pet. If you wanted a pet, we'd see if we could swing that, too."

"If I wanted a pet, it wouldn't be a dog! You know what happens when dogs see me, Georgia. They freak out!"

"Not this one."

"How do you know?"

"Because you've already met."

"When did—? Oh, no you didn't! You didn't bring home the dog that stole my arm."

"Yeah, I kinda did." It was love at first sight for Madison—by the time I realized she wanted to adopt the late Dr. Kirkland's Akita, her heart was set on him. "I know he ran off with your arm that night, but at least he didn't wet the floor and whimper like that Rottweiler we saw that time. I'm sure we can train him not to chew on you."

He just glared at me.

"Honestly, I feel sorry for him. I heard Kirkland's daughter-in-law say they'd gotten rid of him, which is just mean.

The poor dog's owner dies, and then her family just dumps him. The woman running the shelter said he was heart-broken."

"That is pretty cold," Sid admitted. "Getting rid of a dog isn't like selling a house or old furniture. You don't abandon a member of the family!"

"Exactly." I stopped. "Wait. Did I miss some subtext, Sid? Do you feel as if I abandoned you when I left you here?"

"No subtext," he said firmly. "We both know you couldn't take me with you."

"Okay, but—"

"No, I mean it. I was thinking more along the lines of a clue. If the dog saw Dr. Kirkland murdered, the murderer might not want him around."

"They say the police always look at family members first. Of course, the police probably have done just that, and haven't found anything."

"But they don't know what we know."

"Do you suppose that old TV trope is true, that when a dog sees a person who attacked their owner, they'll react somehow?"

"I don't know. If Byron had been here when our burglar showed up, it might have proven it."

"I thought we'd decided that it wasn't burglars who killed Dr. Kirkland."

"Of course it wasn't, any more than a burglar just happened to break in here."

I sat down hard on the couch. "You think that was connected to our search for Sid?"

"Of course they're connected. Honey, I know connections. 'Cause, you know, my foot bone's connected to my ankle bone. My ankle bone's connected to my leg bone. My leg bone's connected to my—"

"Let me know when you make it to your head bone."

"Better a head bone than a bonehead," he replied with a lipless sneer. "I mean, we just happen to get broken into the day after you took me to JTU, a few days after the break-in at your office? And you didn't see a link?"

"I've been trying not to see links," I admitted, "but now it's looking like somebody else has made the connection between me and you."

"And between us and the late Dr. Kirkland."

"Oh God, Sid. I'd been thinking that, as bad as it was, at least Madison hadn't been in danger, because the local burglars weren't killers. And now you tell me she was in the house with the real murderer? She could have ended up like that poor woman!"

"Hey, hey!" Sid said. "It's okay. You've got an alarm now, and a dog. Madison is safe."

"What the hell was he doing here, anyway?"

"It sounds like he or she was searching for something, and I'm guessing that was me."

"That would certainly explain why he was looking in closets instead of running off with computers or televisions. And thanks to Sara, there are plenty of people who know about you."

"Coccyx, Georgia, I never intended to put you and Madison into danger. I should have let that guy find me."

"I wanted to help you find yourself, so I'm just as much to blame as you are." I took a deep breath. "And you're right. We're on our guard now and doing everything we can to keep ourselves safe. And I mean *all* of us." I was so emphatic I almost convinced myself.

"But—"

"But me no buts unless you have a butt of your own."

"Like your reporter beau?"

"Eavesdropping much?" I'd expected the comment, and welcomed it if it would take his mind off of sacrificing himself. "Anyway, now we know that somebody is looking for you—we just need to find out who he or she is first. Speaking of which, I don't suppose you saw or heard anything that could help identify him?"

He shook his head. "I was downstairs when I heard somebody at the back door, and I made a beeline for the armoire. It wasn't until I'd locked myself in that I realized it wasn't one of you guys."

"How did you know?"

"You and Madison use keys, and Deborah picks the lock. Breaking a lock sounds different than either of those. Of course, what I should have done was jump the guy, or at least grab a phone to call the cops."

"No, what you should have done was exactly what you did. If somebody is looking for you, it's doubly important that we keep you hidden."

"I guess," he said, sounding dissatisfied. "Anyway, the guy didn't talk, and of course I couldn't see anything. Georgia, I need a peephole. I tried looking through the keyhole, but the line of sight sucks."

"Good idea. Can you do it yourself while Madison and I are gone tomorrow? There's a drill in the toolbox." I was hoping there'd be no more break-ins, especially with both the alarm system and the dog in place, but it would be a nice change for Sid to be able to spy on Madison and me while he eavesdropped.

"Sure," he said. "Maybe I can do something useful if anything like this happens again. If we'd had the dog yesterday, at least he could have barked."

"Excuse me, but you did warn Madison to get out of the house. You may be the skinniest guardian angel in history, but you got the job done."

"I bet the dog would have kept him from getting in at all."

"Does this mean you're okay with Byron?"

"Do I have a choice?"

"No, but I would rather you be happy about it."

"I wouldn't say happy, but I can deal as long as I don't have to walk him. Or feed him. Or interact with him in any way."

"Insofar as I can control those circumstances, we have a

deal." With that settled, I was ready to move on to the real problem. "I don't suppose you've remembered anything else, like who killed you?"

"No, but I did do some serious thinking, which is why I was downstairs yesterday when our burglar showed up. I was using your parents' computer." My parents had taken their laptops with them but had left their older desktop model in the downstairs den that served as their home office.

"Bone dude, you are rocking the computer age. What were you doing?"

"The other night we were talking about my being a missing person, so I thought I'd look for people who'd disappeared from JTU during the appropriate era. I used some search engines and looked at the files for the local paper, but I didn't find anything."

"It seems like somebody would have noticed a student disappearing."

"That's what I thought, too, but if there was a hue and cry, it's never made it to the Web. Then I went to the site with those JTU yearbooks from before and started looking at pictures, thinking maybe I'd recognize myself."

"Anything?"

"Nothing. But I did get the idea of checking to see if anybody had been in one year's yearbook but not the next. You know, somebody who was a freshman in nineteen eighty-two who didn't show up as a sophomore in nineteen eighty-three, or a sophomore who didn't show up as a junior, and so on. Since that wouldn't help if I was a senior when I died, I found a copy of the commencement program to find students who never made it to graduation. Then I put all that information into a database."

"That must have been tedious as hell."

"Hey, I don't sleep, eat, or work. Tedium is kind of my thing."

Ouch. I reminded myself to go get Sid some more reading material.

He said, "I started in the late seventies and worked up to eighty-two, and ended up with one hundred and seventy-eight students who disappeared between one semester and another. Of those, seventy-four were women, so I scratched them off the list."

"That's still a lot of possibilities."

"The next step will be to Google all those guys to try to track them down. That ought to eliminate a few more. Can I borrow your computer overnight so I can get on it?"

"Be my guest." I brought it to him, then told him good night, checked that the alarm system was armed, looked to make sure all the doors and windows were locked, put my baseball bat next to my bed, and went to sleep.

41

The next morning, my laptop was sitting outside my bedroom door with a note tucked into it:

Down to 85 possibilities.

Eighty-five was still a lot, but the needle-concealing haystack was getting smaller all the time. Maybe we could find out who Sid was without breaking into other houses or finding any more dead bodies. Between Byron and the every-bell-and-whistle alarm system Deborah had installed, I was reasonably sure our house would remain secure while we kept looking. As for Madison, she'd promised to be extra vigilant on the way to and from school and said she'd send me regular texts with her status throughout the day.

I firmly shoved all such concerns out of my head to focus on getting Madison to school and myself to McQuaid on time. I thought I was succeeding pretty well with that until I caught myself humming "Dem Bones" as I left my morning class.

Naturally that was when I ran into my favorite anthropologist crossing the quad. "Hey, Yo. How's the dissertation going?"

"Don't ask," she said with a glare.

"Sorry." Belatedly I remembered how aggravated I used to get when people had plied me with that same question. Deborah had been the worst offender. "Is the parking situation better now?"

"It was until some asshole broke into my car. Twice in the past week!"

"Seriously?"

"The first time they jimmied my trunk, and before I had a chance to get that fixed, they broke the window to get to the glove box."

"Did they take much?"

She snorted. "They could steal the whole thing and not get enough to afford gas for the getaway."

I found myself looking at the grad student speculatively, wondering if she was somehow involved in the Sid situation. After all, she'd been the first to find out about him, even before Dr. Kirkland was killed. The car break-in story could have been a cover. Okay, I couldn't think of why she might have wanted to kill anybody, and she was obviously too young to have killed Sid, but . . .

The thing was, everybody was starting to look suspicious to me: all the Kirklands, the other adjuncts, my students, pretty much anybody I'd spoken to since coming back to Pennycross. Even Fletcher was starting to look fishy—why had he been so interested in getting a photo of Sid for the *Gazette* anyway?

Realizing that I'd been silent too long, I said, "This is getting to be a sketchy place. There was a break-in at the adjunct office over the weekend." I was watching her for a guilty flash in her eyes, but what I got was irritation.

"Please don't start trashing this place," she said. "Maybe your life isn't tied to McQuaid, but mine is."

"Excuse me?"

"If the college starts getting a lousy rep, then how much is a degree from here worth? Nobody is going to care that I graduated before things went downhill—they'll just see that I went to a crap school, which will make it look like I've got a crap degree." Her voice kept rising as she spoke, and people were starting to notice.

"I get what you mean," I said. Not that I agreed with her. I'd seen too many academic scandals blow in and out to take them seriously anymore. Even if McQuaid had a dozen robberies a week, nobody was going to look askance at her degree. What I really got was that she was stressed out of her mind trying to finish that dissertation, and as a result, she'd lost all sense of perspective. Hence the outburst. "Don't worry, I won't spread any more rumors."

"Whatever," she said, but it was in a gratified tone, and we went our separate ways.

Even though I'd mentally cleared Yo from suspicion, I still found myself looking askance at everybody else on campus that day. It didn't help when I heard a couple of my students snickering about skeletons having permanent boners when I came into class—obviously the news about me having a skeleton had spread. I was much relieved to get home, with my alarm system and vicious attack Akita to protect me, even if the pooch was trending more toward cuddly than fierce.

Madison requested permission to hang with friends at Samantha's house that evening, and after a brief discussion about the difference between hanging and chilling, I gave her money to pay for her share of the communal pizza they'd be ordering and drove her over. Then I went home to raid the kitchen for leftovers.

Fletcher hadn't called about any kind of rendezvous, and I wondered if he was on assignment or still vexed with me. Since I was definitely still vexed with him, I didn't call him either.

Sid came tiptoeing downstairs just as I was finished cleaning up after myself, and whispered, "Where's the dog?"

I looked. "Right behind you."

"AAAAAAH!" He ran toward me, and Byron, apparently thinking this was a fun new game, cheerfully trotted after him. They made several laps around the room before Sid hopped on top of the kitchen table. Byron barked in good-natured defeat, then sat to watch him. I knew I shouldn't laugh at Sid's predicament, but I couldn't stop myself.

"Georgia!"

"Dude, you two are going to have to coexist." I reached into the cabinet, pulled out some rawhide chews, and handed them to Sid. "Try giving him one of these."

Sid gave me a dark look, then held one out to Byron while maintaining the greatest possible distance between them.

Byron took it and lay down right in front of Sid, who glared balefully down at him. "Now what?"

"Step around him. If he grabs any of your bones, I've got this." I held up a filled SpongeBob Squarepants squirt gun of Madison's that had ended up in the junk drawer. A friend of mine used a spray bottle to train her cats not to climb onto her kitchen counters, so I figured it might work with Byron, should he decide that Sid was looking particularly delectable.

Sid climbed down gingerly, and when Byron didn't lunge at him, stepped around him to get to the living room. Then he opened the armoire door and sat down in the chair closest to it, ready to make a strategic escape.

Byron kept gnawing on the rawhide, but just in case, I took the squirt gun and more chew sticks with me into the living room.

"Just one big happy family," I said brightly. "Imagine the fun you two can have while Madison and I are gone during the day."

"Can I have a squirt gun? One of those Super Soaker ones?"

"Not a chance." To change the subject, I said, "So, you made progress last night?"

"I was working my fingers to the bone."

"Very humerus," I said dryly.

He grinned. "Anyway, I did some more today on your parents' dinosaur while the Hound of the Baskervilles was locked up, but your laptop is a lot faster."

"Educational discounts—it's the only way to go with computer equipment." Then I thought of something. "Hey, wait a minute! How did you get into my computer? I never gave you the password."

"Oh, please. It only took me two tries to figure it out. Seriously, Georgia, using *Madison* as a password? You couldn't at least substitute 1 for the *i*?"

"Fine, I'll change it." Then I stopped. "How did you know how to guess a password?"

"I saw it in a movie or something. It's common knowledge."

"It's not that common."

"Just because you didn't know—"

"Yeah, yeah, I'm a Luddite. But tell me something: Did you think about how to guess my password, or did you remember it from a particular movie or book?"

"No, not really. I just . . . did it."

"Then maybe that's something you knew from before you died. Like how to talk, and cultural stuff, like movie quotes and Shakespeare."

"Why is this a big deal?"

"Because while it's possible I am in fact the only person in the world who is dumb enough to use my daughter's name as a password *now*, I'll bet that bit of common knowledge wasn't that common back when you were alive."

He was still looking blank—which he was well equipped for.

"Don't you see? This is another clue about who you were—you knew about computers in the early eighties when not everybody had a home computer or even one at work. If you knew that much while you were still in college, maybe you were a computer science major."

"Did they have a computer science department at JTU then?"

"Easy enough to find out." I got out my laptop for some quick hunting. "JTU added computer science as a concentration in seventy-four, with a full-fledged major program instated five years later."

"Maybe you're right. I'd never really done much on a computer before these past few days, but it does seem to come naturally to me."

"Of course, that begs the question of why you were associated with Dr. Kirkland. Why would a renowned zooarchaeologist have anything to do with a computer geek?"

"Who are you calling a geek?"

"Please. Anybody who majored in computer science that long ago was almost certainly a geek."

"Of course, many of those geeks are filthy rich now."

"True enough."

Sid yipped, and I saw Byron walking into the room.

"Why didn't Madison take the mutt with her, anyway?"

"Her friend has allergies. He's not going to bother you." As if to contradict me, the way everybody else in the household did, Byron picked that moment to look at Sid and lick his chops. Sid hastily tossed over another rawhide stick while I wondered if there was another treat we could use if we ran out. Byron accepted the bribe readily enough, but he kept watching Sid as he lay down to work on it.

Sid and I got to work on his list of possibilities and got it down to sixty names in fairly short order. He was willing to keep going all night, but I talked him into a movie break instead. We finished watching *Harvey* just in time for me to go get Madison, and Sid took my laptop to his room before Byron could get any ideas involving teeth.

42

The next morning started out well, especially since I got to sleep in. Madison, on the other hand, had to be up early to walk Byron, a fact I couldn't resist rubbing in when I came down and found her slouching on the couch with what we usually referred to as her grumpy face, watching reruns of *Gravity Falls*.

"You're up bright and early," I said.

She looked at Byron with no great affection. "*He* woke me up at eight. On a Saturday!"

"Dogs aren't big on clocks or calendars."

"Then he kept sniffing and scratching around the attic door. Did you do anything about that squirrel up there?"

"I checked thoroughly, and there's no squirrel," I said. "I don't know what he smells." I really didn't. Sid didn't smell. Well, he could smell, but he didn't have an odor I'd ever noticed. Though he didn't bathe, he did give himself regular wipes with hydrogen peroxide to keep himself clean.

Madison, still disgruntled, turned back to her cartoon,

and I figured it wouldn't hurt to treat her to eggs and bacon, heavy on the bacon. The siren scent soon attracted both her interest and the dog's, and they came to watch me put the meal together. Mom always said that the scent of bacon wafting through the house would wake a dead man, and though I didn't think it had had anything to do with Sid's revival, he did admit that it was the one food he missed most. I thought about telling him to cross any kosher Jews off of his database.

Madison cheered up enough to offer to wash the dishes, and the phone rang while she was at it. It was Fletcher.

"Hey," he said a bit diffidently.

"Hey."

"I thought you might want to know that I've found an editor who's interested in my adjunct story."

"That's great."

"Without the stuff about Charles."

I smiled, even though he couldn't see it. "Thank you."

"No, thank you. I get carried away sometimes—thinking about the story and not the people. You reminded me, and I appreciate that."

"Just call me Jiminy Cricket."

"I know it's short notice again, but I was wondering if you'd like to go to dinner tonight."

I was tempted, but Madison had already told me she didn't have plans for the night, and I didn't think she was ready to be left at home alone so soon after the break-in, even with the alarm and the dog. And I was sure I wasn't ready to leave her by herself. "I've got a better idea. Do you like chili? *Hot* chili?"

"Love it."

"Then come to my house for dinner, and I'll fix you my specialty: Enamel Chili."

"Enamel Chili?"

"It's so hot it'll melt the enamel off of your teeth."

"I'm there!"

When Fletcher offered to bring dessert, I made sure he knew where Arturo's Ice Cream Shoppe was and what our favorite flavors were. This was going to be his first meal with Madison, and I wanted him to make a good impression.

That meant the rest of the day was less relaxing, as we made a quick trip to the store to pick up the ingredients, then cleaned the public areas of the house. Plus we had to fix ourselves up a little, too—Madison and I even painted each other's nails.

Since my computer was missing, I figured Sid had plenty to do on his own, so other than making sure to speak loudly enough for him to overhear, I didn't attempt to talk to him.

As it turned out, I should have blown off all the prep work and spent the day playing Angry Birds. The phone rang a few minutes after Fletcher had been due to arrive.

"Georgia? It's Fletcher. Look, I hate to do this, but I've got to cancel dinner tonight. A big story is breaking!"

"Not another murder." I didn't think either my nerves or Sid's could take that.

"No, but they may have solved the first one. The cops caught two guys breaking into a house on Wannamaker Lane—some kids out playing saw them and called 911. After the arrest, the cops searched their van and found loot from previous break-ins. They're the ones, all right."

"That is big news."

"I thought you'd want to know so that you and Madison wouldn't be worried about them coming back to your place."

"Absolutely." Of course, I didn't think that the break-in at my house was related to the rest of the burglaries, but it was good that the break-ins were over. And that Fletcher was thinking of us.

"Want to know the best part? One of the guys works for a locksmith! So not only was he getting the money from fencing the merchandise, but every theft got him that much more business. They picked targets by checking their database to find out which houses didn't have alarms, and afterward called all the houses nearby to try to sell them systems."

"Which locksmith?"

There was a burst of noise. "The press conference is starting. I've got to go. Rain check on dinner!"

"Which locksmith?" I asked again, but he'd already gone.

I immediately dialed Deborah's number. "Deborah? Georgia. I just heard that they caught the burglars."

"It was *not* my assistant who was involved. It was a guy at ABC Locks and Security."

"That's a relief."

"Only slightly. Most people are still going to think that all locksmiths are shady and that every time we install a lock or security system, we're casing the joint. Which reminds me: thank you so much for assuming it was me."

"Cut it out. I knew damned well you wouldn't be breaking into houses."

"No, you just thought I'd hire the kind of crook who would."

If she hadn't been having such a bad day, I'd have answered that in the way it deserved, but under the circumstances, I let it go. "Is there anything I can do?"

"Only if you can help me improve the reputation of locksmiths."

"Sorry, that's not—" Then I got an idea. "Here's a thought: call Fletcher and tell him you're available for an interview about how you and other reputable locksmiths screen employees. There must be some industry statistics you can toss into the mix to show how few bad apples there are in the field. Maybe he can write a sidebar or something."

"That's not bad. I'll give it a shot. Gotta go." She hung up.

"You're welcome," I said to the dead phone.

I told Madison the bad news, put Fletcher's share of the chili into the freezer for another night, and resigned myself to throwing out any of the salad and fresh French bread we hadn't eaten before it went bad. I meanly hoped that Fletcher had bought ice cream before getting the story lead, and that it was melting all over his backseat.

After dinner, Madison suggested going to a movie, so I left Sid to Byron's tender attentions and headed for the theater. The movie we wanted to see was sold out, the one we picked instead was lousy, and the popcorn was stale. Then, to put a capstone on the evening, when we got home there was a note from Fletcher on the front door. He'd come by with the ice cream, but since we hadn't been there to accept it, he'd taken it to his sister's house for her kids.

I was trying to cheer up Madison with Mom-ish aphorisms when we got inside, and might have succeeded had I not seen another note waiting. This one was from Sid and was sticking out of my laptop.

No luck. Back to square one.

After that, I gave up trying to comfort Madison and settled for making us each a big mug of hot cocoa before bed. Sometimes chocolate is the best part of the day.

At least I didn't have to wait until Sunday night to go see what was up with Sid. Deborah called Madison the next morning and told her she'd be over in an hour to pick her up. She had some emergency calls and wanted Madison to come along and start earning back some of the money spent on Byron's accessories. I felt a little guilty about Madison having to work on the weekend, but only a little. I had a stack of essays to grade, so I wasn't exactly going to be loafing.

But first things first. As soon as Madison was gone, I lugged my satchel up to the attic. Sid was in the middle of the sixth Harry Potter book, and I had a hunch he'd been reading ever since he'd left me that note. His bones were still together, but they were definitely more loosely connected than usual.

"What's going on?"

"Nothing. Which is what's inside my skull."

"You went through all those names?"

"I tried to, but I've got forty left."

"Then why are you stopping?"

"Because I don't know what else to do. I've Googled them, gone on Facebook and LinkedIn, checked the alumni lists—nothing. Maybe I'm one of those guys, but I don't know how I can ever find out for sure."

"You want me to take a stab at them?"

"What's the point? Besides, you've got work to do." He pointed at the essays I'd brought up with me. "I may not eat, but you and Madison still need you to make a living."

"Let's trade. You go through the essays for misspelled words and grammar problems, and I'll research some of your names."

I thought he tightened up a bit as he put down his book. "If you think I can help."

"Hey, you've got a great eye socket for typos."

"Do I get to use a red pen?"

"Absolutely."

While he got to work, I opened his database of Sid candidates. There were forty-one left, and I stifled a sigh so he wouldn't start losing bones all over the essays. At least he'd organized the data thoroughly. Each name was hot-linked to its appearance in the online JTU yearbooks, and any other information he'd been able to scrape up—club memberships, majors, and so on—was carefully noted.

Since he'd already tried the obvious places, I tried some less familiar ones: archives for the *Pennycross Gazette*, and when I knew a student's major, membership rosters for applicable professional organizations. I was able to cross off two men via the *Gazette*—they'd both joined the Army—and found two CPAs, an actuary, and even a guy who was a fellow adjunct.

It was encouraging, but it took over two hours of hard work to cross off those six names, and I couldn't help but wonder what we'd do if we crossed everybody off of the list. Where would we go next? I stifled another sigh.

At least Sid was having a good time marking up essays. He really was a good proofreader, sometimes annoyingly so when peering over my shoulder. That may be why I took such pleasure in finding a mistake in his database. "You made a typo."

"Where?"

"Here." I pointed to an entry. "You spelled that guy's name A-L-L-E-N Reece. It's A-L-A-N."

"No it's not."

I clicked the link to the yearbook where Alan's sophomore picture was printed. "A-L-A-N."

"Then whoever entered the caption into the yearbook spelled it wrong."

I should have let it go, since it didn't matter anyway, but I was tired and cranky. "Would it hurt you to admit that you're wrong once in a while?"

"You tell me—you're wrong so much more often than I am."

"Sid, if all you want to do is fight, I'll go downstairs and play with Byron. I thought it was dogs who snapped at people, not skeletons!"

"Fine!" he snapped—and it was definitely a snap. "I'll go sit in the corner and twiddle my thumbs. Excuse me, my phalanges—wouldn't want to get that wrong."

I resisted the impulse to tell him where he could put his phalanges, and started hunting for information on A-L-A-N Reece while I waited for him to apologize. He went back to the paper he was correcting, and I suspected he was waiting for me to apologize.

Neither of us spoke.

We'd probably still be there—not speaking—if I hadn't received a text from Deborah that she and Madison were on their way back to the house.

"I've got to go." Then I made myself say, "Thanks for helping with the papers."

"No problem," he said with enough hesitation that I knew he was forcing himself to be civil, too. "Thanks for taking six more names off of my database."

"I'll come back up after Madison goes to bed and work on some more."

"No, that's okay," he said. "I think we need a break."

"Are you sure?"

"This has been going on for weeks—another night won't make any difference."

"Okay, but let me know if you change your mind."

He picked up the book he'd been reading, so I packed up my stuff and went to meet Madison and Deborah. I didn't like leaving it that way, but I figured he was right. A night off wouldn't make any difference.

Wrong again.

43

Deborah and Madison had stopped by Darrow's, a local temple to the art of chicken pot pies, so all I had to do was pull out the leftover salad from the night before and dinner was taken care of. Madison had enjoyed her day of having a real job, especially flirting with various comely young men while Deborah did the actual work. I wasn't worried—I knew my sister wouldn't put up with loafing for long, and would soon have Madison earning her pay. And having a daughter who could pick locks could come in handy.

Deborah was in a good mood, too, because Fletcher had run a nice piece on her extra-careful methods of investigating employees, and that cop she knew had even thrown in a quote about her integrity. As a result, she wasn't going to lose a thing from her competitor's woes. In fact, she was picking up business as his monitoring clients switched to her.

After our early dinner, we took Byron out for a walk in the brisk fall afternoon, kicking at fallen leaves and wondering when the first snow of the year would fall. While we walked, Fletcher called on my cell to apologize once again for canceling at the last minute and promised to make it up to Madison and me—both chocolate and ice cream were mentioned. Plus he had me thank Deborah for her interview. We all agreed he was a great guy.

Back at the house, I whipped up hot chocolate for the humans and pulled out the last rawhide chew for Byron. Deborah and I didn't argue once.

It would have been a perfect afternoon and evening if I hadn't kept thinking of Sid up in the attic alone. No matter how many times I told myself that it was his own choice, I still felt like a heel.

So, despite what Sid had said earlier, I had every intention of visiting him once Madison was asleep, but I found a note on my pillow, presumably left while we were all out with the dog.

> *Borrowed a couple of books from your parents' office. Planning to read all evening. Don't come up.*

I should have gone up anyway, but it was late and I was tired and, truth be told, relieved that I was going to be able to get to bed at a reasonable hour. So I took him at his word and turned in for the night.

I did leave my laptop outside my bedroom in case Sid wanted to borrow it again, but the next morning I could tell it hadn't been disturbed. I shrugged and got the week started.

In handing out the essays to my first class, I felt guilty all over again because of Sid's good job proofing them. That was why I started work on his list of possibilities when I went to the adjunct office afterward. I got lucky and eliminated three more names in an hour.

Next up on the list was the contentious Alan/Allen Reece, and I decided the first thing I needed to do was confirm the spelling of his name. In the 1980 yearbook, it was definitely Alan in the sophomore-class listing, but when I went through the activities section, I found Allen Reece was a member of Film Fans and the Computer Connection. I went back to the 1979 edition—it was Allen in both the class listing and the club membership rosters, plus Allen worked tech in a production of *The Night Is My Enemy.*

Sid was right.

But how had he known? If he'd checked those other places, he'd have told me so. All he'd had to go by was the sophomore yearbook listing.

I looked down the list of names in his database, and didn't see a single other name misspelled, even though there were two other Alans, one Allan, an Allen, and even an Aleyn. Obviously Sid wasn't automatically changing the spelling on all versions of the name.

I went to the yearbooks where he'd found those other names and compared. In each of those five other instances, Sid had spelled the names exactly as they'd appeared in the yearbooks. I picked more names at random, and most of those matched the yearbook, too. The only exception was where a guy named Robert had his name misspelled as Rboert in the yearbook, and in that case, Sid had noted the discrepancy.

It was as if he'd known that A-L-L-E-N was the proper spelling without even thinking about it. Just as he'd known about passwords even though that had hardly been common knowledge back in his day; just as he'd known the word zooarchaeology, which I'd never heard before, despite being around academia my whole life. Maybe Sid had known Allen Reece. Or maybe Sid was Allen Reece.

Maybe I'd found him at last.

44

I was staring at the picture of Allen Reece, trying to decide if he looked the way I thought Sid would have looked, when there was a tap on my shoulder.

"Hey!" Fletcher said, leaning down to give me a kiss. "Here's the first part of my apology for missing dinner the other night." He placed a sparkly pink gift bag, complete with sparkly pink tissue paper peeking out, on my desk.

"You didn't have to do that."

"I wanted to. The wrapping is leftover from my niece's birthday—hope you don't mind."

"I had no idea sparkle technology had improved so much since Madison went through that phase. Can I open it now?"

"Please." He rolled his desk chair over and sat to watch.

I ventured in among the sparkles and pulled out a silvery tin, shaped vaguely like a skeleton, with a purple skeleton embossed on the top. At first I had a crazy thought that he'd found out about Sid, but then realized it must be a reference to my bringing a skeleton to school. I chuckled to show my appreciation, and since the tin was too heavy to be empty, pried it open. Inside was a luscious assortment of chocolates. "What time is it?"

"Just after eleven. Why?"

"I'm trying to decide if I'll spoil my lunch if I eat one now."

"Live dangerously! And speaking of lunch, if you don't have other plans, I'd like to take you out."

"If I did, I'd change them." I carefully selected a dark chocolate morsel, hoping it held something yummy. It did, and I sighed happily. "Now you take one."

He went for a milk chocolate. "I've got reservations for us at twelve fifteen."

"Reservations for lunch?" Very few of the places I frequented even took reservations for dinner. "Am I dressed okay?"

"You always look wonderful."

"You're laying it on mighty thick," I said, "but I like that in a man."

"Good." He leaned forward for another kiss, and I heard a smattering of applause from some of the other adjuncts. I was a little embarrassed, but Fletcher went with it. He even bowed, and returned a salute from Charles.

Sara, who'd come in when I was busy, neither applauded nor saluted. She just looked dyspeptic. Since I figured I had her to blame for spreading the news that lead to somebody breaking into my house, I hoped she had an upset stomach for the rest of the semester.

Fletcher said, "I've got a little work to do before lunch, so you can go back to what you were doing." He wheeled back to his desk and pulled out his laptop.

I looked at the picture of Allen again, enlarging it as much as I could. Allen had been lanky, though maybe he'd have filled out later on. His hair was dark, and he had a strong nose and nice eyes. I wouldn't have called him gorgeous—he wasn't as handsome as Fletcher—but he was good-looking in an unfinished, college-student kind of way. But he didn't look familiar.

The sophomore yearbook was the last one in which he appeared, so I started hunting for more mentions of him, either associated with JTU or Film Fans or any computer-programming organization I could find. There was nothing. Then I looked at the local paper's Web site, but their online archives didn't go back that far. If only I had a newspaper specialist nearby . . .

"Fletcher?" I said. "Can I pick your brain?"

"Sure."

"I'm trying to find information about a guy who was a student at JTU in nineteen eighty, but there's nothing online, so I'm stuck. Any suggestions?"

"You could go to the North Ashfield Public Library, where they probably have dusty files or, if you're really lucky, nearly legible microfiche versions."

"Joy," I said weakly.

"Or you could access one of the online newspaper archive sites designed for genealogists and amateur historians, and hope there's one that includes the *North Ashfield Times*. Of course, you'll have to pay a fee."

"How big a fee?"

"It varies pretty widely. Or, best of all, you could find a friendly reporter who has a friend at the *North Ashfield Times* who would be willing to check their files."

"I like that last one."

"Of course, that would also require a fee. Of sorts." He waggled his eyebrows, presumably going for lascivious.

"What kind of fee?"

"I'm sure we can work something out." He reached into his pocket for his cell phone. "Give me the name, and I'll call my friend."

"Allen Reece: A-L-L-E-N R-E-E-C-E. Or possibly A-L-A-N. He was a sophomore in nineteen eighty, but I don't know if he actually graduated."

Fletcher called his friend, and the friend promised to have something to him that afternoon.

"You're amazing," I said.

"Reporters like to trade favors. He does this, and I give him a heads-up on something sometime." Then, ever so casually, he said, "So what's the story on this Allen Reece guy? Anything for me?"

"No wonder you were willing to lend a hand." Before he could insist that he'd done so purely for the pleasure of helping me, I said, "There's no story, just curiosity. If that changes, I'll let you know."

"Fair enough."

By then it was time to leave for lunch, and he escorted me to his car to drive us to the River Inn, the nicest place in town. It's not gourmet dining by Boston or New York standards, but it's got staid New England charm, wonderful food, and enormous portions. The Yankee pot roast and sweet potatoes smelled too good to pass up, and I figured I could take the leftovers home. I would have, too, if there'd been any.

"How are you enjoying crime reporting?" I asked Fletcher.

"It's a lot more exciting than soccer tourneys," he said. "Catching the murderers was really satisfying—the cops were high-fiving everybody in sight. There aren't that many murders in Pennycross, and they were afraid they'd blow it."

"Are they sure the burglars killed that woman?"

"No doubt about it. The guys haven't confessed to it, mind you—they're saying they didn't go near her house."

"Isn't it odd that they broke into a place with a burglar alarm? I thought their M.O. was to target places without security systems."

"How did you know Kirkland had an alarm?"

Oops. "Read it in the paper, I guess."

"Not in any of my articles."

"Maybe on TV?"

He looked a touch perturbed, but went on. "The guys' lawyer is saying the same thing, but nobody buys it."

I felt kind of bad for the burglars. They were thieves, but

they weren't murderers. I just didn't know how I could convince the police of that without bringing Sid into the conversation. Hopefully their lawyer was good enough to make a case for them—even if they were thieves, there wouldn't be any evidence tying them to Kirkland's house.

Fletcher said, "I don't know if you want to tell Madison this, but it's possible that these guys weren't the ones who broke into your house. They had an alibi for that afternoon—they were installing a system at a house across town, and the homeowner was with them the whole time."

"The police did speculate that it might be somebody who thought the house was empty. We'll stay on guard, just in case."

"And if you should feel the need for a man around the house . . ."

I tried not to make a face. I'd received so many similar offers in the past, men thinking that because I was a single mother surely I needed a big, strong man to protect me. Instead I just said, "I'll keep that in mind."

Conversation wandered down other paths, and we had such a nice time that I really regretted having to say, "This has been lovely, but I've got classes to teach."

"Can't you blow them off?" Fletcher coaxed. "We could go over to my place for a while. . . ."

I smiled, though honestly I thought that was a bit pushy. We hadn't been dating that long yet. "I can't. If I don't show, I don't get paid."

He took it gracefully enough, and admitted he had some work he needed to do at the *Gazette*. So he drove me back to McQuaid, and I thanked him for our lunch with what I judged to be one of my better kisses. Since he repeated his suggestion about indulging in afternoon delight, I daresay he agreed, but I turned him down again.

Two dreary sessions of English comp later, I was wishing I'd taken Fletcher up on his offer. Students argued with the corrections I'd made on their work and disputed my description of what they were supposed to have turned in. One indignant student stridently insisted that he'd e-mailed me his essay on time and it had to be my fault that I hadn't received it.

Feeling more than a little aggravated, I stayed in the classroom long enough to boot up my laptop and check my e-mail while the student watched. No paper. I felt that after then looking in my spam filter and scanning every file on my computer, I could authoritatively say I'd never received his paper, but then he had to pull out his laptop to prove that he'd sent it. Except that he'd sent it to the wrong e-mail address, which he should have realized—I always send a confirmation that I've received an essay via e-mail.

A tussle ensued. He asserted that since he'd finished and e-mailed the essay a whole ten minutes before the deadline, he should get full credit. I reminded him that the rule was that a paper had to be *received* on time. I agreed to accept the essay if he sent it to me on the spot, and he agreed to accept an automatic ten-point deduction to his score.

When I checked to make sure the essay had actually arrived in my e-mail box, I found a note from Fletcher's friend at the *North Ashfield Times*. If I could give him a fax number, he'd send over the information he'd found, but he was leaving the office at five o'clock.

I checked my watch. Four forty. If I ran for it, I had just enough time to get to my parents' office, with their personal fax machine. I got there at four forty-eight, called the *Times* reporter, and breathlessly gave him the fax number. A minute later, pages started churning out, and I sat down to read them.

Then I read them again.

I was convinced.

Sid was Allen Reece.

45

Technically, it was more correct to say that Sid had been Allen Reece, and while I was convinced of it, I wasn't sure Sid would be. I needed more than the bare facts from the newspaper articles and police reports Fletcher's friend had sent me.

One of the people interviewed had been Allen's roommate Edward Vinton. I realized that name sounded familiar, so I checked Sid's database of possibilities and, sure enough, Edward was on the list. Even better, there was contact information for him, including a phone number. He'd become a Realtor and had an office just outside San Francisco. It was after five by that point, but not in California. Maybe I could catch him at work.

First I called Deborah and asked if she'd pick up Madison from the house and feed her dinner. I wasn't sure how long the call would take, and I didn't want Madison worried after last week's scare. If I thought she'd have done it, I'd have asked Deborah to tell Sid what was going on, too, but I knew that would never happen.

Before dialing, I spent a few minutes devising a cover story, hoping that at last I had a convincing one.

"Hello, Vinton Realty."

"May I speak to Edward Vinton, please?"

"Speaking."

"Hi. This is Grace Taylor. I'm a student at McQuaid University."

"Always glad to hear from the alma mater. Unless you're asking for money, that is." He chuckled.

I chuckled back. "Actually, I'm working on an assignment for my journalism class. My teacher, Mr. Fletcher, dug up some old news stories, and told us to cover them as if they had just happened. I ended up with one about Allen Reece's disappearance."

"Wow. Allen Reece. That's a name I haven't heard in a long time. That goes back to, what, nineteen seventy-nine?"

"Nineteen eighty," I corrected him. "That's the last time anybody saw him, anyway. Most of my classmates are just using the previously published accounts and police reports for their source material, but I thought I'd get a better story—and a better grade—if I dug deeper. That's why I'm calling you."

"There isn't any new information about Allen, is there?"

"Not that I've been able to find." That was a lie, but it was considerably more believable than the truth. "Do you mind if I ask you some questions about the case?"

"Sure, why not? I had some crazy homework assignments back in the day, too."

"Great. According to the information I have, Allen was a junior in computer science, and he disappeared over Christmas break, but the investigation didn't start until January."

"That's right."

"Why didn't his family report him missing?"

"He didn't have a family—his parents and his baby sister had died in a fire the year before. Allen was away at school at the time."

"That's awful."

"Yeah. The sister was only six years old."

Six years old. The same age I'd been when I'd found Sid.

I went on. "So he'd been planning to go home for Christmas with his girlfriend, only they had a fight the week before, and he decided not to go."

"What happened is, he caught her with another guy. I asked him to come home with me instead, but he said he needed some time alone. He was thinking of going skiing or something. I left a couple of days before the end of term and told Allen to call if he changed his mind, but he never did."

"The last day of the term, Allen attended all of his classes, but that was the last anybody saw of him."

"Yeah. When I got back to school after the first of the year, there was no sign of him. I thought he might still be licking his wounds, so I didn't tell anybody at first, but after a week, I told our RA, and he called the cops."

"I understand that his suitcase and some of his clothes were gone from your room."

"Right. The cops figured he'd taken off and would show up again eventually. When he didn't, they looked at the whole picture: unfaithful girlfriend, Christmas alone, still mourning his family. It looked like suicide."

According to what I'd read, the cops had fully expected to find a dead body out in the woods, probably during the next hunting season. When no body was ever found, the assumption was that Allen had killed himself elsewhere. With no family around to push the case, the disappearance had eventually been forgotten.

"Do you think it was suicide?" I asked.

"I don't know. I guess you never really know what's in another guy's head, but I wouldn't have expected Allen to kill himself. I knew he'd lost his family, but he was seeing a counselor down at Student Services to help him deal. He was keeping his grades up, and he wasn't worried about money because of insurance, and he had an internship to help with tuition. I thought he was doing okay, or as okay as anybody could be in that situation. I swear I would never have left him alone if I'd thought that would happen."

"What about the breakup with his girlfriend?"

"If everybody who'd ever been cheated on committed suicide, there'd be nobody left. I don't think Allen was that serious about Corrie anyway—obviously she wasn't serious about him."

"Corrie?" The name hadn't been in the *Times*.

"Corrie Melville was the girl. They'd only been dating a few months, and I could have told him it wouldn't last. She had her eye on another guy and only started dating Allen to make him jealous. It worked—she just forgot to tell Allen about it. I hear she even married the second guy, so I guess she really was serious about him."

"Was Corrie upset about Allen's disappearance? Did she blame herself?"

"Not so you'd notice. Mostly she was mad because everybody on campus found out about how she'd treated Allen, but the next week there was something else to gossip about."

"If Allen didn't kill himself, what do you think happened?"

"I kind of hoped he just ran off, maybe joined a circus or hitchhiked around Europe, and he'd show up someday with great stories, but I never heard from him again. Of course, I transferred schools the next year myself, but as far as I know, he never came back. So I guess he's dead after all." He paused, and had to clear his throat before saying, "Is there anything else I can tell you?"

"I was wondering . . . What was Allen like?"

His voice warmed, and I could tell he was smiling. "He was a great guy. Funny, too. It didn't show all the time because of what he'd been through, but you could see the real him now and then. Liked to watch Monty Python and the Marx Brothers, stuff like that. He didn't have a lot of friends—he'd just transferred to McQuaid after the fire—but he was the kind of guy who'd do anything for you. I'd only been rooming with him since September, but I didn't hesitate to ask him to spend the holidays with the family."

After that, I was completely convinced, and that was before what came next. "One other thing: You mentioned Allen's internship. Was that through the computer science department?"

"I think so, but he wasn't actually working with anybody in computer science. He was doing something for an archaeologist or paleontologist, something like that."

"The police reports mentioned a Dr. Jocasta Kirkland," I said, which was a flat-out lie—Kirkland's name hadn't shown up at all.

"That sounds right," Vinton said.

I'd have cheered if Vinton hadn't still been on the phone. After all the time and effort, I'd finally linked Sid to Dr. Kirkland. I restrained myself long enough for the requisite amount of politeness, then hung up.

I was about to shut down and zoom home to share the news with Sid when I remembered one thing that had rung a bell as I spoke to Vinton, something about Allen's unfaithful girlfriend. I went to the online yearbook and found her picture. Corrie was pretty enough. Maybe her hair was a little over-sprayed, but not too bad. It was just that she looked familiar. Where had I seen her before?

I found the JTU alumni site, and searched for her name. "Here we go," I said to myself. "Maiden name: Corrina Melville. Married name: Corrina Melville Kirkland."

Corrie was Corrina, Dr. Kirkland's daughter-in-law, the woman who'd snubbed me at the memorial service. She'd dumped Allen for Dr. Kirkland's son Rich.

46

After that I shut down my laptop and packed it away, then locked up and headed for my van, but I did so purely on autopilot. Too many ideas were running through my head for me to pay any attention to what I was doing. I'd set out to find out who Sid was—had I found out who'd killed him as well? Or at least why?

The killer could have been Rich, getting rid of a romantic rival. Or maybe Allen had confronted Corrina about her infidelity, things got out of hand, and she accidentally killed him. In either case, once Allen was dead, Rich could have gotten rid of the body. Making it into a skeleton would have been easy with his access to his mother's lab. Then he could have sold it to the carnival to muddy the waters still further.

Or maybe one or both of the twins had taken on the gory job to protect their little brother. That would explain why they'd been so intent on getting Sid back. Unless one of the twins had been the killer instead—I didn't have a motive, but that didn't mean there hadn't been one. Maybe Mary had a crush on Allen and become angry when rebuffed. Ditto for Donald—neither of them were married, so I had no idea what their orientations were.

Any of the Kirkland siblings or Corrina could have broken into my house to try to get the skeletal evidence back. But what about Jocasta Kirkland? What reason would any of them have had for killing her? How could that murder be tied to Allen's death? Could it have been a coincidence?

I realized I was at the house and parked in the driveway despite having no clear memory of making the trip, so I grabbed my stuff and went inside. Then I stopped. The alarm system hadn't beeped when I opened the door. A quick look at the control panel showed that it wasn't armed. I'd have to talk to Madison about that, especially since Byron wasn't on duty either. I'd asked Deborah to take him along, since I hadn't been sure how long I'd be. That was all to the good. I wouldn't have to find some way to distract him while I spoke to Sid—we'd run out of rawhide sticks.

"Sid, it's me!" I called out. There was no response, so I assumed he was still sulking. I tapped on the armoire in case he was in there, but he didn't tap back. Next I checked my parents' office. He wasn't in there, either. "Sid, come on down! I've got something to tell you."

When he didn't reply, I started for the attic, lugging my laptop. The attic door was unlocked, which I took as an invitation.

Sid wasn't up there. I looked around, but there was nowhere to hide, not even for a skeleton.

"Sid?" I said, going back to the second floor. I went through all the bedrooms, even opening closet doors in an echo of our burglar the previous week. No Sid.

Back downstairs, I went to the armoire and opened it. No Sid. Then I went through every room, even the basement.

"Sid! Where are you?" But I knew he wasn't there. An

empty house has a kind of hollow feel, but I'd never expected to feel it there. I don't think I'd been completely alone in that house since I was six years old and Sid came to stay with us.

Sid was gone.

47

Sid was missing, and I had no idea where he'd gone or how he'd gotten there.

Okay, Sid wouldn't have just walked out. He wouldn't have risked exposing us that way. That gave me an idea, and I went back to the attic. Sid's bacon-patterned rolling bag was missing, too. So somebody had carried him out, somebody who knew about that bag.

I yanked my cell phone out of my pocket and dialed. "Deborah? Sid's gone."

"Hallelujah! It's about time you got rid of him."

"I didn't get rid of him! I came home and he was gone."

"You mean he just left? Do you think anybody saw him? Could he be traced back to you?"

"He wouldn't leave—somebody took him!"

"Why would anybody steal a skeleton?"

"Because he's evidence in a murder." As briefly as I could, given the many interruptions from Deborah, I explained what Sid and I had been doing since he first recognized Dr. Kirkland.

"You're insane," Deborah said. "You've been playing games with a murderer. You must be insane."

"Fine, I'm insane. The point is, I think the murderer has Sid and he's going to kill him."

"Georgia, it's already dead. How could anybody kill it again?"

"Crush him with a sledgehammer, put him in a garbage disposal, use acid, give him to the dog pound—I don't know what he's planning, and I don't care. All I know is that Sid is in trouble!"

"Sis, I know you're fond of the old . . . You're fond of Sid, but don't you think this is for the best?"

"How could—?" I stopped and thought. "Deborah, did you take Sid?"

"What? No. Why would I—?"

"You have been on me to get rid of him ever since I moved back to town."

"That doesn't mean I stole him. Somebody else must have—Wait a minute! How could anybody get past the security system?"

"The alarm was turned off when I got here."

"Say that again."

"The alarm wasn't on."

"Georgia, I armed that system myself when I picked up Madison. What does the status screen say?"

I carried the phone over to the system's control board by the front door and followed my sister's instructions until she was satisfied.

She said, "It was disarmed thirty minutes after Madison and I left. So, who have you given the access code to?"

"Nobody."

"Not even your honey?"

"No, and Fletcher hasn't been here since you installed it, so he couldn't have seen me do it. The only ones who know our code are Madison, you, and me."

"What about bone boy? Did you tell him?"

"No, but I did leave the instruction manual on the kitchen counter."

"With the code written in it?"

"You told me to write the code in there."

"Yeah, okay. I did."

"So, yes, Sid could have read it and unlocked the door. But he didn't wheel his own suitcase down the sidewalk. It doesn't make any sense."

Deborah gave a kind of barking laugh. "Nothing about that freak has ever made sense, Georgia. Look, I'm sorry you're upset, but I don't know where the skeleton is or how it got there. I'm just glad it's gone."

"You—you—" I was so mad I couldn't even get the words out. "Just keep Madison for a while longer. Can you do that for me?"

"Of course, but I think—"

I hung up on the rest of the sentence. I didn't care what Deborah thought—I was going to get Sid back.

Okay, I had to assume that Sid had disarmed the system to let somebody in. So he must have found something or figured something out while I was at work. If he'd just had a *eureka* moment or had shaken a memory loose, there was no way I could catch up, but if he'd been working on the computer again, I might have a chance. I'd had mine all day, but there was still my parents' desktop system.

When I got to the den, I found the computer turned on and open to a Web page, so I knew I was on the right track. Only the site he'd been looking at was the JTU Web site, which we'd looked at a dozen times before. I experienced no new revelations from the panorama of smiling students, enthusiastic instructors, and earnest administrators. So what other sites had he visited?

I checked the browser history and saw that he'd been going through the JTU yearbooks. My first thought was that Sid had zeroed in on Allen Reece, too, but the pages he'd visited were faculty pages, not student photos. I found several shots of the late Dr. Kirkland teaching classes, showing bones to students, and working in the lab. Could Sid have been hunting for himself in those photos? I looked at the students shown to see if Allen appeared in any of them, but unless he was that one guy with his back to the camera, he wasn't there.

That's where the trail stopped. The browser didn't show any other Web sites viewed for the day, and I couldn't figure out what else he could have been doing.

Time was ticking away.

I decided to stop worrying about what Sid had found so I could focus on what I'd learned.

I knew Sid was really Allen Reece, who'd been romantically entangled with Kirkland's future daughter-in-law and her son. The problem was, while I could link his murder to either of those two, or even to the twins, I couldn't make that match up with Dr. Kirkland's murder.

What else did I know? Allen had recently lost his family in a fire. Maybe that was the link. What if one of the Kirklands had been behind it? What if Mary was an arsonist, and Allen had tracked her down, and she'd killed him to protect herself. . . . Nope, no good. For one, the article about Allen's family had said it was a lightning strike that had caused the fire, and for another, the Allen family had lived in Wisconsin. Why would a Massachusetts arsonist have struck in a random town in Wisconsin? And I couldn't connect that theory with Dr. Kirkland's murder, either.

What else? Allen was a computer guy who'd done some kind of work for Dr. Kirkland. Computers . . . The day Sid recognized Dr. Kirkland, she'd been at McQuaid to enlist a grad student for some statistics work. I hadn't given it any further thought, but now that I did, why hadn't she tried to get somebody at JTU? Maybe McQuaid was closer to her house, but surely she had more pull at JTU—even retired professors of her stature had juice. Could it be that she hadn't wanted somebody at JTU to know what she was doing?

Maybe whatever that was had something to do with what Allen had been doing for her in 1980.

I flashed on Yo and her insistence that I not badmouth McQuaid for fear of cheapening her degree. She'd been overreacting, but it was true that a grad student's thesis advisor could lend glory to a new career or, if a scandal arose, taint it. What if Allen had found something like that in the work he was doing for Dr. Kirkland, and he'd been killed to keep it hidden? Maybe she'd been killed to bury it, too.

I went back to the page of the JTU yearbook that Sid had been looking at last, and suddenly I saw what Sid had seen. He'd seen his murderer.

48

I was close to panicking, but I told myself that panic wouldn't help anybody. So I sat down and tried to think about who Sid was, just as I'd analyzed countless characters in literature.

Once Sid realized who his killer was, he would have known that there might not be any way to catch him. After all, the only real evidence was Sid himself. Had he been the vengeful type, he might have gone after the killer with violent intentions, but I couldn't see him doing that. The only times he'd ever shown real menace or even tried to be frightening were in my defense, either at that carnival or by pulling pranks on people who'd been mean to me.

Nor would he have tried for a preemptive strike to defend himself. All during our haphazard investigation, he'd only been worried that he was endangering Madison and me. Our welfare was more important to him than his own.

Then there was his concern that he was causing me trouble or that I might lose my job because of the time I was spending on his identity crisis. Belatedly I remembered the

argument I'd had with Deborah, an argument Sid could easily have heard. Sid was probably thinking the same thing
as my sister, that he was getting in my way. Plus there was
the dog, the new boyfriend . . . He could have concluded
that I no longer wanted him around.

Adding all that up, I could easily see him deciding to leave.

So maybe he did disarm the security system at the house,
climb into his suitcase, and . . . and what? Somebody must
have wheeled that bag away, and who would Sid have asked?
I couldn't imagine that he'd have invited the killer into my
house. The only people he knew were my parents, Deborah,
and me. Come to think of it, *how* would he ask anybody?

The answer was so obvious, I could have kicked myself:
the phone. I thanked God that I'd used my cell to call Deborah, reached for the landline handset, and pressed Redial.

After two rings, a familiar voice said, "Charles Peyton."

"Charles? This is Georgia."

"Good evening, Georgia. How are you?"

"I'm fine, but—Okay, this is an odd question: Did somebody call you earlier from this number?"

"Why yes, your friend Sid called. He said you were hoping that I could ferry that suitcase back to JTU. He told me
to use the key under the mat to get into your house and get
the case from the front hall, then lock the door behind me."

"Where did you leave the suitcase?"

"Just inside the door of the Turner building, as requested.
Did it not reach its intended recipient? Do you need my
assistance?"

I knew I could trust Charles, but I couldn't imagine him
reconciling Sid with his worldview. It was too much to ask.
So I said, "No, I'm good."

I must not have been overly convincing, because he said,
"Georgia, are you quite certain nothing is amiss?"

"Everything is fine. I'll see you tomorrow." I hung up
gently, though what I wanted to do was throw the phone up
against the wall.

Coccyx! That ossifying piece of sacrum was throwing himself onto his sword to protect Madison and me, and had enlisted Charles to deliver him to the killer.

At least I knew were Sid had to be—in the basement of the Turner building. The question was how to get him out of there.

Obviously I couldn't call the cops or campus security. I could have asked Charles to lend me his key card, but after that last conversation, he'd want to go with me, and I didn't want that. I could break into the building, but that would just bring the cops and/or security down on me. What I needed was a way to get in the door. Then I realized that I had a way if I could convince Deborah to help.

I called her back.

"You hung up on me!" she said.

"I know, you're right. I'm sorry, and I need your help."

"If it has anything to do with that bag of bones, forget it. You're better off without him."

"Are you sure? Deborah, do you remember when I decided not to marry Reggie?"

"Of course," she said, startled by the apparent change of subject. "You went from 'I want to spend my life with this man' to 'Who needs men anyway?' overnight, with the wedding less than a week away."

"That's because Reggie was cheating on me."

"Son of a—How did you find out?"

"He used our phone to call another girl to make a date."

"Where you could hear him?"

"No, I was upstairs, but Sid heard him. He'd gotten caught downstairs and was hiding in the armoire."

"And you never considered the idea that the skeleton was lying because it didn't like Reggie?"

"Of course, but Reggie admitted it."

"Are you serious?"

"He said marriage and the baby were scaring him, so he'd been sowing a few wild oats, but he really loved me and the baby and he would end it with the other girl."

"Did he?"

"I have no idea. After that, I couldn't trust him, and I was pretty sure I didn't even love him anymore."

"No wonder you broke it off so suddenly."

"That's the thing. I didn't break up with him until a month after I found out."

"What? Why not?"

"Because I was in grad school and I was pregnant. I figured I had to marry him for the baby's sake. The only reason I didn't was Sid. He found me crying late one night, and wouldn't leave me alone until I told him the truth. I wanted the baby more than anything, but I was dreading being stuck with Reggie so much I was barely sleeping. It's just that I figured there was no way I could handle raising Madison alone. You thought I was nuts to try it, didn't you?"

She hesitated. "I did think it would be difficult."

"Difficult or impossible? Honestly, Deborah, if I'd asked you back then if I'd be able to have a baby, finish grad school, and support the two of us, what would you have said?"

"I wouldn't have thought you could do it," she admitted.

"I knew that, and I knew Mom and Phil would have the same doubts. Sid never did. When I told him I couldn't do it alone he thumped me on top of my head—hard—and said I could do anything I wanted to. If I wanted to raise a baby by myself, I should stop my ossifying whining and do it. There were plenty of women who didn't have half my brains who were bringing up half a dozen kids by themselves, and if I couldn't figure out a way to make it work, then what use was all my education anyway?"

Deborah chuckled in spite of herself.

"He believed in me when I didn't even believe in myself. And because of that, I have Madison. Now are you going to help me get him back or not?"

"Tell me what you want me to do."

49

After a quick stop at Deborah's house to pick up what I needed, I headed to JTU. Luckily, JTU didn't have a walled campus like McQuaid—the classrooms were interspersed with homes and businesses. I parked as close as I could get to the Turner building without actually being on campus and strolled across the street. There were still a few people around, which I hoped meant that Sid was still safe. The kind of work it would take to totally destroy him was best done when nobody else was nearby. That was if I was right and the killer wanted to destroy him—I was working on a tottering tower of assumptions, but it was all I had.

I tried to be casual as I approached the building. The door was locked, as I'd expected, so I pulled out the key card that Deborah had given me.

Since the reputation of locksmiths with shaky integrity was exactly what Deborah had been trying to dodge, it was a testament to her change of heart that she'd been willing to help me get past JTU security. No matter what else happened, I had to make sure it didn't get traced back to her.

So as soon as I got in the door, I started breaking the card into pieces, and each time I passed a trash can, I dropped in a piece until they were gone.

The hallway was empty and the classrooms I passed were dark, so every footstep echoed. There weren't even any cleaning people around. Though I'd grown up around colleges, I can still get creeped out by a school building at night. It was even worse in the dimly lit stairwell, but I knew how much noise an elevator makes in an otherwise unoccupied building, and I didn't want to warn anybody that I was coming.

I slowed to a crawl as I got to the basement, trying for utter silence as I crept toward the lab where Donald and Mary Kirkland had examined Sid. The door wasn't closed all the way, and light was leaking around the edges. I peered through the crack when I got there, but didn't see or hear anyone. I did see the suitcase on the floor. It was empty, and there was a haphazard pile of bones on the worktable that I was sure were Sid's.

I watched for what felt like an hour, but was probably more like five minutes, waiting for movement or sound. Nothing. Finally I hissed, "Sid."

There was no response.

"Sid!"

What was the matter with him? Couldn't he hear me? Why was he just sitting there? Surely he wasn't dead. Deader? I was afraid to call out again, so I just kept waiting for him to move. After another eternity, I stepped into the room, and finally I sensed movement. Except it wasn't from Sid—it was from behind me. Before I could turn, a hand reached over my mouth, and I smelled something sickly sweet before passing out.

I woke up feeling vaguely uncomfortable, as if I'd fallen asleep at my desk. When the fog burned out of my brain, I realized I was propped in a desk chair, but not mine. My arms were tied to the armrests, and my feet were fastened to the chair legs. I blinked away the rest of my confusion and saw a man looking at me with what I had to admit was a convincing expression of concern.

It was Jim Michaels, the chairman of the JTU anthropology department. And unless I'd totally blown it, he was Sid's murderer and likely Dr. Kirkland's as well. Knowing that, I wasn't buying his concerned face.

"How are you feeling?" he asked.

"Kind of dizzy, and my eyes are burning."

"It'll pass. I thought the use of chloroform would be preferable to something more damaging."

I looked over at Sid's remains. "Good to know that you've refined your methods."

I'll give him points—he didn't pretend not to know what I meant. "I was so young then, so caught up. I didn't even know what I was doing when I hit that boy."

"Did you know what you were doing when you used that knife?"

"I tried to make it painless, but I really had no choice. If I'd been arrested for assault, I never would have finished my dissertation on time."

"You must have been cutting it close on the deadline."

"Dr. Kirkland would have given me more time, but not my parents. I was out of money, and they weren't going to give me so much as a month more. You don't know how lucky you are to have parents who understand academia."

I wasn't feeling overly lucky at that moment, but he did have a point. "What did Allen find anyway?"

"I was afraid you'd discover his name. Might I ask how?"

"Does it matter?"

"Only if someone else is involved."

"Neither my daughter nor my sister know," I said quickly. "Just me, and Allen, there in the suitcase."

He raised one eyebrow at the part about Sid, but let it pass, perhaps attributing it to the lingering effects of the chloroform.

I went on. "It was mostly guesswork. I had a list of

students who'd never finished their degrees at JTU, and went through it until I got to Allen's name. The story of his disappearance matched the timing for the skeleton. I promise that nobody else knows."

"I'm glad to hear that. And I must say that you have excellent research skills. You should really consider publishing some papers."

Great. Even murderers had career advice for me. "One thing I didn't find out is exactly why you killed him. Was it something to do with Dr. Kirkland's data?"

"Precisely. You may know she made her reputation with her own dissertation, a seminal work about migratory patterns of early man as shown by the remains of prey animals. Computers weren't easily accessible then, at least not to zooarchaeology grad students, so she had to calculate her statistics by hand. Somewhere along the way, she made a mathematical error, and without realizing it, invalidated her results."

"So her premise was wrong?"

"Completely. But nobody knew that in the nineteen eighties—the study wasn't replicated until just a few years ago, and everyone assumed the original study was flawed by not having a statistically significant sample." He stopped. "I'm sorry, I realize this isn't your field. Let me just say that it was an honest mistake, one that Dr. Kirkland never realized."

"But Allen did."

"When computers became more common, she decided it would be worthwhile to have her data input for future scientists to use. She hired the boy to take care of it for her, and just before Christmas break, he realized there was something wrong with the results. Dr. Kirkland wasn't on campus that day, so he came to me."

"You were her research assistant, right?" The picture Sid and I had both spotted in the JTU yearbook was of Kirkland and Michaels in a lab bent over a tray of fossils.

He nodded. "I told him that she couldn't have made a mistake like that, but he showed me the numbers. I was horrified! If word had gotten out, she could have been accused of falsifying data on purpose. At the very least, every study she'd ever done would have been reviewed, and there was no telling what else they'd find. In the meantime, she'd probably lose her privileges as a professor and I'd be without the head of my thesis committee. Even if I'd had time to find another, who would have wanted me? My thesis work was based on hers—if hers was faulty, so was mine. My career would have been over before it started."

"But Allen didn't care about that?"

"Oh, he was sympathetic, but he was an undergrad. He didn't really understand what it meant. Nobody who hasn't been through it really understands."

Once again, he had a point.

"He wanted me to call Dr. Kirkland right away, and when I tried to stall, he said he'd find her number himself. Then he turned away from me, and—"

"And you hit him."

He nodded, looking ashamed. "I had to stop him. Dr. Kirkland was completely devoted to science. If she'd learned there were discrepancies in her data, she'd have been the first to report it, no matter what the cost to her own career."

"Or to yours."

"Not just to mine. She'd advised other students, and all of them would have been affected. Even her own children's research would have come under scrutiny."

"So you hit him out of desperation, and killed him to hide that. And the skeletonization?"

"To hide him, of course," he said, as if it were the only reasonable thing to do. "With Dr. Kirkland gone for the holidays, I had all of Christmas break to get the job done. It took time away from my dissertation, of course, but that couldn't be helped."

"Then you marked him with the ID of another skeleton."

"I'm impressed—you have figured it all out. Yes, I replaced our specimen with the new one, and donated the older one to a high school for gifted students. Anonymously, of course."

"Of course."

"I admit that I panicked when the new skeleton went missing from the classroom, but now I realize that Dr. Kirkland had it all along. By the way, how did you find out she had it?"

"What?" I'm sure I looked confused—Dr. Kirkland had never had Sid.

"You must have known," Michaels said. "I saw this suitcase in her office before you stole it."

"I didn't steal it."

"Come on, you didn't exactly keep it a secret. One of your McQuaid colleagues sent an e-mail about it, and I immediately recognized the ID number. Then when I looked at the photo she included, I recognized the suitcase as well. How did you know to steal it?"

"I told you, I didn't steal it!"

"Then how did you get it?"

I couldn't think of anything reasonable to say, so I went for the unreasonable. "It followed me home."

He looked pained by what he clearly thought was inappropriate humor. "If I'd had any idea that Dr. Kirkland had the skeleton in there, I'd have taken the case myself when I first saw it. It would have saved me a lot of trouble."

"You mean like breaking into the adjunct office at McQuaid? And into my house?"

"And the car."

"Which wasn't even mine," I said, thinking of poor Yo's battered Corolla.

"How was I to know? It was your parking pass. I don't know about McQuaid, but at JTU only the person to whom a permit is assigned is supposed to use it."

I was momentarily bemused by his indignation for what

seemed like a pretty minor offense compared to murdering two people.

"While I was trying my best to get the skeleton back, your colleague was trying to use it to get a job. When I didn't respond to her note, she got in touch with one of the professors here and told him about it. I only found out after the fact that it was actually here in this room. If I'd known, I would have bought it from you on the spot."

I didn't bother telling him that I would never have sold Sid.

Michaels said, "I was considerably relieved when I got the phone message that the skeleton would be left for me in the vestibule." He cocked his head quizzically. "I'm confused by what you intended. First the obviously faked voice on the phone, then leaving the suitcase as promised, followed by sneaking back into the building. Did you mean to trap me? Blackmail me? What exactly did you expect to accomplish?"

I'd been wondering that very thing ever since I'd woken up tied to a chair with a murderer in front of me, and my reasoning would make no more sense to him than it was currently making to me. "I was going to give the skeleton back, but I changed my mind." Then, to distract him from the utter inanity of that statement, I asked, "What about Doctor Kirkland? You killed her, too, didn't you?"

"I had to," he said almost sadly. "Once she retired, she decided to finally finish putting her data into digital form—she'd given up the attempt after her intern disappeared. She wanted to use one of our students, but knowing what she'd find, I blocked her."

"So she went to McQuaid."

"And soon enough found the mistake. She called to tell me, and as I suspected all those years ago, had no concept of the damage the revelation would do to me, her children, or her other students. Even to the university. I hope you don't think me any less of a scientist, but human costs outweigh a minor scientific error, certainly in this case."

He didn't want me to think he was a bad scientist? I'd thought that living with a skeleton had resulted in some of the strangest conversations of all time, but this one was raising the bar.

"So you've got me, and you've got the skeleton. Now what?"

"I'll destroy the skeleton," he said calmly. "Pulverization and then an acid bath should take care of it. Then there will be nothing to tie me to the boy's death."

"What about me? A fresh body won't be nearly as easy to get rid of as a skeleton. Or are you going for another skeleton approach?" Would I wake up like Sid some day?

But Michaels made a calming gesture. "There's no need to be concerned. Just sit there quietly until I'm done, and then I'll let you go."

"Seriously?"

"You're no threat to me. You have no evidence, and the police won't listen to you—no offense, but you're the oddball who carried a skeleton around in a suitcase. You can go about your life on the fringes of academia as long as you stay away from JTU."

It was all totally reasonable, given his twisted frame of logic, but I'd been deceived by too many college administrators in the past not to be able to see the signs. Besides which, I wasn't going to let him destroy Sid.

"You're lying," I said flatly. "As soon as you're done with him, you're just going to kill me, too. HELP! HELP! HELP!"

"Stop that," he said, but I could hear the edge in his voice. "Nothing is going to happen to you if you just cooperate."

"HELP! HELP! HELP!" I was yelling as loudly as I could, even though I really didn't expect anybody to hear except Sid, and he wasn't moving. For the first time, I really started to believe that my friend had gone on to . . . wherever . . . leaving his skeleton behind at last. Since there was nothing to lose, I kept on yelling.

Finally the facade of the rational academic broke, and

the desperate man showed his face. "Stop it!" He grabbed Sid's thighbone by one end and lifted it over his head. "Shut up!"

I refused to die with my eyes closed, which is why I saw when the bone swiveled in his hand and the end Michaels meant to bring down on my head conked him on his instead.

He staggered, and blood welled up in his hair. He shook himself like a dog, and raised the bone again, this time gripping it with both hands. Again it came down on him and not me, and he bellowed in pain.

The motion was unmistakably a Shinigami chop.

"Sid?" I said.

There was a horrendous clatter as the bones went over the edge of the table, and then Sid rose up behind Michaels. Most of him anyway—Michaels was still holding his thighbone. But Sid managed fine without it as he wrenched the bone out of Michaels's hand and brought it down on top of his head yet again. The man's eyes rolled up and he fell to the floor with a satisfying *thunk*.

"Sid!"

"Not Sid," he said. "The Bone Ranger!"

"Coccyx, Sid, is that why you waited so long to move? Were you trying to come up with a joke?"

"A hero always shows up in the nick of time."

That was Sid. "Well, the Bone Ranger better stay around long enough for me to thank him."

50

"What did you tell the police?" Deborah asked after expressing her disgust at Sid's pun.

It was several hours later, and we were back home. Deborah had actually spoken to Sid more than once, and was sitting next to him on the couch, while I was in the armchair near the armoire. Deborah and I had hot chocolate, Byron was snoozing on the rug, and I'd caught Sid patting him once. It was like a Norman Rockwell painting, if he'd ever painted the Addams Family.

I said, "I wanted to keep it simple—the simpler the lie, the harder it is to disprove. So I told them how I'd figured Michaels was the killer, and that when I got home and found the suitcase with Sid missing, I went out to JTU to get it back."

"Didn't they ask why you did something so stupid?"

"Of course, so I admitted that it was extremely stupid. I'd hoped I could sneak in and get the skeleton without being caught. Which I almost did, after all. And I didn't call them because they wouldn't have believed me, and your pal Louis admitted that was true."

"What was he doing in North Ashfield?"

"He was visiting another cop when the call came out, and he tagged along. He sends his best, by the way."

Deborah pretended not to be pleased.

"Anyway, I just kept saying I'd been an idiot—"

"Which was true!"

"—and they just kept shaking their heads, but they believed me. Who lies to make herself look dumb?"

"No comment. So Michaels supposedly caught you and—"

"And drugged me, tied me to the chair, and was about to hit me when I yelled for help—all of which was true. The untrue part was when I said I'd wriggled partway out of the ropes and shoved him, making him slip and hit his head. Then I worked myself the rest of the way loose. Of course, we put a different bone into his hand to make the cops think he was planning to use that instead of Sid's femur."

"When, in reality, Sid untied you."

Sid grinned, obviously delighted that she was actually calling him by name. "I thought it would look more realistic if I let her get herself out."

I said, "Not only did he just watch while I wriggled and squirmed, he gave 'helpful' advice, too."

"And I was watching Michaels to make sure he didn't come to."

"You just wanted another excuse to hit him," I said, and Sid didn't deny it.

"Then what?" Deborah asked.

"I sent Sid out to hide in the van before I called for help. When the cops showed up, I told them that Michaels had already destroyed most of the bones by the time I got there. All that was left were a tooth and a bone from the wrist that had gotten pushed under a table."

Sid said, "I donated a tooth with a filling, so maybe they can compare it with Allen's—I mean my dental records. And the wrist bone was the one that was broken and healed when I was alive, so it might show up in my medical records.

Or they may be able to scrape up enough DNA to test, if they can find a sample to compare it to."

"I doubt they'll bother," I said. "They were really more interested in Dr. Kirkland's murder. I don't know what kind of physical evidence they'll be able to put together for that, but I'm hoping there's enough to charge him. Just kidnapping me should get him into enough trouble to lose his job, and I imagine university officials are going to be looking into that research data now. I bet he even loses his doctorate."

"Is that enough?" Deborah asked.

"It might be all we can get."

"What did Michaels say while you spun this fairy tale?"

"Not a word. He lawyered up immediately. He probably doesn't remember everything anyway. Head blows tend to cause amnesia of the events right beforehand. Besides, if he did see Sid, he's not going to admit it unless he's aiming for an insanity defense."

"So that's it?"

"Well, I may have to perjure myself if it ever comes to trial, but if it keeps Sid safe, I can live with that. Otherwise we all live happily ever after."

"More or less," Sid said. "I can manage the happy even if I suck at living."

Deborah rolled her eyes. "Geez, you two deserve each other. I'm going home now. I suppose this is a hugging occasion."

"If you insist," I said, but I gave her a good firm hug anyway.

Then she looked at Sid. "Well?"

He jumped up so fast, he left a couple of phalanges on the floor. I tried not to tear up while they hugged—briefly—but failed. Then Deborah said in a slightly too-loud voice, "'Night, all," and headed out the door.

"Wow," Sid said happily. "Wow."

"I know."

"Do you think she'll let me come stay with her sometimes?"

"Not in a million years."

"Yeah, I didn't think so. Well, I suppose I should be getting back up to the attic."

"There's no rush."

"Are you sure? When is Madison due home? Or is she spending the night at her friend's house?"

"Actually, she's here right now."

"What?"

Madison pushed the door of the armoire open—from the inside—and stepped out.

"Hi, Sid."

51

"But—but how—" was all Sid could get out when he saw Madison.

I said, "I called Madison before I got to the van and told her about you. I'm not sure if she believed me—"

"Of course I did!" Madison insisted.

"Okay, she did, but I figured seeing would really be believing, so I told her to hide in your armoire. I hope it wasn't too stuffy in there."

"It could use a few more air holes."

"But—but—" he stammered.

"By the way, this is for thinking I'd freak out over you." She reached over and thumped him on the skull, then winced. It was a maneuver that required practice, but I suspected she'd have plenty of time to perfect her technique.

I demonstrated it on him myself and said, "And that's for not telling me why you really wanted to hide from Madison."

"Ow!" he lied.

"You were afraid she was going to pull a Deborah,

weren't you?" It had taken a ludicrous amount of time for me to figure that out, but in my defense, I'd been mightily distracted.

"Maybe—I mean—and the murder stuff—" He hung his skull in embarrassment. "If I'd had a heart when Deborah quit talking to me, it would have broken. I didn't want to go through that again."

"And when I left you here? Did you think I was abandoning you?"

"No, not really. I understood why you had to go, and why you couldn't take me, but . . . it hurt. I didn't want to get to know Madison and then lose her, too. Or what if she'd hated me and you had to choose between us? Of course you'd pick your daughter—you wouldn't want to be stuck with me."

"Sid, get this through your thick, empty skull right now: You are not going to lose us! We're not stuck with you— you're stuck with us."

Sid couldn't cry, not really, but he came as close as he could—he was speechless. So I took the opportunity to fill him in on who he'd been before. "Just like I said, Sid, you were always a nice guy. I mean, Allen."

"Give it up, Georgia. You're never going to learn to call me Allen."

"It'll just take some time," I said stubbornly. "I only found out your real name a little while ago."

"My real name is Sid. I don't remember being Allen, and I've been Sid longer than I was Allen, anyway."

"If you're sure," I said, though I was kind of relieved. Calling him Allen made it feel as if I were talking to a ghost. Which I was, maybe . . . Oh, coccyx! I'd grown up with Sid the skeleton, and I didn't want to change his name or my perceptions of him.

That's when I noticed how late it was getting. Since it was theoretically a school night, I said, "Madison, you'd better hit the sack."

"I will if you will."

I yawned. "No arguments here—I'm beat."

"I'm sleepy, too," Sid said.

Madison didn't react, but I sure did. "Excuse me? Since when do you sleep?"

"I feel tired, Georgia. I think . . . I think I've done what I was here to do. It's time for me to go."

"Go where?" Madison demanded.

"Good-bye, Madison. Good-bye, Georgia. Have a great life, and thanks for everything." Sid laid himself down on the rug, and then his bones slowly loosened, falling apart so that he was nothing but a pile of isolated bones.

52

"Sid? Sid!" Madison said. "Mom! Do something!"

I shrugged. "Sorry, sweetie—I think he's gone. But on the good side, there's all that space up in the attic up for grabs. You know how you've been wanting a TV in your room? You can have his!"

"Hey!" Sid said, swiftly coming back together. "You keep your ossifying fingers off of my TV."

"Sid!" Madison hugged him as hard as she could without breaking anything. "You're alive."

"More or less." He gave me a dirty look. "You could have at least pretended to be upset."

"Please! You call that acting? Madison played a better death scene than that when she was eight years old."

"Hey, that was a great death scene!" Madison countered. "Sid, you'd have loved it. Hey, I know! I'll see if I can get my drama coach to let us do *Hamlet*—you can play Yorick!"

Over the next week or so, life settled out. I found out Dr. Parker had a long-standing rivalry with JTU, and was so pleased with the school getting a black eye that he'd already promised me another year at McQuaid. Madison might graduate from Pennycross High after all.

Of course, eventually my parents would return and want their house back, meaning that I'd have to find somewhere else to live, and it wouldn't be easy to find an affordable three-bedroom apartment that allowed dogs.

Yeah, three bedrooms. Madison and I had decided that Sid was going to stay with us from then on. Byron, too, even if Sid wasn't overly fond of him.

As for Fletcher, I hadn't told him about Sid and never would. We'd broken up. He'd stuck around just long enough to get the interview for the *Gazette* that I'd promised him, but with those journalistic instincts of his, he could tell I was leaving out parts of the story. He hated that. If it had just been personal pain about my lack of trust, I might have relented, but he was just mad because he'd wanted more of a scoop.

Apparently he was particularly annoyed that I hadn't let him take pictures of Sid when he was thinking about his funky-things-found-in-people's-attics feature. Since Sid had supposedly been destroyed, he'd had to sweet-talk Sara into letting him use one of the photos she'd taken of him. Not only was the resolution dreadful, but he'd had to give her a photo credit. One evening of him pouting about that was plenty. I got one last look at his butt as he left, and that was enough for me.

Of course, Deborah thought we were crazy—me for letting Fletcher get away and Madison for accepting Sid into the family—but she'd resigned herself.

As for Sid, to make sure he got the message that he was part of the family, we'd taken a photo of Madison and me with Sid between us. Then I framed it and added it to Mom's picture wall.

Even then, I could tell he didn't completely believe that he wouldn't be left behind like Andy's toys in *Toy Story*, but if there's one thing being a mother and a teacher has taught me, it's patience.

One night a couple of weeks later, Madison was out with friends and Sid and I were watching TV, when he suddenly asked, "Georgia, how did you know?"

"How did I know what?"

"How did you know I hadn't really died? Again. More. How did you know that I hadn't died that night after we solved my murder?"

"Because I remember the night you came to life. It wasn't to catch a murderer or get vengeance—it was because I needed you. Right?"

He nodded.

"That's why you didn't leave. I still need you."

New York Times Bestselling Author

Charlaine Harris

introduces a southern librarian whose bookish
bent for murder gets her involved in a real-life
killing spree...

REAL MURDERS

The First Aurora Teagarden Mystery

"Charms and chills."
—Carolyn Hart

"Ingenious...an engrossing tale...a heroine
as capable and potentially complex as P.D.
James's Cordelia Gray."
—*Publishers Weekly*

"One of the most original premises I've ever
come across in a mystery, and the whole
book is great bloody fun."
—Barbara Paul

penguin.com

Discover the Aurora Teagarden
Mysteries from

Charlaine Harris

the author of the Sookie Stackhouse,
Harper Connelly, and Lily Bard series

Real Murders

A Bone to Pick

Three Bedrooms, One Corpse

The Julius House

Dead Over Heels

A Fool and His Honey

Last Scene Alive

Poppy Done to Death

penguin.com

WELL-CRAFTED MYSTERIES
FROM BERKLEY PRIME CRIME

- **Earlene Fowler** Don't miss these Agatha Award–winning quilting mysteries featuring Benni Harper.

- **Monica Ferris** These *USA Today* bestselling Needlecraft Mysteries include free knitting patterns.

- **Laura Childs** Her Scrapbooking Mysteries offer tips to satisfy the most die-hard crafters.

- **Maggie Sefton** These popular Knitting Mysteries come with knitting patterns and recipes.

- **Lucy Lawrence** These brilliant Decoupage Mysteries involve cutouts, glue, and varnish.

- **Elizabeth Lynn Casey** The Southern Sewing Circle Mysteries are filled with friends, southern charm—and murder.

M5G0610

P.O. 0003689396